WHAT BOYS LIKE

THE METCALF-ROOKE AWARD:

WHAT BOYS LIKE

(stories)

Amy Jones

BIBLIOASIS

FIRST EDITION

Library and Archives Canada Cataloguing in Publication

Jones, Amy, 1976-
    What boys like and other stories / Amy Jones.

ISBN 978-1-897231-63-0

    I. Title.

PS8619.O525W53 2009   C813'.6   C2009-904130-8

Readied for the press by John Metcalf.

Canada Council   Conseil des Arts
for the Arts   du Canada

Canadian   Patrimoine
Heritage   canadien

ONTARIO ARTS COUNCIL
CONSEIL DES ARTS DE L'ONTARIO

We gratefully acknowledge the support of the Canada Council for
the Arts, Canadian Heritage, and the Ontario Arts Council for our
publishing program.

This book is printed on Rolland Enviro and is 100% PCW recycled
content.

PRINTED AND BOUND IN CANADA

for Cory

ACKNOWLEDGEMENTS

Earlier versions of some of these stories have appeared in the following publications: *The New Quarterly*, *Maisonneuve*, *Event*, *The Vagrant Revue*, *Room Magazine*, *enRoute*, *Prairie Fire*, and *The Coast*. My appreciation to the editors of each, and to the Nova Scotia Department of Tourism, Culture and Heritage who provided me with funding while I worked on this collection.

A huge thanks goes to my editor, John Metcalf, and to Dan Wells and Dennis Priebe at Biblioasis, for making this dream a reality, and to Zsuzsi Gartner, for all the feedback and support. As well, thanks to my early writing mentors, Linda Little and Richard Cumyn, for getting me started on the right path.

To my family: Bonnie Jones, Richard Jones, Erin Jones and Shelagh Hagen, for buying all those literary magazines and managing to tell people "she's a writer" while keeping a straight face. I love you guys.

To Jessica Linzey, my first real editor, for knowing me better than anyone else in the world and never using it against me. To Dr. Heather Davis-Fisch, for finding typos and wrapping everything in bacon, and to Scott Davis-Fisch for helping me eat it all. To Aaron Collier, for the excellent photographs and the equally excellent conversation. To Jeff Nichols, for helping me engage with the cultural zeitgeist. To Lindsay Sangster, for Rock Nights and McDonald's runs. To Shawn Duggan, for being awesome. I love you guys, too.

And finally, to the MFA Superstars: Adrienne Gruber, Matthew J. Trafford and Cory Josephson. For the nothing. And for everything. I . . . well, you know.

Contents

A
Good Girl

The night Alex met Leah, he had been drinking with his boss, Yousef, on board Yousef's boat. The boat was called *Serendipity*. She had three sails, but Yousef only ever used one. Alex didn't know which one. He was just along for the rum and Cokes.

Yousef owned a restaurant called Tahini, and sold his kibbee and fatouche Saturday mornings at the Brewery Market, where he turned on the ethnicity for all the earnest yuppie types with their baskets of fresh herbs and their unpronounceable cheeses. On weekends he drank Moosehead on the *Serendipity*, ate Oreo cookies. Listened to Radiohead. Alex was a server at Tahini, and had become friends with his boss when he saved Yousef from losing the *Serendipity* in a game of pool with some of the kitchen staff. Afterward, Yousef took Alex out drinking and they discovered their mutual love for mid-nineties rock and smoking weed and – even though Alex was thirty-two and Yousef was pushing forty-five – their similar taste in women.

The first weekend in June, Alex and Yousef sailed the *Serendipity* from Hackett's Cove to Mahone Bay, where they got stuck on a shoal and had to call the Coast Guard to tow them off. "Thank you! Thank you!" Yousef said, in his thickest accent, raising his can of vodka-spiked Diet Coke to the surly-looking officer who boarded the *Serendipity*. "I love sailing. I'm just not so good at it!"

The officer gave a terse wave. "Fucking fascists," Yousef said as they motored off.

When they were safely ashore they had steaks and beer at the Rusty Mackerel, which, as it turned out, closed despicably early. Yousef talked the bartender into selling them a forty of Captain Morgan then tried to convince their waitress to come back to the *Serendipity* with them for rum shots and bong hits. The waitress was tall, round-faced, barely eighteen.

"Come on," Yousef said, laying on the accent. "I'll make you a breakfast you won't believe. Have you ever had the chicken livers?"

"Nice try," the waitress said. "But I'm a vegetarian."

So they went back alone, sitting in the cockpit until three in the morning, listening to the Counting Crows and exchanging ideas for ways to work marijuana into the menu items at Tahini. Alex thought his idea, olive oil infused with hash oil, was superior to Yousef's plan to dice the weed with the parsley in his tabouli salad – and it turned into a heated argument that only ended when "Mr. Jones" came on the stereo for the second time and they both had to sing along.

The next day, hung over, they sailed the *Serendipity* through pea-soup fog back to Hackett's Cove. "What was the point of that?" Alex asked as they lugged their gear back up the hill to Yousef's summer house. "Really, we could have stayed and drank on your back deck."

"We had an adventure," said Yousef.

"No, we didn't," said Alex.

*   *   *

That afternoon, while flaked out on one of the three leather sofas in Yousef's living room watching *Dawson's Creek* reruns on the 48-inch LCD screen, Alex got a call on his cell from the waitress at the Rusty Mackerel.

"You left your wallet here," she said. "This number was on the contact card."

"Damn, that's bad timing," Alex said. "Dawson just found out that Joey kissed Jack."

"Who?" the waitress asked.

So Alex drove all the way back – over an hour from Yousef's. When he got there, the pub was closed. There was a note on the door that said *meet me at the government wharf*. It was signed Leah Silver.

She was sitting on the end of the wharf in jeans and a windbreaker. "Leah?" Alex said.

"It's Lay-a," she replied, without turning around. "Like in *Star Wars*."

"Okay," said Alex. "Lay-a." He sat down next to her. When she looked at him, he saw that she had freckles all over her face.

She pulled his wallet from her pocket and handed it to him. Alex took it and instinctively opened it. "You don't trust me?" Leah asked.

"Never trust a girl with freckles," Alex said. "That's what my Mama taught me."

Leah laughed. "Do you want to go for a boat ride?" she asked. She pointed to a weathered skiff tethered to the wharf, a huge outboard hanging ludicrously off the stern. Alex's hangover still pulsed quietly in the background. "Come on," she said. "I have rum." She pulled a flask from her pocket.

"Um," said Alex. His tongue receded back into his throat.

"What are you worried about, sailor?" she asked. "I can handle myself on the open water."

"Do I look worried?" Alex said.

"Yeah," said Leah. She took a swig of the rum and licked her lips. Then she leaned over and softly licked Alex's. "Come on," she said. She stood up.

"Yes, ma'am." Alex looked down at his wallet. "Hey, there was forty bucks in here." But Leah was gone, her rubber boots clomping down the wharf, her ponytail swinging behind her.

*   *   *

The next morning, Leah woke Alex up at five. "Why so early?" Alex asked, groaning, reaching his hand up behind her neck. "You're too sexy to not be in bed."

"Mom's on the night shift at the hospital," she said. "Gets home at six." Alex dropped his hand. Leah shrugged. "I'll make you breakfast," she said. "No chicken livers, though."

"You still live with your mom?" Alex asked. He stood up and began pulling on his pants.

"Just until I graduate high school," she said. She smiled. "Dirty old man."

"Not funny, *Lee-ah*," Alex said, fumbling with his zipper.

Leah stared at him. "It's *Lay-a*," she said. "God, Alex."

After toast and scrambled eggs, Alex drove home along the 103, rehashing the weekend in his head and slapping himself to try and stay awake. He turned the AC on full blast and cranked the radio, singing along to every crappy classic rock song they played. When he felt his eyelids closing, he smacked himself across the face. "Here I am," he belted. "Rock you like a hurricane."

The road stretched on and on. Soon, Leah seemed far away.

*   *   *

"You banged the waitress," Yousef said, the next day at work.

"Twice," said Alex. He grabbed a wine glass from the dish rack and began polishing. "It would have been more, but her mother got off work at six."

Yousef grabbed Alex's face in his hands. "You're my fucking hero," he said.

*   *   *

The rest of the summer was busy at Tahini. Yousef and Alex made one more trip on the *Serendipity*, with a couple who lived in Yousef's condo complex in Halifax. Jim was an architect, and his girlfriend, Martine, worked for some kind of non-profit. Yousef was good friends with Jim, but Alex thought they both seemed a little stuffy. When he offered them drinks, they looked shocked.

"Hey, man," Jim said. "I thought we were going sailing."

"We are," Alex said, chipping away at a block of ice. "Rum and cokes are *de rigueur*."

Martine snickered. Jim glared at her. "Not while I'm on board," he said. "It's against the law."

Alex stopped, mid-chip, and stared at Jim. "Right," he said after a while. He went back to chipping.

Later, while Yousef was showing Jim his new state-of-the-art navigating equipment, Martine came over to Alex, who was manning the wheel with a rum and Coke in one hand and a cigarette in the other. "Your French is terrible," she said. Alex noticed she had the slightest hint of an accent.

"Yeah, well, my English isn't much better," he said.

Martine ran her finger along the bottom of Alex's glass "Could I have a little sip?" she asked.

Alex lowered his sunglasses on his nose and looked over them at her. "Are you sure? Big Jim might get mad."

"I won't tell if you don't."

Alex shrugged and handed her the glass. With her thumb and forefinger she pinched her nose, tilted her head back, and downed the rest of the drink. "Hey," Alex said. "That's good rum. The least you could do is taste it."

She wrinkled her nose. Her nose was very cute. "I don't like the taste of rum," she said. "I like many other drink, but not rum."

"Well," said Alex. "We have many other drink. Let me get you something you'd like." He stood up on the captain's bench and grabbed hold of one of the stays to pull himself up and around Martine. Martine smiled at him, and he felt the stay slip from his hands. Seconds later, he was in the water.

"Really smooth, my friend," Yousef said later, after he and Jim had managed to haul Alex back up. "Chalk up another one for responsible boating."

"I'm done with the *Serendipity*," Alex said. "Sailing's for chumps." Yousef kicked him lightly in the shin. A drop of water trickled down Alex's face like a tear and wobbled on the edge of his jaw. Jim opened his mouth, and then closed it again. Martine, eyebrows knitted, pulled a neatly folded Kleenex out of her khaki capris and wiped it away. They sailed for home.

* * *

Three months after the night he spent in Mahone Bay, Alex heard from Leah again. "I just got a fake ID," she said. "Wanna buy me a drink?"

At the bar, she was wearing a short skirt and tall boots. She swished her hips and all the men looked at her. She sat across the table from Alex and crossed her legs. Alex noticed she had a run in her stocking just above her knee. "Nice place," she said.

Alex felt people staring at them. "They have twenty-seven kinds of beer on tap," he said.

"Wow," Leah said. "I'll have a vodka and cranberry."

While they waited for their drinks, Alex sat there trying to think of something to say. Leah crossed and uncrossed her legs, fiddled with her earring, reapplied her lip gloss several times from a tube she kept stashed in the waistband of her skirt. When the server arrived with their order, Leah smiled at him, touched his arm as he put her drink on the table in front of her. After he left, Leah looked at Alex and raised her eyebrows. "Are you going to just sit there staring at me?" she asked. "Or are you going to ask me what I'm doing here?"

"Probably just sit there staring at you," Alex said.

Leah rolled her eyes. "I'm leaving with him, then," she said, jerking her head towards the server.

So Leah had graduated high school, and had moved to Halifax for college. "Community college," she said, fiddling with her straw. "I'm not wasting my time at some fucking university."

Alex, who had wasted a total of six years at some fucking university, nodded understandingly.

"I'm doing Applied Communication Arts," Leah continued. "I'm thinking actually of majoring in digital imaging, even though it means being stuck behind a computer all day."

"Cool," said Alex.

"You have no idea what I'm talking about," Leah said. She giggled. "You're such an old man." Alex must have flinched, because then Leah touched his hand under the table. "Not ready to joke about that yet, huh?"

"Maybe when hell freezes over," said Alex. "Or the Leafs win the Stanley Cup."

Leah smiled. Then she grabbed his hand and slid it between her legs, pressing it against her crotch. "Would an old man do this to me?" she whispered.

Alex inhaled sharply. "I sincerely hope not," he said.

*   *   *

Usually Alex saw Leah late at night, after he got off work. Some nights she would show up at his apartment after going to the bars with her school friends. "It's your BC," she'd giggle over the intercom. Booty Call. Not something Alex was used to being on the receiving end of, but he wasn't complaining. They rarely went out together, and when they did, there was always drinking involved. Alex had the suspicion that without liquor and sex, the two of them would have very little to talk about. Normally this would bother Alex, but with Leah, he tried to put it out of his head. She was young, she was fun, she was hot, and when he was with her, so was Alex.

There were all these strange little things about Leah that Alex quickly picked up on. She would never commit to plans with him, ever. As far as Alex could tell, she ate frozen dinners almost exclusively. And she cracked the cartilage in her ear when she was bored. "What the fuck is that?" Alex asked, the first time he heard her do it.

"Nothing," Leah said. Then, defensively: "It doesn't hurt, you know."

And the first time he saw her room, which was in a house she shared with four other girls, he was shocked to discover that she didn't have any furniture. Just a futon, unmade, shoved in the corner. Her laptop sat in the middle, open on a pile of blankets.

Alex flopped down on the futon. "Are you doing penance?" he asked her.

"No," said Leah. "I just don't like stuff. It's boring."

"There's no boring stuff, Leah," Alex said, jokingly. "Only boring people."

"Fuck off," Leah said. Her face hardened. Alex suddenly remembered how young she was.

"Don't listen to me," he said. "I'm just an old man, remember?"

The things Alex found most interesting about Leah were the things she didn't want to talk about: the year she spent in South America with her mom when she was eleven, her Uncle Jeff, who played the mandolin in Gordon Lightfoot's backup band in the seventies, the fact that she knew how to use a weaving loom. Then there was her copious list-making. Alex discovered this one day when he was looking for music on her laptop.

"What's 'Lists'?" Alex asked, opening the folder without thinking about it.

They were in Alex's apartment, and Leah had just come from the shower. She stood in the doorway of the living room, naked, toweling her hair – even though the blinds were open and they were only on the second floor. "Duh," Leah said. "What the fuck do you think it is?"

"Lists of what?"

Leah shrugged. "Whatever," she said. She stretched her arms over her head.

Alex motioned toward the window. "You know, everyone out there can see you."

She crossed the living room, holding the towel around her like a cape. She stood in front of the window and stared out into the street. "Do you think anyone's looking?" she asked.

"Oh, undoubtedly," said Alex.

Leah let the towel drop to the floor. At first Alex thought she might have been looking up at the sky, but then he realized she was only looking at her own reflection in the glass.

*   *   *

A few days later, Alex called Leah's cell and got her voice mail. "Hey, sexy," he said. "I want to see you all dressed up. How about dinner this weekend?" When he didn't hear back from her for three days, he called again. "Hi, Leah," he said. "Just wondering if you got my message." The weekend passed, into the next week. Alex waited, feeling like a stalker. The following Thursday, he called again, for what he promised himself was the last time.

She answered on the fifth ring. He could hear some crappy dance music in the background. "Hey, old man," she said. "What's up?"

"I've been trying to call you," Alex said.

The music grew louder in the background. "Sorry, Alex," Leah said. "What did you say?"

"Oh. Um, do you want to have dinner with me this weekend?"

"Sure," Leah said. "What did you have in mind?"

"Well, I thought maybe the restaurant where I work . . ."

There was a loud crash on the other end of the phone. When Leah came back, she was laughing. "Sorry," she said. "You work at a *restaurant*?"

"Yeah, well, when I'm not out running Special Ops for the CIA. Tahini? Remember?"

"Sure," said Leah. "Tahiti. I remember. I'll bring my bikini."

*   *   *

They planned to meet the next night at seven, but Leah never showed. Alex sat at the bar, getting drunker and drunker. "I told you she is trouble, my friend," Yousef said.

"You did not," said Alex.

After the restaurant closed, they went back to Yousef's condo, where Yousef confiscated Alex's cell phone. "Just in case you have the urge to call that psycho bitch," said Yousef, lighting a joint and passing it to Alex.

"Come on, man," said Alex, inhaling deeply. "That's harsh."

"What do you care, anyway?" Yousef asked. "You're just fucking her. Right?"

"Right," said Alex. "Right."

*   *   *

Three in the morning, she was at his door. "It's your BC," she breathed into the intercom.

Alex, still bleary from the joint, rested his head against the wall. "Where were you tonight?" he asked. "I waited at Tahini."

There was silence on the other end, then a burst of laughter. "Oh, fuck," Leah said. "I fucking forgot." A pause. "Do you hate me?"

Alex felt the urge to hang up on her, and then stopped himself. Come on, Alex, he thought, you're acting like a girl. "Never mind," he said. "Come on up."

*   *   *

"How come I've never met your friends?" Alex asked Leah the next morning.

She rolled over and grinned. "How come I've never met yours?"

"I wanted you to, remember?" He poked her shoulder, gently. "You. Never. Came."

"What can I do to make it up to you?" she asked, reaching between his legs.

"Leah, I'm serious." He moved her hand. "I really want you to meet the guys at work. You know Yousef? The one with the boat? He really wants to meet you. And Jordie, he . . ."

"Okay, Alex, whatever," Leah said. She rolled away, and that's when Alex heard it. The cracking cartilage. He reached for her hand again.

*   *   *

A few weeks before the school term ended, Leah called him at five in the morning. "I'm going to Florida for Christmas," she told him. "I forgot to tell you."

"Okay," said Alex, half-asleep. "When are you leaving?"

"Tomorrow," she said.

Alex sat up in bed. "But it's not even December yet," he said.

She laughed. "I know. But my ride's leaving tomorrow."

Alex felt strangely panicked. "What about school?" he asked.

"Mmm," she said. "I don't know about school." Her voice started to fade. "I'll talk to you when I get back," she said.

"When's that?" Alex asked. "Leah?"

But by then she was gone.

*   *   *

"You're never going to see her again, you know," Yousef told him, sitting at the bar in Hell's Kitchen, Alex's throat still burning from the Liquid Cocaine shots. Leah had been gone for two weeks. Alex had barely slept since she left. Yousef ordered another round. "She's down there fucking some old dude," he said.

"Some *rich* old dude," Alex said. "Some fucking *lucky* rich old dude. With a Viagra prescription." His mouth began to sweat. He swallowed hard a couple of times, trying to keep from throwing up.

"No, no, no. You're the lucky one," Yousef said. "You. You are." He paused. "Know what? You should ask out Martine."

"Martine?" Alex asked.

"You met her on the boat. With Jim. He moved out a few months ago."

"Right. Jim. The fun police." Alex spat onto the floor under the bar. The girl sitting next to him gave him a dirty look.

"Fuck Leah. You're done with chicks like her," Yousef said, banging his fist on the bar. The girl sitting next to them got up and left.

Yousef had never liked Leah, Alex realized. "Chicks like her?" he asked.

Yousef moved down the bar and draped his arm around Alex's shoulders. "My friend," he said. "In many ways, you and I are a lot alike. But not when it comes to women." Yousef shook his head. "This one, Alex, she will fuck up your life." He tousled Alex's hair. "You will find a good girl, someday, eh?"

"Sure," said Alex, wiping the back of his hand across his mouth. "A good girl. Right."

*   *   *

The next morning, Alex saw Martine at the bus stop outside Yousef's condo complex, where he had ended up crashing on the couch the night before. Alex was still slightly drunk, stumbling, thinking about how vile the inside of his mouth tasted. Martine appeared to be on her way to work. It was raining, and she was wearing a beige trench coat and black trousers, smart-looking heels. Over her head she held a pert black umbrella with a wooden handle.

It occurred to Alex, who had been shuddering inside the bus shelter, that she was standing outside to stay away from him. He pulled his hood over his head and stepped out into the rain. "You can go in there, if you want," he said.

"That's okay, really," said Martine. "I like it out here."

"I like your coat," Alex said. "Very chic. Did you get that around here?"

"No," she said. "Montreal. Where I am from. They have many special store there."

"Ooh la la," said Alex.

Alex never really knew why Martine agreed to go out with him. She was beautiful and blonde and French, and often forgot to pluralize her nouns. In fact, he thought it demonstrated a rather conspicuous lack of judgment on her part.

"It was because of your eye," Martine told him later. "I looked into your eye and saw you were a beautiful person."

You should have looked into the other one, Alex thought at the time. You might have seen something else.

*   *   *

For a while, with Martine, he slept well. Her bed was wide and feathery, and she kept the windows open, even in winter. The first few times he found himself awake, he wandered around Martine's condo, running his hand over her cool, sleek furniture, staring out her tenth-storey window to the lights on the harbour. But Martine always woke up and forced him into the kitchen to drink some kind of godawful tea – a dream suppressant, she called it, but Alex thought it tasted like mouldy bread. Eventually, Alex just stayed in bed, staring at the ceiling until he could hear the early morning delivery trucks rumbling below her bedroom window.

"You are sleeping better?" Martine asked.

"Yes," Alex said. "Thanks to you."

That seemed to make her happy. And right then, that was all Alex wanted to do.

*   *   *

On Valentine's Day, Alex was in his own apartment, getting ready for dinner with Martine, when the phone rang. "Hey, old man," she said. "Guess who?"

Alex nearly dropped the phone. "Leah," he said. "You're back."

"Yeah," she said. She sounded sad. "Got any plans tonight?"

"Well, I . . ."

"I really want to see you. Please."

He told Martine he was getting sick. "I think it's a migraine," he said. "They usually start with me throwing up."

"Ahh," said Martine. "I didn't know men got migraines."

"Some do," he said, feeling like a jerk. "I just need to rest."

Half an hour later, he was fucking Leah. She still had remnants of a fading tan, and she had gained a little weight around her hips. It drove Alex crazy. As soon as they were finished the first time, he was ready again.

"I guess you missed me, huh?" Leah asked when he finally rolled off her. She was smiling, but her eyes were dull.

"I did," Alex said. He pushed back a strand of hair from her face. "Of course I did."

Leah brought her knees to her chest. Alex could see she had deep bruises on her shins. "Drinking accident," she said, when she saw him looking. "Florida was a little crazy."

"Well," said Alex. "Did you miss much school?"

Leah picked at her toenail. "Yeah," she said. "I'm sorta done with school."

"Oh." Alex sat up and kissed her delicately on one shin, then the other.

"It's okay though," Leah said. "I've been working at this salon, you know, as a receptionist?"

"Cool," said Alex, kissing the inside of her thigh.

"And one of the girls there, she's going to do my hair, for a hair show."

"Excellent," said Alex.

"I'm going to be a hair model."

Alex's tongue was too busy to respond.

*   *   *

The next morning, while Leah was in the shower, Alex saw her laptop and couldn't help himself. He opened up the "Lists" folder.

Inside the folder there were dozens of files, most of them titled something fairly mundane: "Things to Do" or "Birthdays" or "Places I'd Like to Visit." When he came to a list called "People I've Fucked," he opened it without even thinking about it. He found his own name, nestled about halfway down the page. He frowned. Somehow, he thought he'd be at the top. He wondered if the list was chronological. Taking a sip of his coffee, he looked down to see what name came after him.

Yousef.

He held the coffee in his mouth. It just wouldn't go down, no matter how hard he tried to swallow. He could hear Leah turn off the shower. He imagined her in there, reaching for a towel, her body glistening with water as she dried herself off, and then Yousef's hand reaching for her small, round breasts, his mouth on her nipple, his dark hair brushing against her chin . . .

Alex swallowed the coffee. Got dressed, put on his shoes, and went home.

*   *   *

The next day, Alex called in sick to work. And the day after that. Martine called a couple of times to see how he was feeling, but Alex didn't answer the phone. After the third day, Yousef showed up at his apartment. Alex was eating a bowl of Honeycomb cereal in the same pair of sweats he had been wearing for the past three days. The Foo Fighters blared through his shitty computer speakers. "Let me in," Yousef said through the intercom. "I've got some medicine for you."

"I'm not sick," said Alex. But he let him in anyway.

"I know you're not sick, my friend," Yousef said when Alex opened the door. "You've never called in sick a day in your life."

"You said you brought medicine," Alex said.

Yousef pulled a joint from his pocket. "Of the spiritual kind," he said.

Alex waited until after they finished smoking the joint. Yousef was relaxed, telling Alex a story about a party of drunken middle-aged women who had been at the restaurant the night before. "You really missed out, Alex," Yousef was saying. "Jordie made some big tips just for letting them grab his ass a couple of times."

"Yeah," said Alex. "So when'd you fuck Leah?"

Surprise flickered across Yousef's face. Then he leaned back and spread his arms across the back of the couch. "Ahh," he said. "I see. She told you?"

"Sort of," Alex said.

Yousef took a pack of smokes from his pocket and began tapping them against the arm of the couch. "I thought you were finished with her," he said.

"I thought so too," said Alex.

Yousef pulled out a smoke and lit it. "Listen, my friend," he said. "That girl, you don't need her. She's fucked up."

"I know," said Alex. He rubbed his temples. "I know."

Yousef offered him a smoke. Alex took it.

"You know," said Yousef, taking a drag off his cigarette, "she's fucked up, but she sure can . . ."

"Too soon," said Alex.

"Right," said Yousef.

*   *   *

After Yousef left, Alex dumped his bowl of soggy Honey-combs in the sink and opened the fridge to look for the good apple juice – the fresh-pressed stuff that you had to buy in the refrigerator aisle at the grocery store – but all he could find was the shitty kind in the Tetra Paks. Then he remembered it was Martine who bought the good apple juice, and that it was probably sitting in her fridge next to the sparkling water and the little bowl of olives stuffed with goat cheese that she had bought for their Valentine's dinner. Fuck, he thought, staring into the abyss of his refrigerator. What am I doing?

The next day, Alex proposed to Martine. It was too soon, he knew. He didn't care. Neither did she. "Of course," she said, wrapping her arms around him. He breathed in. She smelled like coconut. "Can we have the wedding in Montreal?" she asked. "My parents would be so thrilled . . ."

"Sure," Alex said. "Anything you want."

That night, they made love without a condom. "It takes a while," Martine told him. "We should start now." Alex didn't argue. But three weeks later, she missed her period. When she came back from the doctor, her eyes were shining with happiness, and Alex knew. "I'm pregnant," she whispered.

Alex bent to kiss her, but she pulled away. "Are you happy?" she asked.

"So happy," he said, without even thinking about it.

They were married in Montreal in July. They ate some kind of chicken, and Alex gave a toast to Martine in French, which was a big hit with the relatives. They shook hands with everyone. They cut a cake. They danced to "She Will Be Loved" – Martine's favourite song, although Alex had a hard time getting through it with a straight face.

They had rushed the wedding so Martine wouldn't look pregnant in the photos. She was barely five months along, but already Alex could see a little bump forming on her soft, white belly. He often found himself staring at it stupidly. It seemed too delicate to survive.

The night before the wedding, Alex had called Leah. He had had several drinks, and was alone in their hotel room. "I'm getting married tomorrow," he said when Leah answered. "I don't know why I called."

"Married, huh?" He could hear the Black Eyed Peas thumping in the background. "Just a sec." He heard a door close, and the music went away. "That's fucked."

"I know."

Silence.

"I miss you."

Leah sighed. "I miss you, too," she said. "Wanna come over?"

"I'm in fucking Montreal," he said.

"Oh."

Silence.

The sound of cracking cartilage.

Alex hung up the phone.

*   *   *

At the end of October, a month before the baby was due, Yousef offered Alex a partnership in Tahini. It was late, and the restaurant was closed. The two of them were sitting having a drink at the bar. "I'd be honoured to have you aboard," he said.

"A partner," said Alex. "I never thought I'd see the day."

Yousef smiled. "You know the business as well as I do, my friend," he said. "And you're a family man now, right? Very responsible."

"I'll think about it," Alex said. But he knew he'd say yes. He swallowed the last of his beer. "Another?"

"Go ahead," said Yousef. "I'm going to head home. You lock up, partner."

Yousef left, and Alex called Martine. "That's great!" Martine said when he told her the news. She was trying to sound excited, but Alex could tell she was tired. "We'll celebrate when you get home. You can have champagne and I will have water with sparkles in it, and we'll have a toast. I'll even change out of my pajamas!" She sighed. "That's a pretty sad celebration, isn't it?"

"Are you kidding?" said Alex. "I haven't seen you out of your pajamas in weeks!"

"Nice one, Mr. Smart Guy," said Martine. "Make fun of the pregnant lady."

After he hung up the phone, Alex poured himself a half a glass of draught and walked around the restaurant, running his hands over the tables, along the bar, scanning the ceiling, the light fixtures, the walls, as if he were seeing them for the first time. He turned out all the lights, locked the door and began walking towards home.

Partner, he thought to himself. Father. Partner. Father.

He stopped, turned, and started walking in the other direction.

*   *   *

When he got to Leah's house, there was some kind of costume party going on, cowboys and pirates smoking and drinking on the front lawn in tight little groups. Alex remembered it was the night before Halloween. Shit, he thought to himself. When did I start forgetting about Halloween? He wandered around the outside of the house. It was still warm for October, and most of the party seemed to be happening in the backyard. It looked as though a significant portion of the living room furniture had been pulled out onto the lawn and draped haphazardly with battered strings of patio lanterns. He felt the glare of young eyes on him as he wandered through the crowd. Alex tried to picture himself the way they must be seeing him. Narc, he thought. Parent. Perv.

He found Leah in the backyard. She was lying on a couch in the middle of the lawn, her head in the lap of a stocky blonde boy in a wetsuit who had a blue-painted face and a bunch of seaweed draped around his neck. She was wearing a leather jacket, tight jeans. It seemed as though her hair had grown out a bit. She looked really pale. When she saw Alex, she smiled but didn't get up. "Hey, old man," she said. "Or should I say, old *married* man?"

"Hi," said Alex.

"Still miss me?" she asked. She was still staring at the sky. She took a cigarette from the blonde boy, blew a smoke ring into the air, and then reached up and ran her fingers through his hair. The blonde boy looked down at her with what might as well have been little cartoon hearts for eyes. Alex resisted the urge to wrap the seaweed tight around the little fucker's neck and pull.

"Leah . . ."

Her eyes narrowed as she turned to look at him. "Yes?"

He didn't know what to say. He could feel Leah's hands in his own hair, imagine the weight of her head in his own lap. Then, suddenly, the smell of her breath, the curve of her ass, her hip bones pressing against his. He felt the urge to run, but his feet wouldn't move. "I'm going to have a baby," he said, finally.

Leah laughed. Her voice was hoarse. "You mean, your *wife* is going to have a baby," she said. "You're not going to do shit. You're not going to do *anything*."

"Right," he said.

"Are you?" she asked.

"What?"

"Going to do anything?" She sat up. Her hand snaked down the front of the blonde boy's thigh, but she was staring straight at Alex. He felt himself shiver.

The blonde boy put his arm around Leah protectively. "He's not going to do anything, babe," he said, staring at Alex as well.

Alex rubbed the back of his neck. At one time in his life, he would have taken the guy down, just for the hell of it. But really, what was the point? "What the hell are you supposed to be, anyway?" he asked.

The boy tugged at the seaweed around his neck. "A dead fucking surfer. What the fuck do you think I am?" Later that night, in some dark corner of the house, Alex knew Leah would laugh while the blonde boy fumbled with the buttons on her jeans – his beer breath in her face as he grunted up against some wall somewhere, or hot on the back of her neck with her face in the mattress – the red-knuckled fingers of one of her small hands toying with the top of her ear, waiting for the crack.

"What about you?" Alex asked, turning to Leah. "What are *you* supposed to be?"

Leah smiled, and her eyes were slits.

"Myself."

How to Survive a Summer in the City

1. Stay in the shade

It is hot, sticky hot like the whole world is inside a steamed-up bathroom. For the first time this summer Stacy has promised she'd take Marie to the beach, but at ten o'clock she is still asleep, one naked leg twisted around the sheet like she's wrestling with it. Soon it will be too late, and all the other kids will have taken all the good spots on the sand. Marie has a new pail and shovel that she found a few weeks earlier in the garbage room of the apartment building where she and Stacy live. Marie knows that she is too old to play with plastic beach toys, but she has been thinking about sandcastles ever since she found them. Secretly she imagines she will pack the ordinary-looking pail with regular old sand, and when she turns it over it will transform into something else.

Other people's mothers don't sleep in until ten o'clock, Marie thinks, poking Stacy's heel with her finger. Stacy's foot jerks away, but she doesn't wake up. Marie goes to the kitchen and pours herself a bowl of Froot Loops. She sits on the balcony, pushing them around with her spoon until the milk turns warm and pinkish. Then she drinks the milk straight from the bowl, leaving the Froot Loops in a mush at the bottom.

Inside, Marie tiptoes to the side of Stacy's bed. She thinks about dumping the soggy Froot Loops onto Stacy's head, but she knows Stacy would never take her to the beach then. So instead, she scoops out a handful of mush and flings it at Stacy's foot.

"I was getting up," Stacy says later, scrubbing the sheet under the faucet, her eyes bloodshot. Marie looks at her. "I was. Swear to God, check my alarm."

Marie helps Stacy hang the sheet on the clothesline stretched across their balcony. They are not supposed to have a clothesline, the same way they are not supposed to smoke in the apartment. But Marie knows that Stacy does, sitting on the counter in the bathroom and blowing smoke out the window above the toilet, a little train of o's that float lazily past Marie's window. The sheet is heavy, and bends the clothesline down so that standing Marie can peek her eleven-year-old head over the top. But sitting in the rusty lawn chairs she is invisible to the world. It is nice to have a bit of privacy, but Marie still thinks it looks suspicious, as if they have something to hide.

2. *Take out your garbage every day*

Stacy goes to take a shower. Marie follows her into the bathroom, sitting on the toilet seat and biting at her fingernails. She likes them short so they are easier to keep clean, especially now that she's not taking showers. A week ago Marie found four spiders in the bathtub at one time. She ran into the kitchen crying, begging Stacy to kill them.

"The spiders eat all the fruit flies," Stacy said. She waved her hand over the garbage can, where a thick cloud of them constantly hovered, sending the cloud directly into Marie's face. Marie screamed and kicked over the garbage can, tipping out its putrid contents: week-old coffee grounds, leftover Beefaroni, empty airplane-sized booze bottles, an unidentifiable lump of furry mould. And four more spiders, crawling among the mess.

Marie gagged. "There wouldn't be any bugs in here if you took out the FUCKING garbage!" she screamed, and Stacy spun around and slapped her across the face with a crack like a cap gun, stunning them both into silence. Marie touched her stinging cheek. Stacy stared at her hand. Then they both started to cry.

Now, Stacy gets out of the shower and stands in the middle of the bathroom, untangling her hair with her fingers. Marie concentrates on her own toenails, sneaking an occasional look out of the corner of her eye at naked Stacy. Marie thinks that Stacy is beautiful, even though she would never tell her that. Not in a million years. But Marie admires the way Stacy's dark, freckly skin clings to her, hugging her bones, rib cage rising and falling, hip bones jutting above a tuft of downy black pubic hair. The C-section scar just below Stacy's belly button, glaring white and puckered on her otherwise perfect stomach.

"Are you having one?"

"What?"

"A shower."

"You know I'm not showering with no damn spiders," Marie mumbles. "Not until you kill them."

Stacy wraps a towel tightly around her head, pulling her scalp so taut her eyebrows look surprised. "You know that killing spiders makes it rain, don't you?" she asks. She doesn't mention the fruit flies.

"I'm not showering with no damn spiders," Marie repeats.

"Fine," says Stacy. "But I don't care how hot it is outside, I'm still not gonna be the one to make it rain."

3. Don't go outside between ten and two

Marie has eaten all of the Froot Loops and there is nothing for lunch. Stacy tries to get her come to the supermarket with her, but if they're not going to the beach then Marie would rather stay home and watch Ricki Lake. She loves the way Ricki's guests talk: you go girl, talk to the hand, I ain't hearing that. When Ricki's guests talk like that, everyone applauds.

Marie tries it on Stacy. "I ain't hearing that, bitch."

Stacy laughs. Then she says, "Who do you think you're talking to? I ain't no bitch." She draws the last word out, so it sounds like bee-atch. "I'll throw a chair at you."

"They don't throw chairs on Ricki Lake," says Marie. "God, don't you know *anything?*"

"And I suppose you know *everything*. That's why you failed grade six math?"

Marie turns back to the TV, rolls her eyes. Who needs math anyway? "At least I know the difference between Ricki Lake and Jerry Springer," she says, rubbing at a patch of dirt on the inside of her ankle. But her ears are burning. Stacy *is* a bitch. Other people's mothers don't make fun of them for failing. Other people's mothers ground them, or make them do summer school. Also, other people's mothers let their kids call them Mom, even in public.

"You wouldn't want me to call you Daughter all the time," she told Marie once.

Not all the time, Marie thought then. Once might be enough.

4. *Drink Lots of Fluids*

When are we going to the beach when are we going to the beach when are we going to the beach WHEN ARE WE GOING TO THE BEACH . . .

In her head, Marie is torturing Stacy, Simpsons-style, a non-stop barrage of whining. But it is already two o'clock, and Stacy is lacing up her sneakers, her ugly, falling apart Zellers sneakers, and then she is dumping the change jar out on the bed, so Marie knows they really are going to the supermarket after all.

"See if you can find any good change, baby," Stacy says, disappearing into the kitchen. By good change she means the silver stuff. Nickels, dimes, quarters. Marie is good at it. Once she even found a loonie, a smooth flat flash of gold in a sea of copper, and they were both so happy they went out and spent the whole thing on penny candy, even though penny candy actually costs a nickel.

This time there is no loonie, but she finds eight quarters, eleven dimes and twenty-three nickels. $4.30 when Marie adds it on her fingers. See, she thinks. I can do math. She cups them in her hand and runs to the kitchen. Stacy is leaning against the counter drinking from a tiny glass bottle, her lips wrapped around the miniature neck like she's a baby sucking on a nipple. It makes a popping sound when she pulls it away.

Stacy stares at Marie. "Damn airplane bottles. Barely nothing in them." Marie steps forward, but her foot catches on the peeling linoleum and she comes tumbling down, eight quarters, eleven dimes and twenty-three nickels spraying everywhere. It sounds like they hit the jackpot. Marie hears every one of them hit the floor.

By the time they are finished picking them up, they have seven quarters, nine dimes and seventeen nickles. Added to the damp clump of fives in Stacy's pocket, they have $18.50. Eighty cents, gone. Sixteen pieces of five cent penny candy.

"It's okay, baby, it's okay," Stacy says as Marie cries, wiping the under-the-refrigerator dust from her hands onto her shorts. "One day we'll find it. That'll be a really fun surprise."

5. Seek out free air conditioning

Stacy makes Marie hold her hand as they walk to the grocery store, all the way up to the Sobey's on North Street even though there are plenty of places to buy food on Gottingen, the market with rows of apples and oranges in wooden bins outside on the sidewalk, the restaurant that smells like spices when you walk by, the Middle Eastern store that sells little bags of nuts that taste like candy. "Four bucks for a couple of lousy nuts," Stacy says, dragging Marie up the hill by her hand.

There is even a place to buy food at the bottom of their apartment building, but Stacy says the people who own it are drug dealers and whores so they are never ever going to shop there. But Marie knows this can't be true, because Jin wears glasses and Olivia is pregnant, and sometimes Olivia even gives Marie things, like an apple or a glass of milk. Pregnant ladies and babies need milk to grow, little one, she says to Marie, and even though Marie is no baby, the two of them stand behind the counter and drink their milk together, comparing milk moustaches afterward before licking their lips clean.

"Did you drink milk when you were pregnant with me?" Marie asks.

Stacy looks at her. "What the hell are you talking about?"

"Nothing," Marie says. Marie knows the real reason they can't shop at Jin and Olivia's is because Jin caught Stacy trying to steal some Tylenol. "Do you think there'll be lots of other kids at the beach?" Marie asks. Stacy doesn't answer.

At Sobey's the first thing they do is go to the freezer aisle and open the door to the ice cream freezer. Stacy lifts Marie up and holds her just inside the door so close to the shelf all she can see is a picture of a giant chocolate ice cream cone. She breathes very slowly, feeling the stale icy air freezing her windpipe on the way down.

"Can we get some chocolate ice cream?"

"Maybe," Stacy murmurs. Marie can feel Stacy's nose pressing against her hair, her strong fingers like bones in her rib cage. Stacy breathes in deeply. "God," she says. "Your hair smells like shit."

Stacy holds her there until Marie starts to shiver, then she puts her down and steps forward, peeling her shirt away from her beautiful belly and holding it up like she is flashing the ice cream. Other people's mothers don't have beautiful smooth bellies like that. Marie watches as she gives a little sigh, the creases on her hard-lined face momentarily melting away, her lips parted in a half-smile.

6. *Keep something cold against your skin*

Stacy pushes the cart very slowly down the aisles, shaking her head at everything Marie wants. She fills the cart with tins of tuna, which are on sale for forty-nine cents, and Marie makes gagging noises.

"I ain't eating no tuna," she says, screwing up her face in disgust.

Stacy looks at her. "You fail English too? You *isn't* eating *any* tuna."

Marie giggles. God Stacy is so stupid. "I *isn't* eating *any* tuna, ok?"

"Yes you are."

"No I'm not."

Stacy grabs her wrist. "Yes you are."

Marie kicks the wheel of the cart. "NO I'M NOT!"

An old lady is staring at them, but Stacy stares back until she scuttles away. "You are eating the goddamn tuna," she hisses.

Marie tries to slip Stacy's grasp. "I'm not eating tuna without cheese."

"Cheese?"

"Yeah. Cheese."

"Cheese? You want cheese? Jesus Christ." Stacy's fingers fumble with the money in her pocket. "I don't have money for cheese."

"I need it." Marie is whining now. "Cheese has milk in it, and pregnant ladies and babies need milk to grow. DO YOU WANT ME NOT TO GROW?"

Stacy sighs, blinking back tears. "We ain't getting no cheese, Marie."

"Don't you mean we *isn't* getting *any* cheese?"

Stacy squeezes her wrist, hard. Then she lets go and starts pushing the cart very fast, so Marie has to run to keep up with her. In the dairy aisle, she stops and pulls a block of cheddar off the shelf, one of the really long ones, and holds it out to Marie.

"Put it in your shirt," she says, looking around. Marie shrinks back. "Put it in your shirt!"

Marie feels like throwing up. "No, you," she says. "You do it."

Stacy looks around. "No. They won't come after you. Just shove it in there and cross your arms."

Marie is shaking. "I don't want it anymore," she says, trying not to cry.

"Jesus Christ, Marie. Everyone steals cheese. Don't be such a baby."

Stacy yanks Marie forward by the bottom of her shirt and shoves the cheese underneath. The coldness against her warm skin makes her gasp, and she shivers as they wait in the checkout line.

After a while though, she gets used to it.

7. *Eat lots of ice cream*

"We forgot to get ice cream," Marie says, out of breath. Even carrying the grocery bags, Stacy has been walking very fast, and Marie has to walk double time to keep up with her.

They stop in front of the vet clinic, waiting for the light to turn. Stacy puts the bags on the ground and presses the cross-walk button. A steady line of cars and trucks creep past them, all horns and exhaust, trying to get to the bridge, get out of town. "We'll get some later, baby," Stacy says, wiping the sweat from her forehead.

"Good," says Marie. She stands behind Stacy and reaches for a piece of her hair. Marie loves Stacy's hair because it is so springy, and you can pull the springs down almost to her bum, and then let them go and they curl right back up like a telephone cord. "Where are we going to get it?" she asks, watching the curl bounce back into place.

"Christ Marie, I don't know." Stacy is bouncing too, her leg vibrating like a motor. She swats Marie away with the back of her hand. "At the beach. We'll get it at the beach."

Marie beams. They really are going to the beach, then. "Do you think there will be a Dickie Dee there?" she asked. "Or, like, a canteen with milkshakes and fries and stuff like that?"

"A canteen, probably," Stacy says. She starts jabbing the crosswalk button over and over again.

"What kind of flavours do you think they'll have? Like, Hoofprints or Cookie Dough, maybe?"

"I don't know, Marie. Maybe." She leans against the crosswalk button. "What the hell is wrong with this light, anyway?"

Behind them, a woman with an armful of blankets is struggling with the door to the clinic. Marie skips over and pulls the door open for her, and sees a little tiny kitten head poking out of the bundle. Marie feels sorry for the kitten, who seems to not even know that she is headed for the doctor, with needles and thermometers and probably all kinds of horrible things. Marie smiles at the woman, and then skips back to Stacy.

"Can we get a kitten?" she asks.

"No."

"Why not?"

"Because kittens turn into cats. And all cats do is eat, sleep and shit. And stink. Just like you." The light changes. "Jesus. Finally." Stacy picks up two of the bags. "Get that other one," she says.

Marie grabs it with both hands. There is a sound like a plastic whisper and then there are cans of tuna rolling down the street, and Marie standing with one broken bag light as a feather.

"Jesus fucking Christ, Marie!" Stacy yells, dropping the other two bags and chasing the tuna. "Stop standing there and help me! What the fuck is wrong with you?"

Marie doesn't move. Through the glass door of the vet clinic, she sees the woman gently unfolding the kitten from its blankets, the kitten stretching and flexing her claws. Even with all the needles and thermometers, at that moment Marie would give anything to trade places with that kitten. Even if she was diagnosed with some horrible disease, even if she was going to have a brain transplant.

Even, thinks Marie, if she was being put to sleep.

8. *Drink lots of fluids*

As soon as they get home Stacy heads for the bathroom. Marie can smell the cigarette smoke drifting under the door, hear the miniature clink of the airplane bottles. Marie goes into her room and pulls out the pail and plastic shovel. She sits down on the couch and waits, absently banging the shovel on the bottom of the pail. After a while, she turns on the TV.

When Stacy finally comes out her eyes are glazed, and she is smiling. "Are you ready for the beach, baby?"

Marie picks at a hole in the couch. "It's four o'clock," she says.

"So?"

"So, what about dinner?"

Stacy leans against the door frame. "We're getting ice cream at the beach, remember?"

"Ice cream isn't dinner."

"Ice cream has milk in it. It helps you grow."

"What do you know about it?" Marie mutters, shuffling to her room and slamming the door. Stupid Stacy. STUPID, UGLY STACY. Other people's mothers don't feed their kids ice cream for dinner. Marie knows this for a fact. Other people's mothers also don't buy stolen cases of airplane booze from gross Jed down the hall and they don't play VLTs all day long instead of going to work. But Stacy doesn't like to hear about other people's mothers. Other people's mothers make Stacy want to puke.

Marie starts digging through piles of laundry on her floor, looking for her bathing suit. She finds it, balled up under the bed, still damp from that day the week before when Marie stood on the balcony and Stacy splashed water on her head from a bucket, "Just like we're in a water park," she'd said. "Just like we're on vacation or something."

Stacy wobbles in while Marie is changing and sits on the edge of her bed. Marie crosses her arms over her chest and turns her back.

"What are you, shy? You got nothing I ain't seen before." Stacy lies back on the bed.

"I know," says Marie. "Now do you mind?" Marie pulls her bathing suit on in one motion, and then puts on a T-shirt and shorts over top. When she turns around, Stacy is asleep on her back, snoring softly, her arms splayed out to either side. Marie sits cross-legged on the bed next to her. "Stacy," she whispers. Stacy grunts and rolls over to her side, her dark eyelashes resting against her cheeks. Marie pulls a coil of her hair away and lets it go, but it just falls flat, bouncing over Stacy's face and across the bridge of her nose.

While Stacy sleeps, Marie takes the elevator down to Jin and Olivia's store. Olivia smiles at her and gives her half of her peanut butter sandwich. "Protein," she says, and they both laugh at the peanut butter sticking to the roofs of their mouths. Olivia lets Marie lay her head against her swollen stomach and listen to the baby swimming around in there. Olivia will be a good mother, Marie thinks as she feels the soft lovely skin against her cheek, Olivia's hand on her back.

Afterward, Marie goes back to her room and lies on her side on the bed next to Stacy. She lifts Stacy's arm carefully and gently lowers it across her own body. She curls into Stacy's warmth, smelling the sweat and the alcohol on her skin, feeling the bones jutting underneath her clothes. Slowly, she reaches her tongue out as far as it will go, and gives Stacy's nose a gentle lick. Her skin tastes like salt and smoke.

An hour later, Stacy wakes up, springing off the bed and knocking Marie off to the side. She starts randomly picking stuff up off the floor. "Why the hell'd you let me sleep?"

Marie rubs her eyes. "You were tired," she says.

9. *Swim wherever you can*

Stacy and Marie take the number-nine bus to the end of the line, Point Pleasant Park. It is nearly eight o'clock. There are still a few tourists around, but the greasers are moving in, their cars lined up around the edges of the parking lot, hoods popped open, men in tank tops carrying brown Tim's cups circling, leaning up, flexing and boasting. The canteen is closed, boarded up, trash cans overflowing with napkins, chip bags, pop bottles.

"It's closed," Marie says. "I told you it would be closed." Marie scoops some sand half-heartedly into her bucket and tips it over. The sand pours back onto the beach in a little pile.

"Never mind," says Stacy. "Let's go swimming."

Stacy sits on a blanket on the sooty beach while Marie, shivering, picks her way through the rotting seaweed and garbage lining the shore, the clang and crash of the container pier and the seagulls squealing overhead. Marie, turning around with tears in her eyes, toes touching the edge of the oily, putrid water, begging *don't make me do this*, and Stacy waving to her, saying "Go ahead, go ahead, it's fine."

"We used to swim here all the time when we were kids," Stacy says, vacant look in her eyes as she pulls a loose thread on her T-shirt. "It was good enough for us then. God."

Afterward they take the bus home, Marie's still-damp legs sticking to the plastic seats. The old man across from her is chewing his bottom lip, his rolls of belly escaping from beneath his grease-stained T-shirt. He catches Marie staring at him and gives her a gummy grin. Marie shivers and looks away, scratching absently at her arm, dredging up a layer of sludge with one ragged fingernail. She examines it: dirt and oil and flakes of dead skin, who knows what else from the harbour. She flicks it out with another nail and it lands on Stacy's lap.

Stacy doesn't notice. She is staring out the window, watching the tourists in their Tilley hats and walking shorts, their arms full of shopping bags from stores Marie has never heard of, taking pictures of the doormen at some hotel sweating in their white shirts and kilts. Stacy stares and stares, her bottom lip drawn under her front teeth, her long, skinny fingers absently picking a scab on her kneecap.

When Marie pokes her, she smiles, but her eyes look like they're ready to punch someone.

10. *Take lots of showers*

When they get off the bus, they walk along the overpass through the Cogswell interchange to get to Brunswick Street, cars ripping past them, Marie's bathing suit chafing between her legs under her damp shorts. The layer of dirt on her skin now feels like it is moving, as if it has come alive, grown a mouth and teeth, and will now proceed to eat her. They ride the elevator with the girls from down the hall, their eyelids painted blue and pink and purple, hair sprayed into helmets, arms loaded down with liquor store bags. Marie presses her back against the elevator wall and tries to pull out her bathing-suit wedgie, but one of the girls catches her. She giggles and whispers to her friend. Stacy puts her hand on Marie's head and then quickly pulls it away.

Back in their apartment, Stacy goes straight to the bathroom. Marie plunks herself down on the couch and turns on the TV, waiting to hear the clink of the bottles, smell the smoke. Instead, she hears the *whoosh* of running water in the tub, and then Stacy is at her side, wrenching Marie from the couch by her wrist.

"Hey," says Marie. "It's time for *Wheel of Fortune*." But she follows Stacy anyway, feeling her thumbnail digging into her skin.

Stacy turns the shower on. "Get in," she says. Marie tries to pull away, but Stacy's grip is strong. "Get in the damn shower, Marie," she says again. She yanks on Marie's arm, and Marie's feet slide across the slick bathroom floor.

"No," whines Marie, trying to dig in her heels.

"Come here!" says Stacy. With her free hand, she reaches for Marie's shirt and attempts to pull it over her head. Marie struggles, and Stacy loses her grip on Marie's arm and trips backwards into the tub. Marie falls, skidding across the bathroom floor on her bum and coming to a stop under the sink. A little black spider scurries down the pipe inches from her face. She starts to cry.

Stacy climbs out of the tub. She is soaked, little droplets of water clinging to her ringlets of hair. She lowers herself to the floor and crawls under the sink next to Marie, reaching her hand out. Marie shrinks back, afraid that Stacy is going to hit her. But instead, Stacy puts her hand up to the pipe and squishes the spider with her thumb.

"Your ass okay?" Stacy asks, flicking the bits of spider from her thumbnail and into the trash.

"You're going to make it rain," Marie says. She wipes her face with the palms of her hands. Immediately her eyes begin to sting.

Stacy shrugs. "Might be an easier way to get you washed," she says.

Marie looks at her hands. "I'll wash," she says. "I'll wash, okay?"

Stacy smiles.

Marie steps in the shower, the water scalding on her burnt skin. She begins to scrub. And scrub. When she runs out of soap, she leaves the water running and searches for a new bar. Under the sink, she spots another spider and, holding her breath, squishes it with her thumb the same way that Stacy did, hoping for rain.

One
Last Thing

J ulia's little sister Joey disappeared on the same night Kurt
Cobain died.

The two events are completely unrelated, of course – Joey
was never really all that interested in music, and Kurt, had he
known Joey, had he known she was gone, would no doubt still
have pressed that gun barrel to his head and pulled the trigger.
Still, they are now inextricably linked in Julia's mind: the death
of a grunge-rock superstar and the disappearance of her spoiled-
brat punk kid-sister occupying the same space on her cerebral
timeline, the thread precariously tying her memories together,
her personal Encyclopedia of Monumental Events, or whatever.
Even now, more than ten years later, Julia hears Nirvana on the
radio and all her muscles tighten. She gets a taste in her mouth
like mouldy socks. She sees Cobain's face on the television
screen, in some Behind the Music biopic-docudrama, in one of
those seemingly endless countdowns of the Twenty Most Influential Rock Albums of Our Time, and she gets nauseous and
thinks of Joey.

And now, there is the phone number. The phone number,
scrawled in frustratingly clear black ink on a balled-up, greasy
napkin weighing stone-heavy in the bottom of her purse, the
phone number that Julia has been carrying around with her for

weeks: to work, to the Y, to the Superstore, to her father's house where she goes every evening to cook his supper and do his laundry and help him to bed.

The phone number that Julia can't bring herself to use but also can't bring herself to throw away.

*   *   *

Julia was two months away from graduating high school, and Joey was fifteen – although if anyone asked, she told them she was eighteen (and could pass for it, with her various rings and studs and such, despite her small frame and short, pixie-hair, her breasts like pebbles under her baggy clothes) – and of an indeterminate grade, having dropped out, then been left back, pushed forward and then left back again, passing through the cracks by her charm, by her big, round, sorrowful eyes, her hidden intelligence, her vulnerability, whatever it was that made everyone – parents, teachers, guidance counsellors – all want to protect her, fiercely, to be the one to *save her*, the infamous Joey McConnell.

At the time Joey disappeared, she may have completed some of grade eight, parts of grade nine, but by grade ten, school was long gone from her list of priorities. Their father drove her there faithfully every morning at nine and, on the days she was grounded, picked her up at three, waited while she finished her smoke at the edge of the school property, tapping his fingers against the steering wheel, nervously humming under his breath to some tune on the radio. Waited for her face in the window, *would you stop that fucking humming* as she threw her bag into the backseat and slammed the door. In the mornings she sulked into the car and in the evenings she sulked in her room, but between nine and three, who knows what she did? Certainly not Julia.

Julia was shopping for a prom dress, of all things. It was too early to even be thinking about, but she knew that half of the girls in her Grade 12 class had already ordered their dresses months ago on shopping trips to Montreal or New York. She also knew her boyfriend Nicky's feelings on proms, that they were "an administrative-level reinforcement of the social hierarchy, *the inherent classism* of our modern-day school system," and even though she said she agreed with him she still closed her eyes and saw herself in light blue silk, sitting at a white cloth-covered table in a room festooned with streamers. And she wanted it – the one thing Julia knew she could have that Joey never would. She wanted spiked punch and awkward photographs. She wanted balloons falling from the ceiling while they danced to "Oh What a Night," up-dos unpinning at the napes of their necks, corsages wilting on their wrists. She wanted to stand teary-eyed at the end of the evening, hugging and promising to *keep in touch, really* – and even though they would know it was a lie, even though they had never cared about each other before, and would never think of each other after, they would, in that one moment, be the Class of 1994, and stand together, and be invincible.

She knew it would never happen. Not like that. For one thing, she went into seven stores and not one of them had anything in light blue silk. At a department store on Spring Garden Road the sales clerk said she might be able to order in light blue *taffeta*, but *lavender is really the colour this year*. At another store, a tight-faced woman wearing bright red lipstick and tottering on sky-high heels stopped her at the door, announcing *we have nothing in your price range, dear* as she looked Julia up and down, taking in her bulky sweater, her patchy jeans, her worn-out Docs. Julia ended up going to see a movie instead, sinking down into the back row as the lights dimmed, losing herself in some boring Meg Ryan cry fest and stuffing her face with stale popcorn. Afterward she wandered into a men's store in Park Lane Mall and bought a light blue silk tie for Nicky, just in case. She called her father from a pay phone, almost as an afterthought.

"Joey's gone," he said. He was trying to be casual, but his voice sounded small, tired. Julia knew he had been cleaning, the way he always did when Joey disappeared – schlepping around

47

the house with his cheery little buckets of Mr. Clean to try to make up for his other failures, to bring his little girl home. "She wasn't there when I went to pick her up at school." He paused. "Can you look for her?"

Julia pressed her head against the edge of the pay phone. She pictured her father standing in their kitchen, red-faced and reeking of bleach, clutching the phone with a rubber-gloved hand. "Yes," she said.

"Thanks." Then her father said, "Oh. I just heard on the news. That singer you like? Cobain? He killed himself today."

*　　*　　*

Joey had run away several times before, but she always came home. Julia and Nicky would go look for her, behind downtown dumpsters and in friends' backyards, in parkades and storage units, in dives that passed for underage clubs, in the bathrooms of dirty coffee shops. When they found her, they would clean her up as best they could and drive her home in Nicky's mother's car – spread out on the back seat, on Nicky's A&W uniform in case she threw up – and sometimes she was all unfocused eyes and limp hands and she came with them silently and other times she was hellfire and kicked and screamed and pummelled them with her little fists, or she would pummel *herself*, pull her hair, bang her head against the window in the back seat, claw her legs until they bled. When she turned on herself, that was always the worst.

Now, Julia wonders if Joey remembers these things. She must remember: the back seat of Nicky's car where she pressed her face those nights, the dull grey of the musty upholstery, the crumbs caked in the ripping seams, the stale smell of the innards puffing out through the holes, the empty pop bottles rolling around on the floor. How pathetic their father looked when they brought her home, smiling hopefully through the back door as Julia hauled Joey's body up the steps, trying to hide his horror at her dirty hair, her bloodshot eyes, her cuts and bruises. How he held her while she cried, said she was sorry. Because she always did. Joey always did say she was sorry.

But there *are* things that Joey never knew. How Julia and Nicky fought, how he told her Joey was manipulative and spoiled and worthless, how he wouldn't say these things exactly but Julia would hear them, and she would defend her – Joey was her kid sister, and she knew well enough the things she had been through because Julia had been through them with her, the loneliness and the nightmares, the tension in the house, the months on end the three of them would go without speaking to each other. How their father came into Julia's room one night, drunk, and told her he had dreams about killing Joey, how he dreamed about her blood on the kitchen floor and he didn't know if he could live with himself because of it.

How Julia would lie in bed late at night and feel the music thumping up through the walls from the basement, music Joey didn't even understand, music that was just background noise in whatever scene she was playing out in her head. Julia would hear Joey's laughter, her friends' laughter, and imagine a room full of smoke and noise and Joey, with her feet propped up on the coffee table, her little ears heavy with silver, her little mouth twitching, her fingers dancing across the tattooed forearm of some beautiful, fucked-up boy, her glazed eyes like slits as she leaned towards him in the darkness.

How Julia would lie there those nights, staring at the wall, and wish she could be more like her sister.

*   *   *

Julia tried The Sty first, the most likely place, that café on Blowers Street with the sludge for coffee, all dirty floors and nicotine-stained walls. Julia and Nicky had met at The Sty – had sat together beneath the electric glow of the fire exit sign, drawing pictures of one another on coffee-stained napkins – but that was years earlier, when Halifax was going to be the next Seattle, when even The Sty had live bands playing every night.

Now The Sty was just a bleak room full of look-alike punks with their brand new Etnies propped up against their skate decks under the tables, rolling cigarettes from butts fished from the ashtray – while Uri, the owner, sat silently behind the counter watching CNN. Uri was from Albania and as long as the kids bought his coffee and didn't smoke their dope inside, he left them alone.

"What does your sister look like?" Uri asked Julia, still watching the TV as he poured thick black liquid into a paper cup and passed it across the counter.

"Short black hair," she said, fiddling with a stir stick. "Not very tall. A ring through here, and here." She pointed to her eyebrow, then to her lip.

He stared at her. "You're kidding me, right? Your sister, she is every girl in this place."

So Julia took her coffee and went to call Nicky. The phone was in the basement next to the bathrooms, where exposed pipes leaked drops of rusty water onto the cracked tile floor. On the wall behind the phone, someone had scrawled KILL THE PIGS in what appeared to be blue crayon, accompanied by a crude drawing involving a naked woman and a spectacularly well-endowed dog. Upstairs, the music abruptly changed from punk to Cobain's crunching guitar.

"Are they playing Nirvana?" Nicky asked. His already-thin voice shot up an octave. "What fucking right do they have playing Nirvana?"

What else should I be, all apologies, Kurt sang.

Julia rubbed her sleeve across her nose. "I'm sorry," she said.

"I can't fucking believe this," said Nicky. "This should be a national day of mourning."

But he came anyway – dark and angry, his bony, indie-boy hands shaking on the steering wheel. He parked his car behind The Sty and they walked together up Blowers Street and around Pizza Corner, where a group of people were standing around, giant pizzas slices sliding off greasy paper plates. "This is such fucking bullshit, Julia," Nicky said over and over as they passed in front of the library, watching the little gangs of middle-class teenagers mingling on the lawn with the drunks and the drug dealers, occasionally riding their boards down the patchy strip of concrete or grinding the rail on the edge of the library steps. On the sidewalk, someone had written WE LOVE YOU KERT in spray paint, yellow letters bleeding across the grey.

"There's your national day of mourning," Julia said.

Nicky snorted. "It's just a fucking excuse," he said. "These snivelling, whiny little brats need to justify their own feelings of self-loathing. As if Daddy not letting them stay out late and fuck around at The Sty for hours could compare at all to, well, what can only really be called *the pain of Kurt's genius*, you know?" He rubbed his hands together. "I have a confession to make, Julia. I think I really just hate people."

"I have a confession to make, too," said Julia. "I want to go to the prom."

Nicky kicked at a pop can lying in the middle of the sidewalk. "Very funny."

It was cold for April and all those season-pushers in their flip-flops and bare legs were regretting it, arms crossed around shivering bodies as they passed them, Julia with her hat and mittens, Nicky still in his winter parka, shuffling along without looking at each other because they didn't know what else to do. In Victoria Park they watched while a girl pierced another girl's nose using a safety pin and some ice chips out of a Dairy Queen cup, her friends laughing as she cried out, a bright red bloom of blood growing around the hole.

"Idiots," Nicky said under his breath, but Julia went over anyway and asked if they knew Joey. The girl with the nose ring said she knew one of Joey's old boyfriends – who could have been any number of smelly, mohawked skater boys who slept in their basement and stole their father's liquor, who Joey would turn around and accuse of beating her or raping her when they eventually realized she was too much for them to handle and tried to leave her.

"Ben Greer," she said. "But I haven't seen him in ages, haven't seen Joey either."

"I saw him," one of the other girls said. "Behind St. David's. He looks like shit, if you ask me."

"No one did," the third girl said, the one who had done the piercing. "So fuck off."

"Your nose ring looks cool," Julia told the first girl, even though it looked hideous.

"Fucking right," she said, blood dripping from her nostril. "It's for Kurt, you know."

So Julia and Nicky walked back down Spring Garden towards the church, Nicky still talking fast and breathless, his eyes bright with rage. "The thing not experienced," he said. "It *negates the thing experienced.* For instance, I could say that I wanted to try drugs in order to experience it, to see for myself what it was like, to go through what Kurt went through. But by having that experience, I would be negating the experience of *not* having tried drugs. So, I'm thinking, okay, maybe there is some grand, beautiful secret shared by everyone who's tried drugs. But there could just as easily be a grand, beautiful secret shared by those of us who haven't." He took Julia's hand. "The world is caving in on us, Julia. *Do you understand what I'm saying?*"

"Yes," she said, and folded her other hand over his, warming his delicate bare skin between her wool mittens. She always said yes, and that's why Nicky kept talking, why he slid every thought he ever had out of his brain and into the space between them. But Julia didn't care. So what? So what if maybe he was an arrogant prick obsessed with the sound of his own voice? He was there with her, then, with his cold hands, with his hollow face and his thin, lispy voice, with his little mouth that never stopped moving, his frailty, his unabashed, unending need to be understood. He was there. That was all.

*   *   *

Julia has questions, too – mainly: what is it about teenage girls? She was one herself, once, of course, but even then she couldn't understand the changes she went through. What happens in their brains, at puberty, that makes them hate the people who love them, that makes them want to destroy their own perfect growing bodies, that makes them want to scream obscenities at the world? What part of this is hard-wired – little minds like mush, awash with some dangerous chemical cocktail, absorbing too much too soon? What part of it is *society*, that lets them grow up so quickly, without any clue where they are going, with its pressures and politics and mixed messages etc.?

Could it be rock music, movies, video-game sex-and-violence? Could it be TV? Did they let Joey watch too many commercials that told her to hateyourselfbuyoursoftdrinklove yourself?

Or, was it really *them*? Their mother and father?

Was it her? Was it Julia? She doesn't even want to think about it.

Julia is not only bitter. She hasn't forgotten. She remembers the games they played as kids, the summer afternoons of popsicles and bicycles, Joey and Julia in bare feet and bathing suits at the splash pool on the Commons, the times they slept together in the same bed when Joey had nightmares. She would crawl under the covers next to Julia with her eyes wide and clear, and whisper her dreams into Julia's ear in her calm, oddly detached way: men with broken bones chasing her up and down staircases that never ended, insects as big as cars climbing on top of her in bed, dolls with limbs that grew long and ropey and wrapped themselves around her neck. Julia remembers Joey's cold little feet on those nights, the way she would creep her toes up Julia's leg, under her pajamas, her toenails scraping razor sharp against Julia's skin as she talked and talked, the way she shivered even in the summer, her baby breath on Julia's neck when she finally fell back to sleep.

What gave Joey those nightmares, Julia wants to know. Their house was always warm and full of love. Their childhood was all Frosted Flakes and Saturday morning cartoons, backyard skating rinks and living-room couch forts. Their mother walked them to school in the morning and let them pick flowers from the neighbours' gardens when no one was looking. Their father told them bedtime stories about superheroes named Julia and Joey who saved the world from evil night after night. Together their parents danced in the kitchen on Saturday nights to Johnny Cash while the girls made Jiffy Pop on the stove, the sound of the shaking corn kernels and the aluminum tray scraping against the element in time with the music, their mother beautiful in her moccasins and jeans, gliding across the kitchen with her small hands twisting in the air, their father's soft grey eyes always following her, crinkling at the corners as he watched her.

Then one day she just wasn't there anymore. In the weeks after, Joey and Julia both cried when their father did, because it hurt them so much to see him sad. Was he ever happy after that? Julia doesn't know. She knows he slept every night in the den on that leather loveseat instead of his bed. She knows he made them eggs-in-a-basket on Sunday mornings, the smell of frying butter and sunlight coming in through the kitchen window. She knows he helped them build castles out of Lego. She knows he was proud in the front row of every school play. She knows one year on Easter he gave them real, live bunnies – tiny bundles of white fur and long velvet ears and twitchy pink noses – and cleaned out their cages when the novelty wore off and Joey and Julia forgot all about them.

When Julia was older, she overheard a neighbour talking about their mother: how their father had dropped Julia and Joey off at a birthday party and came home to find his wife's closet empty. At least she waited until those girls were out of the house, the neighbour said. At least they didn't have to see. But Julia doesn't remember any birthday party, and part of her thinks it was a lie – they were there all along, in the next room, playing quietly with their stuffed animals, oblivious to their mother quietly packing her life up into a suitcase, taking inventory of the house she had lived in for more than a dozen years, maybe standing in the doorway of their room, watching her daughters play for the very last time. They could have looked up at any moment and seen her, seen her there with her suitcase in her hand and looked at her with the innocence and guilelessness that Julia knows they surely must have possessed at one point in time, and said something, said "Can Teddy ride in your suitcase?" or "Are you all packed up for our trip to the moon?" and that would be it, the one thing, *the one right thing* they could have said that would have made her put down her bags, that would have made her rush into their room and sweep them up into her arms and kiss their soft baby-hair and swear to never, ever leave them. Ever.

But they didn't. And she left. And Julia still doesn't know why.

Who else is she supposed to talk about this with? Who, goddamn it?

*   *   *

Ben Greer. Julia knows Joey must remember Ben. The one their father threw out of the basement in a rare moment of assertiveness – sick of the dirty-sock smell of him permeating the house, sick of the smoke detector going off at three in the morning, sick of Ben fucking his daughter. Ben didn't argue. He just packed up his knapsack slowly while Joey screamed obscenities. *You fucking hypocrite. You stupid. Pathetic. Drunk. Fuck. The only fucking thing in the world I care about. You. Hate. Me. You're. Fucking. Killing. Me.*

Maybe Joey didn't know Julia was there, sitting at the top of the basement steps where she could see everything. Their father, crossing his arms, clenching his teeth, grinding his brow together to keep from giving in. Joey, with her hands in her hair, face blotchy and red as she screamed and screamed. Ben, slinging his backpack over his shoulder and slinking out the door. Joey, driving her fist into the storage room door. The sick crack of her hand splintering. Joey, collapsing on the floor, screams dissolving into animal moans: low, feral, *rabid*. Their father, leaning over and vomiting on the dirty basement carpet.

Julia could hardly blame Ben for not looking back.

There is still a mark there on the storage room door, a small, half-moon shaped dent made in the wood by one of Joey's rings. Julia sees it every time she goes into the basement to bring up the wood to feed her father's ageing Franklin stove. Once Julia pressed her own fist against it, resting her knuckles against the spot where Joey's had connected all those years ago, and wondered, for a brief second, if Joey could still feel that wood against her fist. These thoughts of a real live, talking, breathing *now-Joey* come to Julia sometimes, before she has a chance to push them out, more clear to her than her memories of *then-Joey*. Even though, until a few weeks ago, *now-Joey* didn't even really exist.

*   *   *

In the dark behind St. David's, people moved like shadows around the edges of the parking lot – Julia and Nicky couldn't see them but they felt them watching as they passed. There was something darker there than on the other side of the library, where the kids only played at rebellion, and then went home to watch *My So-Called Life* and go to sleep under their IKEA bedspreads. Julia had been there before but Nicky hadn't, and she could still feel his hands shaking even though they weren't touching. "What the fuck are we doing here, Julia?" he was whispering. "Ben and Joey haven't seen each other in a long time, it's not like he's going to know . . ."

Julia elbowed him. "Just shut up, Nicky," she said.

And then there he was, Ben Greer, propped up against a doorway, smoking a joint. Ben with his shaved head, his raw knuckles, eyes defiant in the yellow glow of the security light. "Jesus," he said when he saw them. "Julia McConnell. I thought I was hallucinating." He held the joint out to her. "Toke?"

Julia shook her head. Ben flicked the joint onto the pavement and spat, rearranging his face back into a scowl as he fished a flask out of his jacket. Movie tough-guy that Ben was, all grime and attitude, but so pretty underneath, his smooth skin, his heavy-lidded eyes. And Julia remembered how he withered under Joey's glare – he would have licked her feet if she had asked him, would have flung himself from a rooftop.

"Do you know where Joey is?" Julia asked him.

"Fucking cunt," Ben said. "I don't give a fuck where she is." But Julia knew he was lying by the awkward way he rested his hand against the wall above his head. Didn't he know that he was just one in a long line of boys, all willing to fall on their knees and take Joey's abuse? Didn't he know that he could have been anybody?

"Yes you do," she said. "Just tell me where she is."

Ben smiled, lighting a cigarette. "You know, there's a lot of shit I could say about Joey." He exhaled. "But one thing's for sure, that little bitch fucked like an animal." Julia clenched her fists as Ben looked her up and down. "Bet you do, too."

Then Nicky was there, stepping out from the shadows, saying "what the fuck, man" in his little, lispy voice. Ben laughed and he stepped forward, put his face close to Nicky's, and Julia could see his sunken cheeks, his wrists thin as a child's, and she realized for all of Ben's arrogance he really was just a child, just a punk kid, and even though he grunted and snarled, *he knew it*. Julia hated him then, him and all his stupid, sneering friends, and she hated little, ineffectual Nicky hiding behind her, consumed by his own contempt for everything. She hated their father, vacuuming the same spot on the carpet over and over again and pretending nothing was wrong, and she hated their mother and all of her thousands of new possible lives, each one bright and shiny as a newly-minted penny in Julia's imagination.

And most of all, *most of all*, Julia hated Joey.

"You little shit," Ben said, grinning. "You don't even know what to do with her, do you?" He spat on the ground and that was when Nicky hit him, while his neck was bent, so that his head jerked back with the force of the blow. Julia had never seen Nicky hit anyone before. She didn't even know that he was capable of it. He took a step back and clutched his fist in his other hand, staring at it as though he didn't know he was capable of it either. Julia looked at Ben and saw his eyes were dull, unsurprised. He rubbed his jaw with one hand and flung the other out towards Nicky, almost as an afterthought, and Nicky fell to the ground with an obscene-sounding grunt, blood burbling from somewhere, his nose or maybe his mouth. Julia watched his eyes roll, and then close.

"Hell's Hotel," Ben said, walking away. Calling over his shoulder: "May she fucking rot there."

*   *   *

I can't tell this story anymore. Not like this. Let me try again.

You ran away, Joey. You ran away and I went to find you, my boyfriend and I (who never actually forgave me for the dark places I took him, and who left me shortly after, in case you didn't know, Joey, left me and moved to Toronto, where the *world doesn't cave in on him*, where a person could be lost and lost forever); we searched for you the same way we had done in a million other similar stories, a journey that was mapped out in the skin cells on the backs of our necks, steps ingrained in the muscular memory of our calves. Except this story doesn't end like the others – with us dragging you home by the proverbial collar, our fingernails digging into your arms, trying to hold onto you until we finally had to let you go and *you ran*, you ran away and away and away.

No.

This time, we never found you. No happy ending, *no ending at all* if you think about it: we kept looking, it's true, we looked and looked. But gradually the looking slowed – we slept in between, ate lunches, went to school, went to work, met people, ran errands, moved away, got degrees, traveled the world. Even still, we would find our heads turning to look down every dark alleyway, or we would catch a flash of silver out of the corner of our eyes, breathe in a familiar scent in a crowded store, recognize the same slope of your nose on a stranger's face. It's true. The looking slowed, but it never really stopped.

Until. Over ten years later. Sitting at home with my father – *our* father, Joey, the one I couldn't ever bring myself to leave, not after everyone, *everyone* else had, whose loneliness I could never even make a dent in, whose disinfectants, in the end, did nothing but disinfect – eating a butter tart and checking the lottery numbers on the old computer Dad never bothered to replace.

I get an email from Nicky, who I hadn't heard from in years. *Julia. I saw her.*

Followed by ten digits, which I scrawled, without thinking about it, across the greasy, pastry-stained napkin sitting on my lap, in frustratingly clear black ink, butter tart unchewed in my wide-open mouth, watched as the pen formed the numbers seemingly on its own, indelible, tangible, *real* numbers screaming up at me: Joey, Joey, Joey.

Joey.

*   *   *

One last thing. What if it had been different? What if the story had an end? What if I told you I left Nicky there, bleeding on the ground, and ran out of the parking lot, feet flying over pavement to the place I knew I would finally find you? What if I told you that on the night of April 8, 1994, the night Kurt Cobain died, I stood in front of Hell's Hotel – that falling-down shit-hole squat on the corner full of rats and their human equivalents that some jacked-up crackhead would eventually burn to the ground – and looked up into one of the shattered windows, splintered from the centre like a sunburst, and saw your face, fragmented, broken up by the glinting shards of glass, your eyes dull and vacant, looking down on me? What if I told you I knew, somehow, with every ounce of blood, every fragment of bone in my body, that if I left you there, we would lose you for good, and yet still I did it, what I believed everyone always wanted me to do, really, all along? What if I told you I saw you, and left you there? What if I told you that I just couldn't do it anymore, that whatever it was – I was too tired, too lazy, too selfish – I couldn't bring myself to take you back one more time, to try to find the one right thing to say to you to make you stay?

What if I told you I heard Kurt singing then, through the blown speakers of some shitty car stereo – *bruises on the fruit, tender age in bloom* – and I was glad that he was dead?

Places to Drink Outside in Halifax

Not many people know how a cemetery looks in the dark. But Abby does. She knows how the sky turns purple, how the moon looks like an orange. How the headlights from the cars on the road outside shatter through the heavy wrought iron fence and heave into sky. She knows the tombstones look almost fake, as if they were props in a play: Styrofoam cut-outs painted with grey acrylic, sitting on bright green tissue-paper grass. How the Keith monument stands high and mighty, pointing at the sky like a giant middle finger rising out of the mess below.

That mess. It is all wrong. Abby is drunk and indignant. Her head bobbing as she surveys the beer cans strewn all around the base of the monument. You're supposed to drink the beer and then place the can *carefully* at the base of the monument, or if there's room, find a place on the ledge. You kiss the rim of the can or stick a flower in the mouth of the can, roses or daisies or whatever, or if you can't find any flowers you can use leaves or twigs, things lying on the ground. That is what you are supposed to do to honour Mr. Alexander Keith, on his birthday.

Abby has never done this before, but she knows it is all wrong. She knows because Norah told her, and Norah Singh is her finger-pricking, secret-sharing, til-death-do-us-part best friend. They've only been in high school a few weeks and already Norah knows the rules. While Abby hides at the back of her classes – hunched over her desk, trying to tuck in her too-long edges and scowling at the backs of people's heads – there is Norah, smiling at the front of the classroom, chewing on her hair, squeaking away in that piercing, nasal voice that reminds Abby of a cartoon parrot, knowing all the answers and generally being her own annoying Norah self. Then suddenly Norah is sitting with Kelly Lipman in the cafeteria, Norah is playing cards in the hallway with Sarah LeBlanc, Norah is going to football games, Norah is hanging out in the bathroom at the high school dance, Norah is Norah is Norah is.

Norah is invited to Alexander Keith's birthday party.

"Come with me," she said to Abby, that afternoon on their way home from school. "It'll be fun. We can have a sleepover after, sleep out on the trampoline." She jumped in the air, brandished her finger guns, the way she always did when she was trying to talk Abby into something. Like a little brown Annie Oakley. Bang bang.

"I don't want to get drunk," Abby said.

"You're going to get drunk eventually," said Norah, grinning. "Don't you want your first time to be with me?"

Getting drunk is the thing to do in high school. Everyone knows that. Over the summer, Norah and Abby were both excited for high school. Abby would sneak Norah through the staff gate at the Waegwoltic Club, where she worked in the canteen. They'd sit on the grass outside the tennis courts eating french fries and looking down the hill to the lido at the edge of the shore, and beyond that to the boathouse jetties and the sailing kids in their bright orange life jackets rigging up their lasers and pretending to push each other into the harbour, which was so full of raw sewage that on warm days the smell fogged over the whole place. Abby and Norah would watch the high school girls in their bikinis, tanned and blonde as they stretched out on towels around the lido deck, flirting with the cute sailing instructors in board shorts and expensive sunglasses cannon-balling into the pool to show off. It all seemed so bright and sunny, so promising, so different from junior high, where every-one was so stuck-up and immature. In high school, Norah told Abby, they might even get boyfriends.

"I'm going to have me two or three of those," Norah would say after every cute-sailing-instructor cannonball, shoving a french fry lengthwise under her upper lip like a retainer. "Yep, two or three." Abby would laugh so hard that her Coke fizzed up her nose, and she would think that one was probably enough for her, as long as he was kind and maybe had a car.

But in the first week of school, Abby learned her first lesson: that all the cute sailing instructors were potheads and all the pretty girls were mean. Now she thinks high school is a dark and dirty place, full of crowds of loud, leering kids with backpacks slung low on their backs, denim jackets and plaid shirts pulled around them like armour, laughing at inside jokes meant for her to never understand.

What Abby does understand, however, is the way to honour Mr. Alexander Keith, former mayor of Halifax, friend to rich and poor, and above all, brewer of fine ale, or what Abby assumes must be fine ale, as it is the only ale she has ever tasted, and only this time, here to honour Mr. Alexander Keith on his birthday. At this particular moment, Abby loves Mr. Alexander Keith more than anything, and she is disgusted by the cans on the ground. She also feels very sorry for all the other people bur-ied in the graveyard. Most of the graves are so old, no one even knows who the people are anymore. Like Mr. John Foster, Beloved Husband, who Died in 1890. Why, thinks Abby, does-n't Mr. John Foster get any beer cans?

There are about thirty kids in the cemetery. All standing around in little groups. Abby wonders why no one cares that they are there. Norah is sitting on the ground a few steps away, eating pizza. She grins at Abby, cheese sticking to her lip, tomato sauce on her teeth. God, she is gross.

"Nice, Norah," says Abby.

Norah, standing up, stretches her arms towards Abby. "Come here, have some pizza," she says, opening her mouth wide.

"Gross," shrieks Abby. She puts out her hands to stop her. Squeezing her eyes shut in anticipation of the Attack of the Cheese.

Then a boy named Angus with huge curly hair steps between them, saying "I'll have some of that." Angus is a grade ahead of them, and plays hockey, a fact he advertises proudly to anyone he meets: "Hi, my name's Angus and I play hockey." Abby wonders how he fits a helmet over his hair.

Angus comes at Norah with arms extended. Norah sticks out her tongue and Angus chases her around the graves while other people watch and laugh and cheer "Go Angus, go Angus, get her Angus." Angus reminds Abby of one of the sailing instructors at the Waeg, the one who would climb out onto one of the jetties and cannonball right into the Northwest Arm, all the girls shrieking with horror as he chased them around the lido, arms dripping with toxic sludge.

Abby sits down on Mr. Foster's grave and crosses her arms and wonders why Norah is so popular. She's not even very pretty, and she dresses weird, not like the other kids in their Nikes and ski jackets. She's always in long skirts with leggings underneath them, big black boots with different coloured laces. She doesn't play sports and she's smart in math, and she spends every Saturday night playing cards with her *mata*. It must be the trampoline, thinks Abby, taking a drink of her beer. Everyone likes her trampoline. Or maybe it's the nose ring. Nobody else in their high school has a nose ring, and Norah's had hers since she was a baby, so it's not even like she got it just to be cool.

Angus catches Norah around her waist, swinging her off the ground. His hair bounces and sways as if it was an entity all its own – a sea anemone muckled on to his head. Norah kicks her legs against his shins and he lets go, cursing.

All the girls are standing in a circle near the path and they turn their ponytailed heads and blow cigarette smoke through strawberry-glossed lips. "Nice work, Norah," says Sarah LeBlanc, her voice low and scratchy, authoritative. Stupid Sarah

LeBlanc, with her stupid French name that isn't even French, that she pronounces Le Blank. Le Nothing. The other girls are faking, thinks Abby. Copying the way she crosses her left arm in front of her, rests her right elbow there as she smokes. Copying her whatever expression.

"Yeah, Norah," says Michelle Hennigar, her voice higher, sugar-coated. "Come over here and have a smoke with us." Stupid Michelle Hennigar, with her fake tan that looks orange, that everyone knows is a fake tan.

Norah jumps in the air and brandishes her finger guns. Bang bang. The girls dissolve into giggles. "You're fucking crazy," says Sarah.

"Yup," says Norah. She wiggles her butt like a girl in a rap video, her long skirt swish-swishing from side to side. Why, thinks Abby, her face turning red. Why are you doing this now? They used to practice that in the mirror, as a joke. The girls are laughing, though. They think it's hilarious.

Abby gets up off of Mr. Foster's grave and crosses to the pile of empty beer cans. She picks one up. Then another. They keep falling out of her arms but she keeps picking them up again. Abby really likes the cans. They are green and have a picture of a moose or something on the front. Alexander Keith must have drawn that, she thinks.

"Who is that?" asks Kelly Lipman. Abby pretends not to hear her. Stupid Kelly Lipman, star-fucking-basketball-player, with that stupid short boy hair cut.

"This is Abby," says Norah. She grabs Abby's arm. Don't touch me, thinks Abby, staring at the ground. Donttouchme donttouchmedonttouchme. "Come on, Abby. Let's have a smoke."

"You don't smoke," says Abby, staring at her.

"I might want to have one though," Norah pokes her in the ribs. "Lighten up, baby."

Abby watches as Kelly opens her pack of cigarettes and holds it out to Norah. Norah takes one in her mouth, letting it dangle from one corner. Kelly flicks her lighter and holds it to the end. Norah inhales. She looks weird. Like the way a horse or a dog would look with a cigarette.

"Abby," Norah says, "Abby . . ." She pulls another cigarette from the pack and waves it in front of Abby's face. "Want one?"

Abby is reeling. Feeling sick. She looks down at her legs, stick-thin and knobby-kneed, and suddenly thinks that some day she will be beautiful. She is already tall, and she knows her blonde hair will grow longer, her breasts will get bigger, her face will fill out. Not like Norah, with her coarse dark hair and thick dark eyebrows, who will always be short and squat. This thought comforts Abby. She takes the cigarette from Norah.

"Right on, Abby," says Drea Meisner sarcastically. "Way to be a badass." Stupid Drea Meisner, with her perfect curly hair, with her stupid last year's ski passes dangling from her zipper.

Abby stares at Drea. She opens her mouth and slowly stuffs the cigarette inside. The tobacco is dry and tastes like window cleaner, but Abby chews it anyway, until the cigarette is a sticky blob in her mouth, the paper sticking to the roof of her mouth, her teeth bouncing apart on the filter. Then she opens her mouth and lets the mess fall from her tongue onto the ground. All the girls shriek and pretend to make vomiting noises, but Abby doesn't look at them, she just walks back over to her pile of cans and resumes her cleanup.

"What a fucking freak," she hears Sarah say. The other girls mumble agreement, choking on little huff-huff noises in the back of their throats.

"Abby, what are you doing?" asks Norah Singh. Stupid Norah Singh, with her stupid nose ring and stupid trampoline and her thick eyebrows. "Abby, baby, come back."

Abby ignores her, starts placing the beer cans along the edge of the monument. When she runs out of room on the monument, she moves on to the other graves, placing the cans at the base of the headstones like flowers. They all look so unloved, these graves of people who died so long ago no one even remembers them. They deserve cans, too. She places one on Mr. Foster's grave, and gives it a little pat. She can hear the snickering but she doesn't care. She knows Norah is watching her. Abby tries to send her telepathic thoughts. This is me, she thinks. This is me, Norah! She tries to balance the cans but they keep falling. It's like the bottoms are rounded, uneven. She picks them up and they fall again, and again, and suddenly in front of her eyes there are bright lights, spots spinning around and around and then Abby herself is falling, head full of hate and misery. Then she is retching, puking into the grass, her eyes welling up with tears, the grass flattening under the weight of her vomit. Oh please God, she thinks, let this all be over.

Then Norah is there, whispering something in her ear. "Abby," she says, "Abby, are you okay?" She pushes Abby's hair out of her eyes.

Abby spits on the ground. "I guess," she says.

Norah surveys the mess. "You must have had the pepperoni pizza," she says.

"Gross, Norah," Abby says. She rests her head against the gravestone. She thinks back to when she and Norah were younger, when they used to pretend to be different people every time they left the house. Norah would be an exchange student from England, Norah with her terrible British accent, and Abby would be the daughter of a rock star. Once they even pretended they were blind. Put Band-Aids over their eyes under dark sunglasses, stumbling around, bumping into everything, laughing like their sides would split. I want to go back, she thinks. But she can't say it. She traces a finger along the names on the gravestone. Mary and George McLaughlin, Died 1875, May God Watch Over You. "I just wanted them to have some cans, too," she says.

"Sure," says Norah. "Why should Alexander Keith get all the trash?" She takes a can and sticks it upside down in the pile of vomit.

Then, suddenly, the cemetery explodes with light. Frenzied kids pop up from the ground, flying between the gravestones in twos and threes, people yelling, loud voices and dogs barking. And Abby and Norah are running. Norah drags Abby by the hand along the gravel path and out of the graveyard, past the gates of the Public Gardens, past the CBC building with its digital sign flashing 11:14, 10°, CBC, 11:14, 10°, CBC. Abby's stomach churning, Norah grinning, her dark hair flying out behind her like a superhero's cape, her army boots making a clack-clack sound on the pavement, running around the edge of Citadel Hill and down Sackville Street, picking up speed as they soar down the hill through downtown Halifax, past the people in the window at Tim Horton's, past the grown-ups drinking out-side, on patios, their faces hazy and serious and old. Past the old boarded-up Tex-Park, across Lower Water Street, around the wave sculpture licking the sky like a giant tongue, and onto the pier, across the weathered boards that bounce and shake with every step, running until they reach the end, until they have nowhere else to go. They stop, breathless, looking out over the harbour glistening with lights from the buildings on the Dartmouth side, the water slick with oil and seaweed and sludge. Abby can still feel her feet flying, can still see the faces of the grown-ups sitting on the patios, but everything else is gone, is a blur, and when she touches her face she is surprised to feel her cheeks wet with tears.

Norah laughs and squeezes her hand. Abby turns around and looks up the hill, trying to take in the distance, knowing she really doesn't want to go back. She breathes in deeply, feeling the salty air stinging the inside of her nose, smelling the rain and the garbage and the rust from the bottoms of the ships, the rats and the fish and the silence.

Abby and Norah look at each other. They don't say a word. They just close their eyes and jump.

Miriam Beachwalker

After hours of thinking and walking, walking and thinking, Miriam Townsend has made up her mind. She is going to run away from home. This isn't a whim, something born of anger or disappointment, run-of-the-mill teenage angst or anything like that. Miriam is going to leave because she wants to have a dream, and because she knows that people in her town think she is A Loser Just Like Her Brothers. And because she knows she will never go to college. Even though her mother says, "Oh Miriam, you're so smart!" Miriam knows she doesn't mean college-smart. At best she means finish-high-school-smart. Not like Ricky and Damon, who both dropped out in grade ten. Certainly not like Jason, who has never seen the inside of a classroom in his life.

So it's very important that Miriam think things out, because a dream that just sits around in your closet and never comes out will eventually rot and stink up the place, and when you finally dig it out it is so gross and deformed that you don't even want to touch it. Or something like that, Miriam doesn't exactly remember, but she's sure she read it on a greeting card once.

*   *   *

Saturday morning, like every Saturday morning, Miriam looks out across the beach, its stubbly contours disappearing into the fog. It is late September and she is in her bare feet walking along the edge of the frigid ocean, looking at the ground. She feels the undertow pull the sand between her frozen toes, watches the pebbles make little rivers like v's behind them as the waves haul themselves back into the ocean.

Up further on the sand, just below the dunes, the Beach-walkers are huffing and puffing along, all big hats and fanny packs, sneakers, men and ladies too old and fat to use a treadmill. Miriam ignores them. Miriam hates the Beachwalkers. She thinks they are ridiculous, and they don't belong at her beach. Also, Dr. Wallace created the Beachwalkers, which is another reason Miriam hates them. He put up signs all over town, at the community centre, at the Pharmasave, at Cormier's Garage: Walk Your Way To Better Health! Lower Your Blood Pressure The Drug-Free Way! Miriam doubts if Dr. Wallace is even a real doctor. Someday, when she is a Poet-Singer-Reporter, she will investigate, expose him as a quack. After all, it was Dr. Wallace who told them that Jason was autistic. But Miriam knows he's wrong. At the library at school she looked up autism and it said that autistic children are "lacking in social skills." But Jason can't even talk, can't even aim his pee into the toilet when he goes to the bathroom. Miriam makes a note in her book, right under her list of potential dreams: *research Dr. Wallace's credentials.*

The three things on her list of potential dreams are: Poet, Singer and Reporter (not the kind that sits behind the desk on TV, but a real *investigative journalist* like the guy who stood out-side on the waterfront during the hurricane, shouting over the wind and rain and really suffering to bring you the whole, true story). These are real dreams, the kind that people sweat and cry over; Miriam knows a dream has to make you cry or else it wouldn't be a dream, but something else, something like what the guidance counselor calls a *career path.* Secretary school, call centres, auto mechanics: these are not dreams.

Halfway along the beach, Miriam sits down in the sand and opens her notebook again. Her plan is almost complete: steal cash from Ricky and Damon's underwear drawer, escape from class field trip to the Art Gallery in Halifax, hop on a bus. Her only major dilemma now is to decide where to go. Toronto seems the obvious choice, since New Brunswick is just as bad as Nova Scotia, and she skipped too many French classes to get by in Montreal. But she really doesn't like the thought of Toronto either, with all those Maple Leaf jerseys and that stupid pointy CN Tower sticking up into the sky like it owns the place. These days, she has her mind on the States. Why only do things halfway? Miriam pulls out her pen and starts a list in her notebook: *United States of America – Good Cities to Live In.*

Before she heads back, she wades out into the ocean, feeling the icy cold water rippling around her bony knees until her legs are numb. New York, she thinks. Boston. Chicago. New Orleans. Florida. Isn't New Orleans in Florida? She can feel the fog creeping into her bones. I bet they don't have any fog in Florida, she thinks.

When she turns back around, she is surprised to see a strange man in a red Speedo pointing a camera at her. When she stares at him, he puts the camera down and waves enthusiastically. The man is short and hairy, with a belly that swells dangerously over his bathing suit. His head is completely bald and has turned bright red with the sun. He looks like a tourist, although Martinique is too cold to be a usual stop for tourists.

"Hey," he calls, "Come here for a second."

Miriam does, warily: not because she is afraid, but because she has a suspicion he might be a Beachwalker. He practically has a whole house set up on the beach, complete with the silly hat and sneakers sitting on top of a cooler. Next to him, another man is lying face down on a towel. His shoulders are broad and there is a string of symbols tattooed across them, Chinese or Japanese or something, the black ink barely visible against his dark skin. As Miriam draws closer, she can see the tendons in his neck running like two thick ropes on either side of his spine, tensing and relaxing as he moves. Miriam feels a strange curdling in her stomach as she stands there, dragging her toe in the sand.

Red Speedo hands her the camera. "Take a look," he says proudly.

Miriam takes it. It's a digital, and on the display she sees herself, standing knee-deep in the ocean, her short brown hair standing on end, her flat, boyish body pushing against the wind. She makes a face and hands it back. "Gross," she says.

"What do you mean?" Red Speedo says, hurt. "I thought it was a great picture."

"The picture's okay," said Miriam. "I mean I look gross."

"Oh, sweetie, don't be ridiculous. You look fantastic. Josh, doesn't she look fantastic?"

The man on the towel rolls over, and takes the camera from Miriam. His eyes are very brown, almost black, and smiling like he's letting Miriam in on a secret. "Fantastic, baby," he says. "She looks like a little nymph. Very European."

Miriam feels herself blushing. "I do not," she mumbles, pinching a few grains of sand between her thumb and forefinger.

Red Speedo laughs, but the man he calls Josh just looks at her. "Oh, you do, honey," he says. For a startling second, Miriam believes him.

*   *   *

It turns out Red Speedo's name is Paul, and he and Josh are from Los Angeles. They came to Canada to get married: after the ceremony in Toronto, they drove down to Nova Scotia in a rental car to have a seaside honeymoon. Miriam doesn't think she has ever met a gay person before, although Paul says she probably has. Truthfully, she is more bewildered by the idea of going to Martinique Beach for a honeymoon than the idea of two men getting hitched.

"You have no idea how wonderful it is here," Paul says, sweeping his arm in front of him. "Look, no people. In LA a beach like this would be wall-to-wall people."

"There's no people because it's always foggy," Miriam says, drawing her knees up. "You can't swim. The only people who come here are the stupid Beachwalkers. It really sucks."

Paul continues waving his hands in the air, like he's not even listening. "LA is all traffic, smog, people, cars everywhere. Everything is go-go-go all the time. You have no idea how lucky you are, living here. It's paradise."

"I hope not," Miriam says under her breath. Josh looks up from his *People* and smiles at her. She pulls out her notebook and, covering the page with one hand, she writes *Los Angeles*.

*   *   *

At home, Miriam's mother is cooking supper. "Potatoes, Miriam!" she bellows from the kitchen as Miriam slinks in the door and slips out of her shoes. Damon and Ricky are both in the living room, playing video games and drinking beer. Miriam sneaks behind the couch, crawling on hands and knees across the puke-green carpet, hoping they won't notice her.

"Jesus fucking Christ!" Damon yells, throwing his controller at the TV. "This stupid cocksucking controller is broken!" He turns around. "Miriam! What the fuck!"

Miriam gives him the finger over her shoulder and crawls faster. She stands up when she reaches the kitchen and pads barefoot across the linoleum. Jason is sitting at the kitchen table, finger painting on the inside of a cereal box Miriam's mother has cut up for him.

"Mim! Mim!" he says, banging his fists on the table.

Miriam takes the cardboard and stares at the blob of paint, stroking her chin. "Hmm. I like what you've done here. You show definite promise. I think maybe it's time we moved you up to crayons, don't you?"

"Mim!" says Jason happily. He bangs his fists again, and the salt and pepper shakers dance their way off the edge and crash to the floor.

"For the love of Christ, Miriam!" her mother says, turning around. "Will you stop getting him all worked up?" In two strides she crosses the room and picks up the salt and pepper shakers. Miriam skulks to the pantry and pulls out the bag of potatoes.

*   *   *

For the next few days, Miriam skips her after-school beach walk to hang out with Paul, who turns out to be really nice. He teaches her how to play Chinese Checkers, which is just moving little marbles on a dented metal board covered with drawings of men with triangular hats on their heads. He even lets her use his camera, and they take pictures of everything – morning glories growing wild in the dunes, her toes in the sand, even the Beachwalkers, dragging themselves purposefully along the edge of the water. Paul says they are tragically ludicrous, like clowns crying. Miriam thinks they are just clowns.

Josh is always there, silent, reading or listening to his headphones. Every once in a while he rolls over on his towel and gives her a smile. Miriam tries not to look at him too much, because whenever she does she gets this weird feeling in her lower intestines, an aching pressure, kind of like she has to pee.

*   *   *

At school the next day, Miriam is at her locker when Maddie Croft throws an empty Coke bottle at her head and calls her "Miriam Beachwalker." Miriam skips fifth period and rides her bike up and down the fire access road behind her house, avoiding the beach, scared to go home.

Later, when she does go home, her mother calls her into the kitchen. Miriam is in the living room with Jason, building a garage out of blocks for their dinky cars. It's not going very well, because Jason keeps trying to eat the cars. Miriam gives up, kicks over the remaining blocks before stomping off.

Her mother is sitting at the table with Ricky, who is flipping through a motorcycle magazine. She has an open bag of carrots and a cutting board in front of her. "Why weren't you at school today?" she asks, banging the knife down on the head of a carrot.

"I was," Miriam lies.

"Hey, Mom," says Ricky.

Her mother sighs. "Miriam, Dr. Wallace saw you riding your bike past the practice. He called me at work to tell me."

"Mo-om," Ricky says a little louder.

Miriam shuts her eyes. That stupid Dr. Wallace. She opens her eyes and looks at her mother, who's got her *or-else* look on, the one she uses when she thinks she's being really tough. Miriam shrugs, sighing loudly. "It was my free period, Mom," she says in her very own patented are-you-stupid-or-something voice.

"Mom!" Ricky yells. "Jesus Christ, Mom, are you fucking deaf?"

Her mother's shoulders sag. "All right Miriam, fine." For the first time, Miriam notices the lines on her mother's face, notices she looks old. She feels a tiny twinge of remorse, just a tiny one, then reminds herself how much better off everyone will be when she's gone.

*   *   *

The next day the sky is grey as concrete. The beach is almost empty, except for Paul and Josh's umbrellas and blankets pushed back against the dunes. Even the Beachwalkers are nowhere to be seen. Wimps, thinks Miriam.

When she reaches the dunes, she realizes that Paul is also missing in action. Josh is lying on a plaid wool blanket in jeans and a sweater, his bare feet sticking off the end, toes resting in the sand. "Where's Paul?" she asks shyly. Josh props himself up on one elbow and points to the ocean. Way out beyond the breakers, Miriam can see a little bald head bobbing in the water.

"He'll swim in anything," Josh says, his voice a deep chocolate brown, vibrating through Miriam's body like a bang on a funny bone. "I think he's a bit insane, myself."

"Yeah," says Miriam, her eyes wide. Even in the middle of summer, the only people in the water are the surfers, who all wear wetsuits anyway. "Won't he get, like, hypothermia?"

"Probably. We should be ready to rush him to the hospital when he gets out."

"Yeah," Miriam repeats. She sits down on the sand and draws her knees up under her chin. After a few minutes she turns to see Josh smiling at her. "What?" she asks, a little defensively.

"Nothing," he says. "I mean, don't you have any friends your own age?"

"No," she says matter-of-factly. "I don't really like anyone my own age."

"Me either," he says. Then they both laugh.

Miriam ends up telling him everything. She can't help it. She tells him about school, and about her list of dreams. While she talks, Josh sits with his legs crossed, listening intently. Miriam has never had anyone pay such close attention to her, so she keeps talking, keeping her eyes focused on the water. She tells him about Jason, and Ricky and Damon, about Maddie Croft and Dr. Wallace. She even tells him about her mother, about the lines on her face. Finally, she runs out of things to tell him.

"Poet-Singer-Reporter, huh," he says when she is finished. "That's lofty. Well, I guess if Jennifer Lopez can be a Singer-Actress-Fashion Designer . . ." He pauses, rearranging the plaid blanket to cover his toes. "So can you sing?"

"No," confesses Miriam.

"Well, that never stopped J-Lo either. Are you interested in current events?"

"No."

"Hmm. Have you ever written a poem?"

76

"No."

"Hmm."

They are both silent. Josh studies her face. "Well, I don't know how much my opinion counts, but I think you should start with one thing," he says. "Work your way up. Which one do you like the best?"

Miriam shrugs. "I don't know." She really doesn't. But Josh keeps staring at her, and she doesn't want to disappoint him. "Poet, I guess," she says.

"I can see you as a poet. More an Erica Jong than a Sylvia Plath, though."

"Who?" asks Miriam.

When Paul finally comes back he stands dripping over them, his doughy flesh pimpled with goose bumps. She and Josh giggle as he shakes like a dog, spraying them both with water. Miriam wonders if maybe they'll take her to LA with them, introduce her to some Hollywood people. Take her to parties. Miriam is sure they must go to some parties. She presses her fists to her cheeks, which ache from smiling.

*   *   *

Miriam tries to write a poem. She takes an Erica Jong book out of the library, but she doesn't understand any of it. Josh gives her a box of words with magnetic backs. "Try to make something beautiful," he says. That night Miriam sits down at the kitchen table with Jason and tries to rearrange the words, to make something beautiful.

Wait ing With A Milk y Flower Petal.

Rust y Fields Ache For Sorrow.

Scared Dream s Float Through White Garden.

"Mim," says Jason happily, picking up Scared and swallowing it.

*   *   *

"I can't do it," she tells Josh. It is Friday afternoon, and Miriam and Josh are walking down the beach together. At the far end, where the sand turns to rocks, four harbor seals are lounging, catching a few last rays of sun. Paul has set up his camera on a tripod and is jumping up and down trying to get them all to look his way at the same time.

"I can't believe people hunt these beautiful creatures," he says, waving his arms in the air.

"They have to," says Miriam. "They eat all the fish. Anyway, it's not even the same kind of seal."

"I still think it's cruel," he pouts. "Seals and fish lived in perfect balance before we came along. It's not fair." He lies down on the beach and wiggles his legs in the air. Miriam thinks he looks a little bit like a seal himself; maybe that's why he feels so sorry for them.

"So, can't do what?" asks Josh, picking up a stick and dragging it in the sand.

"Write a poem. I've tried."

"Well, you should write about what you care about. What do you care about?"

Miriam thinks for a moment, trying to stop herself from blushing. "Nothing."

Josh draws a heart in the sand with his stick. Miriam stares at it, imagining her initials written inside. "Sure you do. You care about something. Everyone does."

"I don't know."

Josh looks at her for a long time. "I doubt that," he says finally, jabbing the stick into the ground.

"I'll try again tonight," says Miriam quickly. "I'll bring you a poem tomorrow."

Josh's eyes widen. "Miriam, honey, we're leaving tomorrow."

Miriam starts to feel dizzy. Her mind tries to bend around the words. Suddenly she thinks, now is the time. Ask him if you can come too. Ask him. Ask him, ask him, ask him, her mind screams. LA, Chinese Checkers, Hollywood, parties, Josh, ask him, ask him, ask him!

But she doesn't. Because she already knows what the answer will be.

Then Paul comes running over, breathless and excited, and grabs Josh around the waist. "I got it, baby! I got the most amazing picture!"

"That's great!" Josh says, wrapping his arms around him: Paul's dimply-white belly pressing up against Josh's perfect dark skin, Paul's bald red head barely visible over Josh's muscular shoulder. They look so ridiculous, Miriam doesn't know whether to laugh or cry.

* * *

When Miriam gets home, her mother is sitting alone in the living room. "Where are the boys?" Miriam asks, grabbing an apple from the fruit bowl.

"Jason's upstairs," her mother says quietly. "The boys are out riding their dirt bikes."

"Cool," says Miriam. She sits uneasily in the armchair across from her mother. She begins to get a strange feeling, like she forgot her gym clothes.

"How was the field trip?" her mother asks.

"The . . . what?" asks Miriam, her heart beginning to pound.

"The field trip you took this afternoon to the Art Gallery. How was it?"

"Fine," says Miriam automatically, while her brain screams the kind of curse words Ricky and Damon yell at their video games. She missed the goddamn-fucking field trip . . .

"Don't lie to me," her mother says. "I'm so sick of being lied to. Mrs. Pettipas called."

Miriam shuts her eyes, bracing herself for the yelling. It doesn't come. When she opens her eyes, she is shocked to see that her mother is crying.

"I give up," she says, not looking at Miriam.

"What?"

"I'm done. I give up. I don't care anymore."

"Yes, you do . . ."

"You're so smart, Miriam." She covers her mouth.

Miriam wants to tell her. I'm going to be a poet, Mom. But she doesn't. She can't. She's not going to be a poet, or even a Poet-Singer-Reporter. She's never going to leave Nova Scotia. She missed the field trip. And she can't even write a goddamn-fucking poem.

*   *   *

The next day it rains. Not a huge downpour or anything, just drizzle, a fine mist that makes you feel slightly damp all day, even when you're dry. Miriam is grounded and has to look after Jason after school, but when her mother leaves for work she bundles Jason in his rain slicker and they walk slowly down the road, Jason splashing through all the mud puddles, Miriam dragging her feet along the ground.

When they get to the beach, Miriam takes her boots off, and crunches barefoot across the wet sand. She has brought a kite for Jason, which she unfurls unenthusiastically. Jason plops down on the sand and watches, face red, fists balled up, barely able to contain his excitement. The wind is strong, and after a few tries Miriam raises the kite. She unwinds the string as far as it will go, then she holds the spool out to Jason, who launches himself at her outstretched arm and gleefully tears across the sand as fast as his uncooperative body will carry him.

So that's it. That's life. Stuff happens. People go away. Sometimes they come back, sometimes they don't. Whatever. Miriam looks out over the water contemplatively, although she really has given up being contemplative along with everything else. She imagines she sees Paul's little head bobbing up and down through the waves. She hears a voice and turns around, half-expectantly, and is irritated but not surprised to see two Beachwalkers, in head-to-toe yellow rain gear, pushing themselves along the shore. Miriam plunks herself down on the sand, shoving her hands in her pockets. Her fingers rub against some-thing sharp, the size and shape of one of those stupid magnetic words. Great, she thinks. Might as well let Jason eat this one too.

She pulls it out and looks at it. Long. She sighs. What kind of dumb word is that? Who writes poems about long things, anyway? Long is for hot dogs. Long is for weekends. "Long," she says out loud, to no one in particular. "Long, longer, lon-gest, longing, long, long, song, wrong . . ." Miriam stops abruptly. Longing. Now there's a good word. *Appropriate*, even. With the tip of her finger, she writes the word in the sand. L-O-N-G I-N-G. Then she writes F-O-R E-S-C-A-P-E. Escape from what? T-H-E P-R-I-S-O-N O-F Y-O-U-R E-Y-E-S.

Longing for escape from the prison of your eyes. That's not bad, she thinks, not bad at all. Sounds like something from that weird Erica Jong book. She lifts her sandy finger to her lips, imagining the prison of Josh's eyes, a deep, brown, liquid prison, holding her captive in their gaze. I am captive in their gaze, she thinks. No. *Enslaved. Enslaved* by their gaze . . .

"Mim! Mim!" she hears Jason yelling. She looks up to see her brother, staring skyward with rapt adoration, galloping along at full force toward the backs of the two Beachwalkers.

Miriam jumps up. "Jason!" she yells. "Watch where you're going!" She starts to chase him across the sand.

"Mim!" screeches Jason. This is his favourite game. He starts to run faster, arms flailing wildly, jerking the kite back and forth in the sky. He turns around, shrieking, and smacks right into the Beachwalkers, tipping them forward and tumbling on top of them. She hears Jason laughing, and the two Beach-walkers, tangled in a web of kite string, moaning "oh dear, oh dear" as they try to extricate themselves from each other. Jason stands up. "Mim!" he yells gleefully as he throws himself back on the heap.

Miriam jogs over, grabbing Jason's arm and hauling him up. His clothes are covered in sand and he is grinning wildly, still clenching the kite spool. The kite itself still floats serenely above them, bright against the slate-grey sky. Miriam stares up at it a moment before turning back to Jason, brushing the sand from his face and giving him a kiss on the forehead.

One of the Beachwalkers manages to right himself. "Could you please," he sputters, his face red and sweaty, "control this . . . this . . . *person*! We are trying to enjoy our beach!"

Miriam stares at him and his friend, who is still rolling around on his back like an upended sea turtle. "This is *our* beach, buddy," she says. "Could you please control *yourself*." She gently opens Jason's hand and takes the spool, clenching it between her teeth like a rose and giving the Beachwalkers a curtsey. Jason cackles. Looking back to the edge of the water, Miriam sees that her sand poem has already been erased by the tide.

The People
Who
Love Her

U nder Sephie's arms there are red marks where the tops of the crutches have rubbed against her armpit skin. She'll get used to them, the nurse at the hospital told me last night, but maybe at first she'll get a bit of a rash. Tells her to use some lotion and wear long sleeved shirts. But it is summer and she only wants to wear tank tops. Sephie is my best friend and I know she is stubborn like that. Plus she has really nice shoulders, all soft and freckly and covered in fine, silky hair.

Sometimes I am surprised at how easily things break.

We are going to Cosy's for breakfast because I have no food in my apartment and even if I did it would be too hot to cook. Last night Sephie slept in my bed and I slept on the couch, which is not really a couch but a loveseat and so this morning my legs are cramped up and tired, as if I spent the entire night crouching in a corner. I was supposed to prop Sephie's leg up on pillows before she went to sleep but I don't have many pillows so I ended up propping her leg up on a stack of magazines. Now my bed smells like plaster and perfume.

At Cosy's Sephie bumps into an old man sitting at the counter when she is trying to squeeze between the tables. She is not very good at maneuvering her crutches yet, or maybe she is still a bit drunk. The old man glares at her, but secretly I think he is

83

happy that someone has touched him, that he is sitting on that stool with his butt pushed way out just so someone will.

*   *   *

Sephie once lived in London with a man named Jonah who loved her more than anyone has ever loved anyone. They lived together in a small, cold apartment with rats and did a lot of drugs and Jonah painted pictures of Sephie: Sephie sleeping, Sephie eating, Sephie lighting candles, Sephie in the bathtub, hundreds of pictures, on huge canvases at first, then on loose-leaf when he had no money left to buy canvases, cheap copy paper, napkins. Sephie never left the apartment, and Jonah only went out to buy bread and soup. Jonah loved Sephie so much that he would cry the whole time he was apart from her, and when he came back his tears would be frozen to his face, tiny icicles dangling from his eyelashes.

The last portrait of her he painted with blood pricked from his fingertips on the classified section of the newspaper, pictures of cheery-faced real estate agents peeking out from the dried-brown flakes of her eyes. By then they had only four slices of bread left, and one can of chicken noodle soup. Sephie let Jonah eat the bread and they shared the soup, sitting and staring at each other until their last candle burnt out. Jonah was beautiful, Sephie said, he had kind eyes and pale, parchment skin that cracked in the London winter.

When the candle burnt out, Sephie came home. She still had a five pound note sewn into the lining of her backpack, and a return ticket to Halifax. She said she waited until it was dark because she wanted Jonah to remember her sitting there, in the apartment, her face lit by candlelight; she didn't want him to think of her leaving him. She said she wanted to stay burned on the back of his eyelids. Sephie could be dramatic like that. When I asked her if she was happy in London with Jonah she told me that when someone loved you that much it was impossible to be happy.

*   *   *

Sephie is visiting me from Calgary, where she lives with a man named Albert who owns four cars and is much older than her. Albert is an architect and they live in a brand new house that he designed himself in a brand new subdivision in Calgary, which Sephie says isn't a big deal because most of Calgary is brand new, hard and sparkling like the edge of a knife. Two of his cars are sports cars of some type and one is a regular car and the other is a truck.

"Why would anyone need four cars?" I asked her once. "There's only one of him. He can only drive one car."

"I drive the truck sometimes," Sephie said.

"Okay, that's two."

Sephie rolled her eyes. "Jill, you have more than one pair of shoes, don't you?" From the way she says it I know it's something Albert said to her once. Albert and Sephie have been living together for almost two years and the most I know about him is he's the kind of man who changes cars to match his outfits.

*   *   *

At Cosy's Sephie orders the breakfast special and a chocolate milkshake and a side order of onion rings. "Pain makes me hungry," she says, spreading peanut butter on a slice of toast that is already drowning in regular butter. "I'll probably just throw it up later." When she sees me staring at her she says "For God's sake Jill. Where's your sense of humour?"

*   *   *

Last night at the hospital the doctor told me something about Sephie's ankle but I can't remember what it was. Sephie was playing with the controls on the side of her little hospital bed, raising it up and down, the slick paper sheet crinkling like old newspaper. She had one of the nurses in the room with her, a young woman with short blonde hair and rosy cheeks. The nurse took Sephie's blood pressure and then Sephie took the nurse's. The nurse gave Sephie a lollipop and a tongue depressor, and Sephie stuck both of them in her mouth.

"Josephine can take these in the morning," the doctor said, holding out a bottle of pills. "When she sobers up."

He kept talking. Sephie and the nurse were laughing about something, and then there was an older man in the room, a technician of some kind, and he was laughing too, and I wanted to be in there laughing with them instead of listening to this old doctor talk about pills. I took the bottle and shoved it in my purse, but by then Sephie was up on her crutches yelling "yee haw, baby, let's go!" and the nurse and the technician were gone.

*   *   *

Before last night, the last time I was in the hospital with Sephie was in high school. She had been starving herself almost as long as we had been friends. When she starting having seizures her mother called her doctor, who sent an ambulance to take Sephie to the hospital. By then she weighed ninety-six pounds and had lost two of her teeth, but it still took three paramedics to strap her to the stretcher.

The doctors put her on suicide watch and gave her an intravenous feeding tube, which she named Jean-Claude. "He's the action hero of medical equipment," she told me. "The *Street Fighter* of feeding tubes." Her roommate in the behavioural ward was another tiny girl named Jules with bulging eyes and short hair like straw who was an arsonist and a cutter. Sometimes, Sephie told me, she would wake up to find Jules in bed with her, trying to curl up to her like a kitten. Another time, Sephie found Jules in the bathroom with a lighter trying to burn her own nipples.

When they found Sephie's name carved into Jules's stomach they moved them both to private rooms. Everyone assumed that

Jules had done it to herself but when I went to visit Sephie the next day she told me how Jules had given her the blade, which she kept hidden in a shampoo bottle, how she had touched the tip of it to Jules's belly and watched the blood bloom beneath it, how easily Jules's flesh had yielded, how it vibrated as the razor skimmed across the surface. How Jules had stared at the ceiling, her tongue poking out between her chapped lips, her eyes bright and feverish; how afterwards she lay on top of Sephie and pressed into her bare skin, staining her in blood in the shape of her name.

*　　*　　*

After we finish our breakfasts and share the onion rings Sephie divides the milkshake into two glasses and tops them both off with brandy poured from a flask she pulls out of her purse. I haven't had a brandy-shake since Sephie and I lived together in our second year of university. No one sees Sephie pour the brandy except a couple at the next table who are busy getting their baby to eat some baby mush from a glass jar. The baby has orange hair and a long face and likes to spit out the food his parents try to feed him and chew on the rubber end of the spoon.

Sephie props her foot on the seat next to me, and I can see that her toes are turning purple. I suddenly remember the pills in my purse so I pull them out and Sephie takes three and I take two and we wash them down with our brandy-shakes. One of Sephie's crutches clatters to the floor.

"I wish they had given me a wheelchair instead," Sephie says. "You'd have to push me around. Think of all the fun we could have."

I imagine pushing Sephie up to the top of Citadel Hill, then sitting on her lap and pushing off, rocketing to the bottom like two kids on a toboggan. My stomach drops to the floor.

"I might have to throw up," I say.

Sephie leans back, looking at me like she's daring me. "Go for it, Jill," she says. "I'm here for you." She laughs. I swallow, concentrate on the patterns on the table top. Beige Formica, flecks of green, flecks of brown. A stain that looks like ketchup. There's no pattern. Just flecks of green, flecks of brown.

"We're all here for you, Sephie," the doctor in the behavioural ward had told her, back in high school, when we were all gathered in the common room for Family and Friends therapy. "You're surrounded by all the people who love you."

Sephie stretched her long, bony legs in front of her, brittle and crooked as twigs. "I know that, Doc," she said. "And that's the problem."

*   *   *

Ever since Sephie arrived from Calgary I've noticed things about her. She's been quieter than usual, she looks tired, and she has this new way of staring at me, like she's reminding herself why we're here together. She laughed at me last night when I suggested going to our old favourite Irish pub, said she'd rather go dancing.

"I hate all that fucking fiddle music," she said.

"Me too," I said. "I just thought."

It had only been six months since I'd seen her. There was a new club where all the Toronto kids liked to go, with two big muscular guys out front wearing tuxes and headsets over their bald, fat heads, where you couldn't wear sneakers and had to pay ten bucks at the door. We drank a bottle of Jäger at my apartment while we were getting ready and then stumbled into a cab. At the club we drank martinis that looked like antifreeze and then we lost each other on the dance floor. At one point I looked up and saw Sephie dancing on a speaker, sandwiched between two Asian girls wearing matching silver miniskirts. She was much taller than them, and they slid up and down her, as if they were the strippers and Sephie was the pole.

When I found Sephie again she was on her knees on the wet bathroom floor, retching into a clogged toilet while the two

Asian girls sat on the counter smoking cigarettes. One of her shoes was missing, and her ankle was purple and swollen. I held her hair back and since there was no toilet paper I found her some paper towel, which she wiped across her mouth and then tossed on the floor. I took a drag from one of the girls' cigarettes while Sephie splashed cold water on her face. When I looked in the mirror I realized my makeup looked like a drunk person had done it.

"What happened to your ankle?" I asked. Sephie stared at me blankly, an open tube of lipstick shaking in her hand. "Your ankle. It looks like it's broken."

She raised the tube to her mouth. "Sometimes Albert hits me," she said. The two girls giggled.

"Albert?" I said stupidly. I never thought of Albert as a hitter. Albert was old. He designed houses. He drove four cars at once.

"Yup. *That's* how crazy I make him." She stared at the lipstick for a second, her eyes out of focus. Then she bit off the tip. When she opened her mouth again, her teeth were caked with red.

"Gross," one of the girls said. They giggled again.

Sephie looked down at her feet. "My ankle really hurts," she said. "Maybe I should go to the hospital."

*   *   *

We sit in Cosy's for three hours until the waitress tells us she's closing. I pay the bill while Sephie struggles with her crutches. My heart is beating very fast and my mouth is dry. I cough loudly and the waitress gives me a dirty look along with my change.

Once we're outside, Sephie leans against a tree and lights a cigarette. I sit down on the grass next to her, looking up at her. I've just always done that. I wonder how I would know who I was without her.

"Are you going back to Calgary?" I ask.

Sephie stares at me. "Yeah, of course. Why wouldn't I?" She takes one drag of her cigarette and then butts it out against the tree.

When we get home we each take two more of the pills. I start to feel calmer. Sephie hops around the apartment, her stuff is everywhere. The cat follows her, batting at her foot bobbing in the air.

"Your flight's not until Tuesday," I say. "You don't have to pack yet."

"I know," Sephie says, zipping up her suitcase. "I was just feeling, I don't know, scattered."

I'm sinking into the couch. There is a show on TV about sharks and I watch very closely until the rest of the world fades away. Sephie sits on the couch next to me, propping her feet up on the coffee table. I pull a blanket over us, even though it is still so hot. Under the blanket I can feel Sephie's hipbone pressing gently against mine. On a chair on the other side of the room, the cat follows something with her eyes that I can't see. It suddenly feels as if the room is teeming with things I can't see, thick in the air around us, and as usual, I am oblivious.

An Army
Of One

You promised things weren't going to change between us,
but they did. One night on the phone, a few weeks after Florida,
I said "I miss the little soft spot right behind your ear," and you
said "You know what? I could really go for a hot dog right now."
I thought I knew what you meant, but the next day when I was
standing at the street meat vendor outside the video store, trying
to decide between the seven different kinds of mustard set out
on the little table, it occurred to me that maybe you really did
just want a hot dog, or that maybe I didn't actually know what
you wanted at all.

You weren't married when I met you. You dated a string of
petite, vanilla-scented blonde girls with sweet faces and perfect
teeth before you settled on the sweetest, most perfect of them
all. I didn't know it was coming. The night before I found out,
we had talked on the phone. You had just come home from a
family dinner and were a little bit drunk. You told me about a
fight you had with your mother, about how she had told you,
with authority, that there were no multiple choice questions in
Trivial Pursuit. You laughed, told her of course there were
tonnes of multiple choice questions in Trivial Pursuit, that they
were always the easiest ones to answer. You went straight to her
game cupboard and found a card: "How many muscles does a

bee use in stinging – 2, 22, or 102?" She started to cry and said over and over, "There's no a, b, and c, there's no a, b, and c," and when you laughed at her, she called you an insensitive prick and wouldn't let you finish your slice of pie.

"What was the answer?" I asked you.

"The answer," you said, "is that you should take off your pants and tell me what you're wearing underneath."

Neither of us had ever been good at big conversations. The next day, I got an email. "Proposed to L. The ring was almost $2000.00. Think of the size of the television I could have bought with that." You never told me the answer to the bee question, but I knew what it was, anyway. The right choice is always the middle one, the mediocre one, the one that really wouldn't surprise anyone.

When I arrived in Florida for your wedding, you picked me up at the airport in your rented Prius and on the drive back to the hotel we talked about food. "There's these croissants at the breakfast buffet," you said. "They're unbelievable. This morning I ate, like, four of them." While we were on the freeway, you slid your hand up the inside of my thigh under my sundress and wriggled one finger under my panties until it slipped inside me, and before you would let me come you made me tell you how good it felt, how badly I wanted you.

"Please," I said. "It's all I think about."

Afterward, you licked the taste of me off your finger and then, with your finger still wet, flicked through the radio stations until you found some Avril Lavigne. "This is in case you get homesick," you said, and started singing along under your breath: *Hey, hey, you, you, I don't like your girlfriend.* I punched you in the arm and wondered if you knew how true it really was.

*   *   *

I have been known to not leave my apartment for days at a time. For most of my twenties I had lived with my sister, Kelly, and a revolving collection of third roommates in a three bedroom condo Kelly had bought when she was only twenty-three. Kelly was a *go-getter*. I was more of a *stay-putter*. Kelly and whichever Jennifer/Michelle/Amanda we were living with at the time would monitor the groceries that went into the fridge for their nutritional value, organize "house movie nights" with themes all somehow usually relating to Hugh Grant, and force me out of bed at seven A.M. to do Sun Salutations on the balcony in the summer, or in Kelly's east-facing master bedroom in the winter. When I finally moved out last year, I would spend entire days in bed, sleeping, watching TV, reading magazines.

"The best part about living by myself," I told you on the phone, "is that I can sit on the floor in my underwear and drink seven-dollar wine right from the bottle. I can eat KD and hot dogs out of the pot, and play Army of Two until four A.M. if I want, and there's no one around to stop me."

"You hate playing Army of Two," you said.

"I hate playing Army of Two *with you*. You yell at me too much. Plus you never let me choose my own weapons."

"It's called Army of *Two*, Becca. There's supposed to be *two* of you."

"Well, I am an army of *one*, asshole."

"Uh huh. An army of one whiny chick and one computer-generated replacement of me. Pretty awesome."

When I hung up the phone, I thought about how I could use a computer-generated replacement of you in real life. It would be such a relief, I thought, to be able to turn all this on and off. You were resistant to change, for everyone else as well as for yourself. "Aren't you going to miss having other people around?" you asked me once, just after I moved out. What I didn't tell you was that I didn't miss *anything* anymore, that the part of me designed for missing things was already too busy missing you.

*   *   *

When we got to the hotel in Orlando, I wanted to go straight to my room and shower. But there was a group of wedding guests in the hotel bar and I guess you figured it was best not to prolong the inevitable. "Do you want to meet Larissa?" you asked me.

"Uh, no," I said.

"Well, too late," you said, "cause here she is," and I watched her cross the room. Her presence felt like a bee sting. I wondered how many muscles she was using.

She was beautiful, of course. At first she shook my hand, saying "Eric's told me so much about you!" A second later she threw her arms around me and hugged me close and told me we would be "like sisters. Really, really." And I smelled her soft pink beachy smell and toyed with the end of one of her blonde tendrils, wondering if I pulled it out hard enough I could take a piece of her scalp along with it, if her veil would cover the scabby bald spot that it would leave behind. I smelled like airport and Starbucks, my hands were clammy, and I needed to pee.

"The veil is hideous" you told me later, when you came to my room. You looked past me with your usual vague bemusement, but your mouth was all wet and behind your eyes there was something on fire. "What's the deal with the veil, anyway? It's not like it's some big surprise, what's under there."

"Who knows," I said. I didn't want to talk about Larissa, or veils, or anything. I slid my fingers down the front of your jeans and pulled you down on top of me, feeling the familiar weight of your body pushing me into the pile of clothes I had dumped out of my suitcase and onto the bed. It wasn't until you were holding me down and fucking me – right there on top of all my stuff, with my hair dryer digging into my shoulder and one of my socks stuck to your arm – that I felt Larissa's sting start to fade away.

Afterward, I got up and washed my face, and then brought us two Cherry Cokes from the mini-bar. "Thanks, Becks. You're the best," you said, your body making a little nest of my once neatly-folded clothes. You had the remote in one hand, surfing through the television channels, looking for sports highlights.

You found ESPN and tucked the remote under a pile of socks. I curled up next to you with my soda and rested the cold can on your naked hip. You shuddered. Your leg jerked out and kicked one of my hoodies onto the floor.

"Clearly, I'm not," I said.

Silence. On the television, the Sports Center anchors were making a joke about some basketball player. I watched as the little ticker tape scrawled by on the bottom, squinted my eyes until everything else went away: *Brady works out in Patriots training room. Staal, Pens beat Wings in first Cup finals rematch. Roddick out of Master's Cup.*

"Not what?" you asked, finally. *Giants ace Tim Lincecum wins NL Cy Young Award.*

"The best. I'm not the best." *Knee surgery ends season for Man U's Hargreaves.* "Larissa is the best. Right?"

Struggling Sixers face Raps in Toronto. "Whatever," you said. You took a sideways sip of your Cherry Coke.

"Yeah, whatever." *Price and Higgins put Habs back in win column.* I blinked my eyes away from the television, looked at you. Your eyes were closed. Your cock was still hard. I stretched out behind you, reaching around to grab it. Pressed my face into the back of your neck. Your hair tickling my nose.

"You and your outside spooning," you said.

"Yeah," I said.

"You think you're so tough."

"I am tough."

"Yeah. Tough like a little fuzzy bunny."

"Uh huh."

"Uh huh." You rolled over to face me. And that was all we ever said about it.

*   *   *

I wasn't lying when I told you that meeting you was the best part about working at the video store, even though we were allowed to take home two new releases a week, and try out all the video games before they went on the "Previously Owned" shelf. Our first conversation was in the lunch room, after I had spent a tedious morning being trained on the cash register. I was sitting at the table, playing Tetris on my Game Boy and eating a bologna sandwich. After a while, I realized there was someone else in the room doing the same thing. We both played in silence for a while, until you messed something up and mumbled, "Fuck!" under your breath. I smiled, and I could feel you look up at me.

"What's your score?" you asked.

"What's *your* score?"

"Probably higher than yours."

"Whatever."

Under the table, I felt your foot press down on top of mine. "Stop distracting me," I said.

"What's the matter? Can't play with distractions?"

"I can. But if you win, you know you get an asterisk."

"If you win, *you* get an asterisk for talking to me while I'm trying to concentrate."

You kept your foot on top of my foot. I lost 30 seconds before you did, but when we compared our scores, they were exactly the same. We held our Game Boys side by side and looked at the number: 87,242. I could feel the hair on your arm against the back of my hand. You looked at me.

"Holy shit," you said. "We're the same person."

After that, everything was always Eric and Becca. During staff meetings we passed notes making fun of our co-workers' hair as if we were sitting in the back row of high school chemistry class. "Jamie F. + too much hair gel = John Stamos." "Is that a bald spot under Angie's extensions? Cause if it is, I'm totally taking her home after the Christmas party." Back then, I was dating Todd and you were dating Christine. Still everyone just assumed that eventually we would start dating each other. Maybe that's why we never did. When Todd broke up with me you dragged me over to your house at midnight and we stayed up until five in the morning playing Tekken 4. I beat you three times in a row before you started kicking my ass like you usually did.

"You're supposed to let me win all of them," I said. "I'm the one who got dumped, remember?"

You pressed your bare foot down on top of mine. "I didn't want you getting cocky," you said. "We all know girls can't play fighting games."

Later, you made me pad thai with extra peanut butter, the crunchy kind, because you knew I liked the texture. When you left Christine for Larissa, I picked you up at the bar and drove you to your brother's place so that Christine wouldn't be able to track you down. Larissa was there waiting for you, in her little toque and wool coat, cheeks rosy from the cold, and when we pulled into the driveway you told me you had never been more relieved to see someone in your entire life. The radio was playing "All I Want Is You," and you laughed and said you had been hearing that song in your head all day, that it was the only thing you could think about when you looked at her. "You're the best, Becks," you said as you got out of the car, and I sat in the driver's seat, the engine still running so I could stay warm, and watched you run up the icy steps to meet her.

"All the promises we break, from the cradle to the grave," Bono sang, and in that moment I knew I could never drive you to meet another girl, ever again.

Two months later, without me ever even meeting her, you and Larissa moved back to Timmins together. Four months after that, you and I started sleeping together. You came to see me in Toronto and we went to Canada's Wonderland to ride our favourite roller coaster, the one where your legs hang underneath you while you go around the loops. We sat in the very front and afterward you bought me a cherry ice and I was so excited about everything that I dropped the entire thing down the front of my tank top. I sat there laughing, the ice melting into red, sticky syrup running down between my breasts, and then out of nowhere you leaned over and licked it off with so much hunger that for a moment I thought you must have ripped me open with your tongue – that my body would split open and my insides would spill out right there on the little bench in the middle of the park. We got up and walked back over to the roller coaster, not speaking, not touching, and when we got to the front of the line you pulled me into the back car where no one could see us and before we even reached the first drop, you had undone the top button of your jeans and my hand was in your underwear, my fingers wrapped around your cock as we reached the peak and took off flying through the air.

That was almost five years ago. Five years and I can still feel that trail of saliva your tongue left on my skin, a poorly sewn seam that continually threatens to break open again.

*　　*　　*

Kelly was the only one who ever knew the truth about us. After I moved out, we would get together for coffee once a week and talk about Larissa the way I imagine Jennifer Aniston and Courtney Cox must have once talked about Angelina Jolie.

"She's probably in a book club," Kelly said. "A Jane Austen book club or something, where they all sit around and talk about how in love they are with Mr. Darcy."

I laughed. "She probably has horse posters on her wall. Or dolphins. With little inspirational sayings on them like 'Dreams will set you free.'"

Kelly snorted, and cappuccino foam sprayed across the table. "She probably wears flannel pajamas to bed. Pink ones. With little hearts on them."

"Cotton pajamas," I said, scooping up some whipped cream with my finger off the top of my hot chocolate. "But yeah. With little hearts on them." I had been with you when you bought them for her, the Christmas before you moved away. I had tried to convince you to buy the ones with the little shorts, but you told me Larissa liked to have her legs covered when she slept. I remember laughing to myself at the time, thinking how wrong you were, that no girl liked to have her legs covered when she slept, especially when she had a boy sleeping next to her. But, of course, you were right. She loved them.

"I bet she won't even go down on him." Kelly said. "Or if she does, she spits."

I pictured Larissa's mouth sliding slowly off your cock, her sweet face screwed up with thinly-veiled disgust, then pursing her lips and delicately spitting into a strategically placed paper cup on the bedside table. I wiped my finger on a napkin and shoved my hands down between my knees to stop them from shaking. "Yeah. I'm sure that's exactly why Eric's with her. Her spitting abilities."

Kelly put down her cappuccino and looked at me. "Then why *is* he with her?" she asked.

I didn't say anything. It wasn't because I didn't know the answer. *Because he loves her. He loves her. He. Loves. Her.* It was the middle answer, the one that wouldn't surprise anyone. But that still didn't mean it made any sense at all.

*   *   *

In Orlando I avoided Larissa for as long as I could. At night I would lie alone on my bed and try to imagine the two of you in your room, Larissa in her little pink-heart covered pajamas resting her blonde hair on your chest while you watched the hockey game. Then the afternoon before the wedding, she showed up at the door of my hotel room. In her shy, soft voice she told me that one of her bridesmaids had gotten appendicitis and couldn't make the trip, and Larissa was wondering maybe, if I didn't think it was too crazy or anything, if I would take her place. What else could I do? I nodded numbly and braced myself against the door frame while she hugged me.

"You're Eric's best friend. You should be a part of this," she whispered.

"I thought I would have made a pretty good best man," I said, pulling away from her, trying to keep my voice steady. "Stupid brothers, stealing all the good wedding roles."

That night, at Larissa's bachelorette party, I sat in the hotel bar with her and her other bridesmaids and drank overpriced martinis while they talked about their babies and their home renovations and reminisced about high school. One of the girls joked that she had hired a male stripper to come to Larissa's room later, and her face turned an unflattering shade of bright pink. Eventually, they started talking about the honeymoon.

"I can't believe you're going to Disney World," the tall bridesmaid with the red hair said. "Who's idea was that, anyway?"

Larissa laughed. "Eric's, of course. I would have much rather gone to Paris or Venice or something. But it's what he wanted. Really, really."

"Wow," the fat bridesmaid said. "You must love him. *Really, really.*"

Larissa turned to me. "Becca, you're Eric's best friend. You must know. What is his thing with roller coasters?"

Everyone turned to me expectantly. I took a drink. This is my moment, I thought. This is it. It would have been so easy. I could have taken a sip of my Lychee-tini or Pom-tini or whatever the hell I was drinking, set it down delicately on the coaster, crossed my legs, leaned in to the four expectant faces staring at me from around the table, and said "Because roller coasters turn him on." I could have told her about that day at Canada's Wonderland, about the way you looked at me after you ran your tongue over my skin; then you leading me to the line up, how hard your cock was in my hand, how good it felt when it was all over, the exhilaration, my fingers sticky with your come as we stumbled out the exit gate and back into the bright, pulsating light of the park. Right there, right then, in that tacky hotel bar in Orlando with the black vinyl benches and the mirrored wall behind the bar and the cheesy ambient jazz music playing just a little too loud, that was my moment to tear you open the way you had torn me open that day. Then in a flash I saw Larissa crying, people yelling, a wedding dress ripping, a cake being returned, uneaten; and you, showing up at my door telling me

Thank you and *You did what I couldn't do* and holding me close and everything being all right.

So, yeah. I saw that flash and knew that it was all wrong. That it would never happen that way. So I just shrugged and swallowed down those words along with my mouthful of martini. The girls went back to talking, and everything else went back to the way, I suppose, it was meant to be.

*   *   *

That night, after the other girls had gone to bed, I stayed at the bar and drank three more martinis and went back to the room of the first man who asked me. He was tall and handsome but had a really silly looking goatee and a laugh that made me want to duct tape his mouth shut. He didn't seem interested in fucking me, he just wanted me to suck his cock, for what seemed like hours, bobbing up and down over his lap until my neck hurt and my jaw began to cramp.

"Deeper, deeper," he groaned, then laughed that obnoxious laugh. "Try to touch your nose to my belly button." So I did. I jammed his cock so far down my throat that I gagged, and then suddenly I felt my mouth fill with vomit.

"Hey," he said. "Did you just . . ."

But I shook my head. Swallowed it back down with his cock still in my mouth. And I kept going, harder now, faster, as if I had something to prove, as if at that very moment the only thing that could possibly ever put my world back together was making him come. But when he finally did – with a long, shuddering grunt that sent shivers up my spine – my world was still broken. I got up and put my clothes back on and left without saying a word.

Back in my room, I phoned Kelly from the hotel phone and woke her up. "I just threw up giving some guy head," I said.

"Huh?" said Kelly, her voice gravelly with sleep.

"It was really gross."

"Was *he* really gross?"

"No." I turned on the television, then turned it off again. "Maybe I should move back in with you," I said.

"I already rented out your room."

"Oh." I rolled over on my side and curled up in a ball, squeezing my eyes shut. "I don't get it," I said, barely able to get the words out. "If he loves her, why is he sleeping with me?"

Kelly paused so long that I thought maybe she had fallen back to sleep. "Becca," she said, "I've been asking *you* that for years."

I started to cry. "We're the same person," I said.

Kelly yawned. "Yeah," she said. "But nobody wants to marry themselves."

*　　*　　*

The next day, stomach churning, jaw still aching, I walked down an aisle towards you. And up there on that sandy altar – with all of your friends and family sweating in their seats under the hot Florida sun, stood with the fat bridesmaid and the tall, red-headed bridesmaid and the other bridesmaid who had no distinguishing features at all, and your brother who your mother insisted be your best man even though you hadn't seen each other in two years, and you, in your shorts and flip-flops and your face burned in the shape of your snorkelling mask and wearing a shirt with buttons, real buttons – I watched you marry someone else. I watched you watching Larissa float down the beach, in her silky strapless dress, her tiny shoulders freckled from the sun. I watched you take her hand, and tell her *I do*, and slip a tiny little ring on her tiny little finger. I watched you kiss her tiny little lips. I watched you smile. I watched you marry her.

Later, at the reception, in an air-conditioned banquet room with seashells and polished stones spread out across the tables, we danced together. It was to "All I Want Is You." As soon as I heard it I figured you would be dancing with Larissa. I slipped my shoes off under the table and went over and offered my arm to your father, but just as we were walking away you stopped us and said, "I think it's my turn." And I looked at you and heard the music and my heart broke for the thousandth time that day. But still I held your hand and walked out with you to the dance floor, and when you pulled me into you I thought about how all those people watching us would never know how familiar that was, how many times I had felt your hand on my back, your fingers spread, digging into my skin. I could see Larissa at the head table, smiling stupidly, eating a piece of wedding cake. She waved, and her rings sparkled on her finger. I wondered for a moment if maybe she knew, if maybe there was more to her than I gave credit for, if maybe she really was a super fantastic girl and that we really could be "like sisters," really, really. But I knew I didn't care enough to find out. If I had been doing anything else at that moment other than dancing with you, I might have run over there and pushed her head right down into that cake, just so she could know what it fucking felt like, to have the whole world staring at you when you were that much of a mess.

"So that was weird, huh?" you said.

"What? Yeah."

"Sorry."

I shrugged. "Whatever."

You pressed your foot down on top of mine. When I moved my foot to the side, yours moved with me. "Nothing's going to change, Becca," you said.

"I know."

"You're still my best friend."

"I know."

"I can still beat you at Tekken 4."

"I know."

Over at the head table, the fat bridesmaid poured a drink for Larissa and splashed some of it all over the front her dress. "Good thing it's champagne!" I heard her say. They both laughed. Larissa took one of the cloth napkins and dabbed at her cleavage. I grabbed your head and pulled your ear to my mouth.

"I know what you want," I said.

You didn't say anything back, but you knew. I know you knew it was true. You rested your chin on the top of my head. We just kept dancing, your foot on top of my foot, moving together awkwardly around the room.

Twelve Weeks

J enny comes home on a Saturday. The first thing she notices is the lawn. It is freshly mowed. Jenny's father, Ed, is meticulous about many things. His lawn is not one of those things. But Jenny can smell the cut grass, still tinged with gas fumes. It reminds her of being little. It makes her sick and sad and angry all at once.

Ed is in the garage, tinkering away with some sort of small engine. When he sees Jenny walking up the driveway, he stops tinkering and stands up straight. Jenny hears a crack. She knows this is his top vertebrae. When Jenny was young she used to rub it for him, rocking her little knuckles around the edges until the cracking stopped. She wonders if anyone rubs it for him now.

"Hi, Dad," she says.

"Hi, Jenny," he says. He stares at her.

Ed is not a tinkerer, Jenny thinks. Ed is a newspaper reader. On the weekends, he sometimes reads three or four. He is a baseball watcher, but only in the post-season. He is a log splitter, a hedge trimmer, an omelet cooker, a country music listener. Never a tinkerer. Jenny wonders when her father added this new dimension to himself. If there are other dimensions of her father she has yet to discover. This thought makes her uncomfortable.

She sets her bag down in the driveway and shoves her hands in the back pockets of her jeans.

"Is it okay, if I just, um . . ." She pauses. Then nods at the house.

"Oh . . . yes. Yes. Go on in." He rubs his hand over his face. "I'll be right there."

Jenny picks up her bag and carries it into the house. Not much has changed since she was last home, five years ago. There is dust covering everything, but otherwise the house is clean. On the inside of the front door, there is a sad, brown wreath hanging on a nail, a dusty felt bow at the base, left over from some long-ago Christmas. When Jenny touches it, a few brittle needles fall to the floor. All the pictures have been taken down off the walls, but the wreath remains.

In her old room she drops her bag by the door and lies down on the bed. Her duvet smells musty. Above the bed there are several gummy bears stuck to the ceiling. Jenny remembers being ten or eleven, sitting on her bed with her friend Michelle, sucking on them until they turned sticky then throwing them up in the air. "No way they'll stay up there," Michelle had said, but they did, the sugar and saliva somehow cementing them to the ceiling paint. Jenny's mother never even noticed them there. It was like she never looked up. Jenny wonders if anyone has been in her bed since she left, if anyone has seen the gummy bears up there. It seems like the whole act of sticking them there was futile, if no one ever looked up.

*   *   *

For dinner Ed has made lasagna. He makes it with cottage cheese instead of the ricotta Jenny's mom used to use. Jenny has been a vegetarian for two years, but she eats the lasagna anyway. She has a second helping. And four pieces of garlic toast. Ed has a beer with his dinner. He doesn't offer one to Jenny. They don't talk. When Ed is finished eating, he wipes the corners of his mouth with a paper napkin.

"How long did you say you were staying?" he asks.

"Twelve weeks," she says. He looks at her. She shrugs. "Give or take." She has not told him why she is there, and he doesn't ask.

Ed scrapes his plate with the edge of his fork, collecting all the leftover sauce. "That's three months," he says.

"I hope that's okay."

Ed nods. His hair is still thick and dark in the front, despite the growing bald spot on the crown. Jenny wonders what her father will look like as an old man, with steel grey temples, deep creases around his eyes, muscular arms softening. Then he stands up, and she hears the cracking again – not only in his top vertebrae, but his knees, his back, his elbows – and she realizes he is already there.

"Can I help?" Jenny asks, rising with him.

"No, thank you." Ed starts toward the kitchen with his plate, then stops, turns around, and collects Jenny's as well.

*   *   *

Twelve weeks. Three months. A quarter of a year. The first trimester of a pregnancy, another GST cheque. The length of a summer romance, if you're lucky, from first kiss to the last tearful promise. The length of Jenny's first real relationship, with a boy called Todd who wore Adidas sneakers and wanted to be a rally racer, who dumped her for a field hockey player with red hair and stubby legs. The amount of time they gave Jenny's mother to live when she was finally diagnosed with lung cancer, her huge eyes already sunken into her hollow face, her hands already shaking, her lips cracked and pale. Twelve weeks, they thought. Twelve weeks of trying to say goodbye.

She didn't even make it eight.

*   *   *

The first week is easy. Everything is new and interesting. Jenny spends whole afternoons reading through her old diaries, looking at photo albums, staring out the window. Ed is now partially retired from the law firm where he spent forty years of his life working twelve-hour days, so he only goes into the office in the mornings. In the afternoons he holes himself up in the garage. Every night Jenny offers to cook dinner, and every night Ed refuses. After dinner he watches the news on the new flat screen TV in the den. Sometimes Jenny joins him. They don't talk. They sit side by side on the couch and rest their slippered feet on the unfinished pine coffee table. Then Jenny remembers that was how he and her mother used sit. After that, she sits on the floor.

One morning before he goes to the office, Jenny makes coffee for Ed and takes it to the garage while he works. He looks surprised but takes it from her, wraps his big hands around the chipped mug and breathes in. Jenny makes her coffee strong. Something she and Ed have in common. She watches as he brings the mug to his mouth, slurps loudly. He swallows, and then nods, putting the mug down next to the hunk of rusting metal he's been working on.

As a child, Jenny was never allowed in the garage. Now, she looks around. The space has changed from what Jenny remembers, from those rare occasions her father needed her help with something. Back then, the garage was for storage. Christmas decorations, Jenny's old baby things, old cans of paint, tools, and camping gear, which they somehow accumulated even though they had never been camping. Now there is a workbench in the middle of the garage, engine parts laid out carefully across the top. To the right of the workbench are two lawnmowers. The shelves along the back wall are stacked with tools. Against the left garage wall is her mother's Vespa, sad and old and rusted, sitting up on wooden blocks. Jenny walks over to it and runs her fingers over one of the handles, trying to imagine her mother young and beautiful, tortoiseshell sunglasses, shiny boots, dark hair flying out behind her as she rode. "I was riding that Vespa the day I met your father," Jenny's mother once told her. Jenny wonders why she stopped riding it, if it was Ed who made her stop.

Ed looks at her sharply. He puts down his screwdriver. "Thanks for the coffee," he says.

Jenny drops her hand. "You're welcome," she says. She walks around Ed on her way out the door.

"She has to stay out of the garage," Ed told her mother, back then. "She'll mess things up." Even though Jenny was a neat, precise child, who never messed anything up.

*　　*　　*

The second week is harder. Jenny is bored. She takes walks around the old neighbourhood, listening for familiar sounds. The clang of the school bell, the squeal of the train as it pulls into the station. Helicopters landing on the roof of the children's hospital. When Jenny was young she loved the helicopters, the sound they made, the wind, the excitement. Then her mother told her what they were for. Medical emergencies. Children who slip through the ice, fall off their ATVs, get hit by cars; whose drugs stop working, whose organs fail. After that, whenever Jenny heard the beating outside her window, she pulled the pillow over her head and listened to her heartbeat instead.

"What about your job?" Ed asks her one night, sitting in front of the TV.

Jenny fiddles with the shag of the carpet. "I quit my job, Dad," she says. She flicks a thread of dark brown fuzz from the end of her finger.

Ed makes a noise in the back of his throat. He looks deeply worried. He has never quit a job in his life, Jenny knows. He went from working summers at the fish plant during high school to law-school scholarships and partnership in a firm. He never considered anything else, never wondered if he had made the right decision. Never wandered from bad job to bad job, trying to find some place to fit in.

"It's okay," she says. "I have money."

"Mmm."

"I can find something else."

"I'm sure you can." Ed props his feet on the coffee table. Jenny notices that one of his slippers has a hole in the bottom.

"Give me your slipper, Dad," she says.

"Why?"

"There's a hole in it."

He stares at her. "I know."

"I could fix it for you."

Ed drops his feet to the floor. "If I wanted it fixed, I could fix it myself," he says. His voice is heavy, but to Jenny he sounds like a petulant child.

*   *   *

Twelve weeks was the first semester of classes at the University of Toronto. Twelve weeks of introductions: Introduction to Psychology, Introduction to Biology, Introduction to English Literature. Twelve weeks of Jenny trying to concentrate, skipping classes, failing papers. Six weeks to flunk her midterms, and six more to drop out.

Five more weeks to tell her father, who had already paid her second semester's tuition. Hoping he would tell her she made a mistake, but getting nothing but heavy silence on the other end of the phone.

"It's your life," he said finally, before hanging up. The same thing he always said. Jenny, closing her eyes, wishing that it wasn't.

Twelve weeks might have been the length of her first job in Toronto, at a Baskin Robbins near Yonge and Lawrence. Then more twelve-week increments of other jobs, with frequent breaks in between. Thirteen weeks. Fifteen. Twenty-four. Sometimes she would lose track of where she was, which store, which restaurant. Days broke over one another, awash with boredom.

Then one afternoon, in the cereal aisle of the Dominion on College Street, eating from an unpaid-for box of Corn Pops, there was Devin. When he saw her staring, her price scanner pointed at him like a toy gun, he offered her some. Without even thinking about it, she dug into the box and pulled out a handful of cereal. Her hand brushed against his.

Devin tilted his head as far to the right as it would go. "Jenny," he said. Jenny felt a rush of wind in her ears as he spoke her name. He straightened back up. "Your name tag is on upside down."

Jenny didn't know what to say, so she held the scanning gun up to his forehead and pressed the button. The words Code Not Found flashed across the screen.

"How much do I cost?" Devin asked.

"I don't know yet," Jenny answered.

*　　*　　*

The third week, Jenny calls Michelle, who is still in town, living a few blocks away in a three-storey brick apartment complex with her boyfriend and his Rottweiler. One of them is named Jagger, but Jenny's not sure which one. Michelle picks her up in a souped-up Civic and they drive to the Tim's on Barrington, where they sit behind the glass so that Michelle can smoke.

Jenny is nervous. She hasn't seen Michelle since their party days, since that night five years ago when Jenny drove her mother's car into the side of their old high school. She peels back the tab on the top of her coffee, blows delicately into the cup.

"You look good," Michelle says. She holds her cigarette between her thumb and forefinger, flicks the ash hard into the tinny ashtray.

"You too," says Jenny. It's not true. Jenny looks at their reflection in the window: Michelle with her fried blonde hair and doughy, pockmarked face, Jenny thin as a skeleton next to her, disappearing into her fraying black peacoat.

"I heard about rehab," Michelle says. She butts out her cigarette and lights another.

"Yeah," says Jenny. She looks at the table, at the ring of fuchsia lipstick around Michelle's cigarette butt, at the dirty floor, anywhere other than the window.

Michelle twists in her seat. "I tried to get Jagger to go," she says. Smoke curls out of her nose.

Jagger. The boyfriend.

Jenny coughs. "Do you remember the gummy bears we used to stick up on the ceiling?" she asks.

"Gummy bears?" Michelle asks. She looks up.

"In my bedroom," says Jenny. "On Oakland Road. Michelle?"

But Michelle just stares at the ceiling, her cigarette burning down to ash between her fingers.

*   *   *

Weeks four, five, six and seven fly by in a blur. Jenny starts going to Michelle's in the morning, after Ed goes to work, where they smoke pot and watch daytime talk shows until lunch, when Jagger's seven-year-old son, Friday, comes home from school. Then they watch cartoons. When she gets home in the afternoon, Ed is already in the garage. There is no more lasagna, no more six o'clock news. Jenny spends the evenings in the bathtub, watching the skin on her fingers shrivel like old people's faces.

Sometimes while the cartoons are on Michelle makes lunch for them, grilled cheese sandwiches or tomato soup from a can, mixed with water instead of the milk that Jenny's mom used to add. More often, though, Friday gets his own lunch, packages of pre-made pudding, or peanut butter spread over stale bread heels. "It's just temporary," Michelle tells Jenny, glaring at the back of Friday's head. "Until his mom gets out of jail." Friday is a sullen child with a wet mouth and close-set eyes, who sits and stares at Jenny during the commercials, one dirty finger in his nose, or his mouth, or his ear. If she talks to him, he looks away.

"You're named after the best day of the week, you know," Jenny tells him one day, just to make him stop staring. "Friday means the weekend's here."

"I hate the weekend," Friday says. He takes his finger out of his nose and wipes it on the Rottweiler. The dog pays no attention.

Michelle smacks him on the back of his head. "Don't let your father see you do that," she says. Friday moves closer to Jenny and sticks his finger back in his nose. Then he wipes it on her leg.

"That's it," says Michelle, standing.

Jenny stands, too. "I think I should go home," she says.

*   *   *

Twelve weeks. Not quite the longest of Devin's disappearances. That was seventeen weeks. Seventeen weeks without a word, without as much as a phone call. Then suddenly he was back, body shaking against the door frame, skin pasty, eyes feverish. "Please, Jenny." And she let him in. The same way she always did. He slunk to the kitchen, Jenny trailing behind him, waiting for him to say something else. Instead, he turned on the tap, tilted his head sideways and began to drink. When Jenny pulled a glass out of the cupboard for him, he just stared at it, his pupils dilating and contracting in the harsh fluorescent light, drops of water trickling out of his mouth and over his chin.

*   *   *

Halfway through week eight, Jenny has a breakdown. She has no idea what sets her off. She smashes the mirror in the bathroom and then from the window she screams at her father in the garage. "What are you fucking hiding from?" The next-door neighbour's porch light flicks on, but she gets no response from Ed.

113

The next three nights she stays on Michelle's couch. At night she drinks beer with Michelle and Jagger while Friday plays video games in his bedroom. Every morning when she wakes up, the dog is lying on top of her, his hot breath in her face. She still doesn't know the dog's name. Usually she just pushes him off, but one morning she throws her arms around him, buries her head in his neck. He growls softly, and then licks her hair. At that moment she loves the dog more than anything.

"Dobie likes you," Jagger says the next day, scratching the dog behind his ears.

"Who?"

"Dobie," says Jagger. "The dog?"

"Oh. Right."

"He likes everyone," says Michelle. She humps the back of her chair, and then laughs.

"What's he supposed to do?" says Jagger. "He's got no fucking nuts."

That night Jenny wakes up with Jagger leaning over her. Dobie is on the floor, whining. Then Jagger's tongue is in her mouth, his hand reaching roughly under her shirt. Jenny is half asleep, groggy from the beer and pot. Her hips arch toward him, and she feels his erection pressing against her thigh. She reaches for it, and then stops.

"Fucking tease," Jagger says, his breath ragged.

The next morning, Jenny goes home. Ed is in the kitchen, drinking coffee. They don't speak. Jenny goes straight to the bathroom and runs a bath, then slides herself into the scalding water. She stays in the tub until the water turns cold. Then she manoeuvers the tap with her toe, feels the hot water sluicing through the cold. She can hear Ed still in the kitchen, doing the dishes, the sound of metal scraping on metal. Then she hears the back door close, and a few moments later the light from the garage shines in fragments through the condensation on the bathroom window. She has a sudden, sharp memory of her mother, wrapped in a silk bathrobe, standing at the bathroom counter and staring at a chunk of hair stuck to the palm of her hand.

If I am sick, Jenny thinks. Then stops. She can't get any farther than that.

*   *   *

"You have to wait twelve weeks," the nurse at the clinic told her.

"No," Jenny said. "No, no, no. Test me now." She thought back to that morning, a stomach full of gin martinis and Vicodin, Devin in the bathroom vomiting, whispering *Jenny, Jenny, I'm dead, Jenny*. The track marks on his arms, the emptiness in his eyes. The realization sliding down her spine.

"I can," the nurse said, "but it won't be accurate."

Jenny felt her breakfast rising in her throat. In one instant, her life had become unrecognizable. Her life, which had always been small, insignificant, unattractive, but still *hers*. She swallowed. "What am I supposed to do for twelve weeks?"

The nurse didn't answer, but she held out her hand. It reminded Jenny of her mother's hand, cold and rough. Jenny looked around the small clinic room, the jars of cotton swabs and tongue depressors, the little basket of condoms sitting on the nurse's desk. On the wall in front of her, there was a poster with pictures of several smiling women, of all different ages and ethnicities, all looking very pleased about having a pap test. A piercing antiseptic smell hit Jenny's nose.

"I want my mom," she whispered. Then she ran out of the room to throw up.

*   *   *

"It's none of my business why you left Toronto," Ed says.

Jenny stares out the window. It is week ten. They are in the kitchen. Ed paces in front of the fridge, his back stooped, his fingers splayed. Jenny can see his reflection in the window. She

115

notices that he has hiked his pants past his waist. Has he always worn them like that? She turns around. Ed stops pacing and straightens a magnet on the fridge door, which is holding up a coupon for winter tires. The magnet is wooden and is shaped like a wine bottle, and painted on the front it says *good friends are like wine – they get better with age.* Jenny realizes she can't think of one friend of Ed's.

"It's none of my business why you left," Ed says again. "But I want to know why you came back here."

"I want to be here," Jenny says.

"No you don't," Ed says. He begins pacing again.

Jenny turns back to the window. The garage door is propped open with a cinder block, and Jenny can see the well-worn path across the lawn from the back door to the garage. She understands why Ed wants to be out there all the time. The house feels old and hollow. Broken.

"I had nowhere else to go," she says, biting her lip.

Ed stares at her. "Don't do that," he says. "You look like your mother."

He hates me, thinks Jenny, feeling the teeth marks with the tip of her tongue. He hates me and I hate him, and mom was the glue that kept us together, and neither of us will ever say it. Well, fuck it.

"I wanted to be near mom," Jenny says.

Ed stops, his back to Jenny. She can feel his body tense, his shoulders rising and falling with each breath, his hands clenched tightly at his sides. "She's not here," he says quietly.

Jenny stands and crosses the room until she is standing directly behind her father. She can smell him, sweat and motor oil and the damp, warm wool of his fisherman's sweater. She forms her hand into a fist and raises it to Ed's neck, pressing her knuckles into the muscle around his top vertebrae. Jenny sees his hands unclench. She begins rocking her fist gently, around and around, feeling Ed's leathery skin under her fingers. Ed lets out a long, slow breath. Jenny applies more and more pressure, rocking around and around.

*   *   *

Twelve weeks. Almost the amount of time Jenny will stay at her father's. Near the end of week eleven, she will scrape all of the gummy bears off of the ceiling, pack up her things, and take a cab to the airport while Ed is at work, wondering why she thought she could ever make it twelve weeks. She won't leave a note, but will call from the airport and leave a message. "You're wrong," she will say to the answering machine. "She is here. She's everywhere."

Jenny wakes up early that day, before Ed goes to work. She makes a pot of strong coffee and pours one mug for Ed and one for herself. Then she wanders out to the garage, still in her bathrobe. She feels the grass prickling the bottoms of her feet. I can't be sick, she thinks, raising her face to the sun. There's no way. She takes a sip of coffee. She can hear her heart beating in her ears.

She pushes open the garage door. Ed isn't there. In front of the workbench is her mother's Vespa, down off the blocks, new paint and polished chrome, brand new whitewall tires. It looks just like it did in the old photographs Jenny's mother used to show her. "It was like standing on the edge of a really high cliff," she'd tell Jenny, when Jenny would ask what it was like to ride it. Her hand on Jenny's head, that faraway look in her eyes. "It was like falling in love."

Jenny puts the coffee mugs down on the workbench and runs her hand over the seat and up over the frame, feeling the soft leather under her fingertips, the cold metal. She shuts her eyes. She sees her mother laughing, her small hands gripping the handlebars, and Ed, young and boyish, eyes full of expectation, touching her face with the back of his hand.

What Boys
Like

Audrey knows he has a girlfriend.

She could be a ghost, blonde hair, pale skin, breakable-looking wrists straight as daisy stems, ready to snap in your fist. She comes into the lingerie store where Audrey works wearing expensive jeans and pointy shoes with heels, small earrings that tremble like drops of water from milky earlobes. She prefers push-up bras, white or pink; bikini underwear, low-rise, full back. Never thongs.

"Probably a good thing," Susie said once, watching her wiggle out the front door. "The way she clenches that ass, it might get stuck in there forever."

*   *   *

His name is Paul. Audrey knows this because his apartment is in the same building where Susie and Pam live. Across-the-hall Paul. And he has been in the store, dragged along by the girlfriend, his tall, skinny frame hunched over as she piles his arms full of clothing, standing awkwardly outside the dressing room as she tries everything on. Some girls buy a lot of underwear.

But Monday he comes in alone, in a blue T-shirt and hoodie. He blinks in the light and hunches as he walks between

119

two tables stacked with bras that are on sale three for $36.00, and even though Audrey can tell he is making himself as small as can be he knocks the table with his hip and four bras fall to the floor, then he just kind of stands there until Susie sighs and says "Jesus Christ" and asks if she can help him.

His cheeks flush red and he drops his eyes. As he talks, low and mumbly, he absently toys with a red lace thong in his hands until he realizes what he is doing and drops it abruptly. "She's not that, you know . . ." his hands rise up to his chest to make a gesture. "She's *smaller*. Kind of like her . . ." he says, pointing at Audrey. Their eyes meet and Audrey could swear she feels a little cartoon arrow pierce her in the chest. She ducks down behind the counter abruptly, wondering how long she'll have to stay there before they stop staring over at her.

*   *   *

Audrey Green falls in love with every boy who comes into the lingerie store: every sweet, awkward boy who lurches in jeans or suit and tie between the racks of lacy, frilly things; who touches the fabric reverently, sliding silk between his rough boy-fingers; who lays himself out, vulnerable, exposed, because he loves a woman, because he would do anything for her; and who wears all this so blankly, so nakedly, on his earnest face. This kind of devotion is irresistible to Audrey. Some days she feels like she could die for any one of them.

Audrey is twenty-two years old and still a virgin. She has never even had an orgasm, although she has brought herself close, so close, under the covers in bed at night, stopping just short of climax, her whole body throbbing and breathless. Her sisters think there is something wrong with her, that she just doesn't know what she is doing. They try to teach her what boys like, just in case: a brush of the hand, a lick of the lips. Audrey always pays very close attention to what her sisters tell her. She practices in front of the mirror, wearing the lingerie she buys from the store with her 43% staff discount. She wears high heels and lipstick and sways her hips, pushes her breasts together, runs her hands over her thighs. Thinks about the boys who come to her store, the way they touch the lingerie, the way they breathe in and out, the way their mouths move when they talk to her.

"She doesn't try," Susie says.

"She just doesn't care," Pam says.

"She totally needs highlights," Mandy says.

"She just hasn't met the right boy yet," her mother says, tucking Audrey's short brown hair behind her ears, smiling at her, even though Audrey knows nothing in the world would make her mother happier than to see Audrey with a boyfriend – except maybe to see all four of them with boyfriends, or better yet, married off – big outdoor weddings and honeymoons to the Caribbean, a herd of strong, handsome sons-in-law with stable jobs and barbecues in their backyards who will adore her cooking and call her "Ma" and lift her off her feet when they hug her.

Audrey wishes she could give them all what they want. But the truth is, Audrey doesn't have a boyfriend because she's scared it won't be as wonderful as she imagines; that maybe wanting sex really is better than having it, and after twenty-two years of fantasy, she's not sure she can settle for reality. Because Audrey has seen less-than-perfect. And she knows it's not what she wants. She might not know what boys like, but she knows that, for sure.

*   *   *

On her break Audrey walks down the street to the Tim Horton's and while she is waiting in line for her English Toffee cappuccino she sees Across-the-hall Paul sitting at one of the plastic tables reading a book and eating some soup. He is so enthralled with the book that whenever he goes to scoop out some soup, he has to jab around with his spoon in order to find the bowl. One time he misses his mouth and vegetable beef barley trickles down his chin and onto his blue T-shirt. When he looks up from his book to wipe his face with his napkin, he catches Audrey staring at him and blushes, making Audrey blush too, and then they are blushing together, which Audrey thinks is so sexy she can hear her heart beating in her ears like tiny wings. There is something about Paul that makes Audrey feel brave – even though she has barely spoken to him, even though she knows he has a girlfriend, even though she knows deep down there is nothing different about him at all. But then she finds herself walking over to him, a growing tenderness between her legs, her heels clicking on the tile floor.

The book he is reading is called *Yzerman: The Making of a Champion*. Audrey wants to ask him what an Yzerman is, because the best way to get a boy to notice you is to pretend that you are interested in the same things as he is, even if you're not. From the picture on the cover, Audrey thinks that maybe an Yzerman is a kind of skate. But instead she walks over to the table and says "Did your girlfriend like her present?"

His eyes crinkle at the edges when he looks at her. "I just bought it fifteen minutes ago."

"So you did," says Audrey, leaning against the plastic chair on the other side of the table. She tries to push her cleavage together with the tops of her arms, the way her sister Mandy showed her, but it seems to work a lot better when Mandy does it. "You like Yzermans?" she asks, widening her eyes instead.

Across-the-hall Paul coughs. "Um, yeah," he says. "He's my favourite player. Since I was a kid."

"Really?" says Audrey. "That's totally fascinating." She reaches out and pretends to be examining the book cover. "I haven't read this one. You'll have to lend it to me."

"Um, okay." He prods his vegetable beef barley with the tip of his spoon.

"Okay." Audrey smiles a small, shy smile. "I hope your girl-friend's present fits." She feels a grin spreading like a stain across her face, and she spins around and walks out of the Tim Horton's giggling madly into her brown paper cup.

*   *   *

The rest of the day Audrey is so happy she tells the other girls that she will go in the back and sort the sale bras by size and colour, which is everyone's least favourite job to do. Paul, Paul, Paul, she thinks, holding each bra to her chest, trying to decide which one she will be wearing when he first takes off her shirt. The thought of it makes her feel so giddy she kisses Susie on the way out the door.

After work, when she goes to the nail salon with her sister Mandy – like she does every third Thursday so she can carry Mandy's purse and dig out Mandy's credit card and do all the other things Mandy can't do while her nails are drying – when the nail lady asks her, like she asks her every third Thursday, if Audrey would like new nails too, instead of giggling and shaking her head Audrey straightens her back and says yes.

On the way home, Mandy drives, and Audrey admires her new nails, pink and silver and hard as plastic. She taps them against the window. She draws them lightly across her forearm, humming under her breath.

"What is *up* with you?" Mandy asks.

"Nothing," says Audrey.

But later, after they go through the Dairy Queen Drive Thru, Mandy catches Audrey french kissing her soft-serve. "Okay, spill it Aud," she says, stabbing her Blizzard with a plastic spoon.

Audrey runs her tongue over her lips. "I'm in love," she says.

Mandy flicks her blonde hair behind her shoulder and gives Audrey a sideways look. Then she smiles, that horrible knowing smile. "You're not in love, Audrey," she says. "You just need to get laid."

*　　*　　*

That night, in her room, Audrey lies naked on her bed and lays her hands on her body: her thighs, her stomach, each opposite arm, admiring the way her nails shimmer against her pale skin. Later, she slips on her pink Swept Away Satin Pajamas and joins her mother in the living room. All three of her sisters are over, sprawled across the floor in front of the television set, smoking cigarettes and watching ER. The Invincible Green Girls, their mother always calls them. As though Audrey is a part of it all, and not just standing in the doorway, tapping her new nails against the frame absently.

"Jesus, Audrey, cut that out," Susie says, stubbing out her cigarette and clutching a batik-patterned cushion to her bulky midriff. Susie is the only one of the Green girls who is fat. "You're making me nervous. Can't you see that Dr. Carter is trying to insert an endotracheal tube? It's a very complicated procedure."

"No it's not," says Pam, who works at the hospital. Pam loves watching ER so she can point out all the things they get wrong, even though she only works in the accounting department and really has no idea. "It's totally routine. They just want it to be difficult for it to look good."

"Well, it looks good to me," their mother says, drawing her legs up onto the couch. "Dr. Carter looks good to me, too."

"God, Mom, gross," says Susie. "He's, like, twenty years younger than you."

Their mother ignores Susie. She pats the couch next to her. "Audrey, honey, come sit down with us." Audrey shakes her head. "Oh, come on, sweetling. You never hang out with us anymore."

"Audrey's in love," Mandy says, digging into a little pot of lip gloss with her index finger.

All four women look at her. Audrey shrinks back into the darkness, feeling the shadows folding themselves over the soft blue-green television glow. "In love!" Pam giggles. "Who's the lucky guy?"

"What's his name, Aud?" Susie asks.

"She doesn't know," Mandy says. She looks at Audrey and raises her pencil-thin eyebrows, blowing smoke through glossy lips.

Audrey can't help herself. "*I do too!* His name is Paul."

Their mother looks at her and clasps her hands together. "Well, that Paul is the luckiest boy in the world," she says, eyes shining with happiness.

*   *   *

Since Audrey works all day at the lingerie store with Susie, she doesn't really tend to visit her apartment very much. Susie and Pam are always at their mother's house anyway, eating out of her fridge, bumming cigarettes. In fact, Audrey has probably been to Pam and Susie's apartment less than a dozen times, so when she shows up on a Saturday morning with fresh bread from the market, they are both immediately suspicious.

Pam puts it together first. Pam is smarter than Susie. "Paul is Across-the-hall-Paul?" she asks, leaning against the kitchen counter in her Ultra Deluxe Chenille Robe in Cosmo Red, her blonde hair slipping out of curlers, sipping coffee from a chipped mug. "Really?"

"No," whispers Audrey.

Susie laughs, her body jiggling under her Night 'N Day Satin Sleepshirt. Her blonde hair is piled on top of her head in a messy bun. "He was in the store the other day," she says.

"Doesn't he have a girlfriend?" Pam asks.

"Yeah, but she's a total twat. Audrey's way prettier than her." Susie takes the bread and begins slicing it on a cutting board. "He seems a bit dumb."

"Of course he's dumb." Pam says.

"Did we tell him about our party tonight?"

Pam gives her a look. "Um, did we tell *Audrey* about our party tonight?"

Audrey toys with a ribbon hanging from the front of her sweater. Susie and Pam both tear into the bread, chewing thoughtfully.

"We need Mandy," Susie says finally. "She'll have to lend you some clothes. And do your hair. Do you have any makeup?"

"Um," says Audrey.

"You can borrow some of mine."

"You'd better be here by six," Pam says. "You don't want him to see you in the hall before the party."

"No," whispers Audrey. She turns to leave. Turns back around. "Do we have to tell Mom?"

Pam and Susie both burst into giggles. "Do we tell Mom *anything*?" Susie asks.

Pam pokes her. "Do we tell *Audrey* anything?"

Audrey resists the urge to stick her new nails in her mouth and chew them.

*   *   *

After her sisters are through with her, Audrey feels completely tarted up. It's not an entirely unpleasant feeling. She can't tear herself away from the mirror, from her dark red lips, her shadowy eyes (Mandy calls them "smoky"), her hair swept off her neck and lacquered into place with hairspray. She is wearing one of Mandy's "hooch shirts" – crushed red velvet with spaghetti straps and lace trim around the neckline – and a pair of slim black pants. Her sisters are surprised to discover Audrey has an exceptionally nice ass. "I can't wait to see the look on Paul's goofy little face," Pam says, lighting a cigarette.

It takes them two hours to get ready, clothes piled on Susie's bed, makeup everywhere, overflowing ashtrays and two bottles of wine. By the time they are finished, they are all drunk. Audrey sits in an armchair on top of a pile of laundry, her knees pulled up under her chin. It is the longest Audrey has spent with her sisters since they were in junior high and Audrey was even younger, when their mother would threaten them with early curfew if they didn't take Audrey to the mall with them, where they would promptly deposit Audrey in the bookstore while they went to the food court to hang out with their friends. Audrey would sit on the floor in the back of the bookstore and read magazines: *Cosmo*, *Vogue*, anything glossy with beautiful women

on the cover and articles like "Discover His Secret Sex Zones."
In those days, Audrey would have given anything to hang out
with her sisters – just to be able to sit on one of those plastic
chairs and drink Orange Juliuses with her sisters and their ponytailed, foul-mouthed entourage, listening to each other's Walk-
mans and writing on each others' backpacks, giggling while the
boys from the basketball team in their baggy jeans and high tops
yell at each other from across the mall and pelt each other with
french fries, trying to get the attention of one of those Invincible
Green Girls.

"I hope he doesn't bring that cow with him," Susie says. She
is leaning against her dresser, wearing nothing but her X-treme
Cleavage push-up bra and matching panties in Fuchsia Fantasy.
The bra is too small for her, and her breasts are spilling out the
sides, the underwire digging into the folds of flesh over her
ribcage.

"I don't give a fuck if he does" Pam proclaims loudly. She is
sorting through a pile of clothes on the floor. "Has anyone seen
my *fucking* belt?" she asks.

"I know his secret sex zones," Audrey whispers, and then
giggles.

Mandy, who is sitting cross-legged on the bed, her rye and
ginger pinned against her crotch as she sprays her hair, points
her curling iron at Audrey and waves it in a circle. "You don't
know anything until you've done it, missy," she says.

"Do you know about the ear?" Susie asks, folding her arms
in front of her chest.

"Oh! The ear!" Pam says, throwing her arms wide.

"The ear!" Mandy proclaims, sitting up straight. "You *have*
to know about the ear. The trick is to be *gentle*." She points the
end of the curling iron at Audrey's ear, and Audrey can feel the
waves of heat radiating from it. "Use the tip of your tongue and
just run it along that little foldy part, just like you'd run it over
the end of his pecker." All the girls giggle, including Audrey.
"What?" says Mandy. "I know a girl who made her boyfriend
come in his pants just by doing that."

"Mandy!" says Pam. "You're such a slut."

Mandy rolls her eyes. "I didn't say it was *me*."

"I bet I could do it," says Susie. "I made a guy come once by sucking his finger."

"That's not the same thing," Mandy says loudly, still gesticulating with the curling iron. "That's easy. Anybody can do that. Even Audrey." She jerks her hand towards Audrey and suddenly the curling iron is flying, the cord ripped from the wall socket, tumbling through the air in a slow-motion spin.

Audrey hears the curling iron before she feels it. It slaps her right across her left cheek and sizzles against her flesh for a moment before falling to the floor. Mandy's hands fly up to cover her mouth. Audrey looks around at her sisters, who are all staring at her. She feels a warmth rise in her cheek, then the pain reaches her. But she doesn't cry. She knows instinctively that this will ruin her eye makeup. She grinds her teeth together and clenches her fists to keep the tears back. Her sisters are quiet, moving around the room with their lips pursed together, avoiding each others' eyes. Pam, who has had the most experience with medical emergencies, holds a cold washcloth to Audrey's face. In the sudden quiet Audrey feels her insides begin to quake with disappointment.

After a few minutes Pam pulls the washcloth away to reveal a deep, red burn slicing diagonally across Audrey's cheek. Audrey stares in the mirror while Mandy and Susie discuss, in hushed voices, what kind of miracle makeup techniques they can use to cover it up. Audrey raises her fingers to the burn, still hot to the touch, sending a sharp pain up into her left eye. "I don't think that's a good idea," she says. "Let's, um, just leave it."

Susie tucks a piece of Audrey's hair behind her ear and looks at her with true tenderness. "Maybe Mandy could fire up the curling iron again and do the other side to match," she says.

"Fuck off," says Mandy. Susie and Audrey giggle, and it's almost as though everything is okay again.

*　　*　　*

Before the guests arrive, Mandy positions Audrey on a couch in the living room, where there is the least amount of light but she can still see out into the hall. She tilts Audrey's cheek slightly, so the left side is obscured in the shadows.

"Just hold that pose, Aud," she says. "Okay?"

"Okay," says Audrey. She knows this is Mandy's way of apologizing.

Mandy smiles and adjusts one of Audrey's straps. "Cool," she says. "Let me get you a drink."

Audrey sits and watches as her sisters' friends arrive in little groups, carrying cases of beer, backpacks full of wine and coolers, bags of chips and cheesies. Everyone heads straight for the kitchen. A few people come into the living room, standing uncomfortably in the doorway as Audrey tries to smile at them without moving her head. Nobody comes to talk to her. Around ten o'clock Paul shows up, slouching through the door with the girlfriend floating in behind him. Paul heads straight for the kitchen, but the girlfriend lingers a moment in the hall, fixing her lipstick in the mirror on the closet door. Audrey watches her, with those tiny arms and round, hard breasts, wondering if Paul ever worries about breaking her when he puts his arms around her. Then the girlfriend leaves and Audrey is alone again.

She sits by herself for what seems like forever. Eventually Susie comes over and brings her a drink, then sits down next to her and lights a cigarette.

"They're fighting, you know," Susie says, leaning in conspiratorially.

"I don't care," says Audrey, her voice shaking.

"Sure you do," Susie says. She blows smoke rings into the air. Susie has never had a boyfriend, Audrey realizes suddenly. She wonders why she never noticed. "Come on, for fuck's sake," Susie says. She takes Audrey's hand and drags her out of the living room into the hallway, which is packed with people. Audrey lowers her head, thinking everyone must be staring at her, but after a moment she realizes no one is paying attention to her at all. She relaxes a little as Susie leads her into the kitchen, the strap of her shirt slipping from her shoulders.

"Audrey," Susie says. "Audrey, this is Paul. From the store?" She pokes Audrey. "Remember?"

"What happened to your cheek?" Paul asks.

"Just a little accident," Audrey hears herself say. "No big deal." Then she leans in toward Paul, brushing against his arm. "I'm sure you've got a few old scars yourself," she says.

Paul laughs awkwardly. "I do," he says. Across the room, Audrey can see the girlfriend leaning against the kitchen counter watching them, arms crossed over her chest.

"We all do," Susie says, winking at Audrey.

Audrey smiles. She leans back against the counter and exhales, feeling her sweet breath pushing out into the smoky air, wondering if this is what it feels like to feel invincible.

All We
Will Ever Be

Now that you think about it, yeah. There are things about Emm that worry you. The way she stands outside in the rain, getting soaked. The way she says she agrees with you even when you know she doesn't. The way she seems to focus on your earlobe instead of your eyes when she says she loves you.

And another thing: there is something almost artificial about the way she fucks you. The way she looks up at you while she sucks your cock. The way she fingers herself when you have her on all fours. The way she arches her back when she comes. *Oh James, oh James.* Your name hot and electric on her lips. It's too perfect. As though she learned about sex from watching porn. What would make a man crazy.

It's not that you're looking for problems. But there are just all these things about her. Makes you wonder if you really know her at all.

*   *   *

Emily calls Daniel out of the blue, says his name so tenderly even though it has been ten years since he's seen her. On the phone her voice sounds like summer, fresh and alive, sparkling, reminding him of peppermints, of little kids on a playground.

"Daniel," she says. "I'd love to see you." He is struck with the memory of her smell, a clean, bright, grapefruity scent that used to linger in the room long after she was gone.

Emily was Daniel's first kiss, in the back of the junior high school gym after they had danced together to "I'll Be There," – the Mariah Carey version – her skinny arms, her boyish hips brushing against his crotch, her hot breath in his ear, whispering his name, *Daniel, Daniel*, as if he was the only boy in the room. Later there were those casual make outs in high school, drunk and in the dark, his inexperienced fingers fumbling under her shirt, her jeans hot and damp between her legs. But then she went to Toronto for university and Daniel stayed home, working at a bar and saving money for a Europe trip that never happened, that he somehow knew would never happen – blowing his money instead on a four day, brain-fried road trip to Virginia to see the Dave Matthews Band with two guys from work he barely knew, arriving back at the bar before the postcard he sent to his boss.

Emily comes to visit Daniel at his parents' farmhouse, where he has been living since his divorce. She looks the same as she did in high school and he feels old and tired as he pulls two beers from the fridge and cracks them open, thinking about how long it has been since a woman has come to see him – how pathetic he must seem, with his messy farmhouse, his piano with two missing keys, his sheets of music, his little life.

"Big-city girl," he says, sitting down at the table.

"No way," she says. "Toronto's fun, but it wears you down. It takes hours to get anywhere." She looks at him, gives him a wide, soft smile. "I'm a small-town girl at heart."

Daniel picks at the label on his beer bottle. "I thought you would be married by now," he says.

"Come on, Daniel. You know no one can hold me down." She is laughing but her eyes are far away. Later, he finds out that she has been living with a man for two years, James, that he has moved back east with her. Daniel wonders what being held down is, if that isn't it.

*   *   *

You've decided you don't like it here on the east coast. It's the fog. And all this rock and wind. People who step out into the street without looking both ways. It's too reckless. Too forward. No decorum. But somehow you always knew you would follow Emm back here. It seemed inevitable. In Toronto you knew people from back east. The thing about them was they always ended up going back east. Reckless.

One day she just said it. Folding laundry on your king-sized bed. Blue plaid duvet from page 77 of the Eddie Bauer catalogue. One of her latest obsessions, catalogue shopping. Just said it: "I think I want to go home, James." She didn't look at you. You understood that she would go with or without you. What the hell, you thought. Your job was flexible. You'd been freelancing for the past three years, sports stories mostly, the occasional big interview. Damon Allen. Nik Antropov. A slightly surreal lifestyle piece about Tie Domi's home renovations. Nothing you couldn't take with you. She worked a few shifts a week at an Irish pub, but otherwise her life was your life. Your Thursday night pick-up hockey team would have to find another right winger. Not much else to leave behind.

You and Emm have moved into an apartment with crown moldings. With two big, bricked-up fireplaces. Drafty Victorian windows. You worry about how you're going to afford to heat it. It's only September, and already here is the fucking fog creeping into your bones. Makes your joints ache. But she is happy. Moving her furniture out of her mother's basement. Painting the kitchen yellow. Enlarging old photographs to hang in frames. Babies and puppies, for Christ sake. Her old furniture is ugly, student-dorm kind of stuff. But this new nesting instinct. Strangely attractive.

"Next thing you're going to want to get married," you say. Actually hoping it's true.

She just laughs. Slaps your ass with the handle of a paint brush. "No one can hold me down, James, you know this." Then she's back into those old photographs. Wiping the dust off her former life.

*   *   *

Emily starts visiting Daniel at his farmhouse once every couple of weeks. At first the two of them talk like strangers – they *are* strangers, really – but eventually their friendship falls back into an easy rhythm. Emily shows Daniel pictures from Toronto, from her sister's wedding, from her trip to Costa Rica last spring, and Daniel plays Emily some songs he's been working on, his back hunched over the piano, fingers stiff on the keys. "I've been mostly taking in students," he explains apologetically. "I don't get to play in front of people very often." He can feel her being gentle with him, as if she can tell just by looking at him how badly he has been hurt. Daniel wonders if everyone can see this, but when she looks at him with those dark eyes he remembers that she knows things about him that no one else does, that she can still stare down into him like staring into a clear blue lake.

Emily brings him presents from town: a case of his favourite microbrew, St. John's Wort capsules from the health food store, a copy of *Rust Never Sleeps* on vinyl, which she puts on while he cooks dinner. Daniel chops peppers and mushrooms while Emily dances around his kitchen, blonde hair swinging above small shoulders, pale skin glowing.

"'Powderfinger' is too fast," she complains. "It's not anything like the Cowboy Junkies version, you know, all soft and sultry. Something a girl can sway her hips to."

"Neil Young wrote the song," Daniel says. "So he can play it however he likes."

Emily sticks out her tongue. "Look at your pot," she says, dipping her finger into the bubbling tomato sauce and licking it off. "You need new pots. I'll bring you the fall Paderno catalogue."

Daniel knows her finger must be burnt, but Emily doesn't even seem to notice, and he is reminded of a time in high school when her mother was away and the two of them stayed up all night drinking rum and playing Super Mario 3 – Daniel blowing in Emily's ear, tickling her feet, thrashing around the room to the Ramones, trying to distract her, none of which worked, her face grim in the flickering light of the screen. Then when it was her turn, she just stood next to the TV and licked her finger, slowly tracing it down the front of her neck and into her cleavage, at which point Daniel had forgotten all about the game, transfixed by her finger's journey, his erection straining against his jeans.

He gets that same feeling now, watching her dance around his kitchen: attracted to her but also scared. Scared that she had known that this one little thing would make him want her in a way he couldn't explain – like hot July sidewalks, Neil Young on a Tuesday afternoon, a cool fog bank rolling in over the sand dunes.

Scared that she had known, and had done it anyway.

*   *   *

Life begins to settle. You pick up a few stories. Local college stuff mostly, small potatoes. But you're feeling more relaxed. You take Emm to see the CIS men's basketball tournament when a local team makes the finals. She spends the whole time screaming her little head off at the refs. Adorable. You sit back in your plastic seat, the concrete beneath your feet sticky with beer. Smile. Wonder how it's possible that you've fallen in love with a girl who prefers basketball to hockey.

Emm gets a job waitressing. An Italian restaurant downtown. She's a good waitress. Likes the people. The *social interaction*. Not one of these only-a-waitress-until types. Then after three days she's obsessed with Italy. "Ciao, bello!" She says when you leave for work. Waves her hand in the air like a princess. On the weekends you run together in the park. She shows you

135

places. The spot in the woods where she smoked her first joint. The long, flat slab of rock where she lost her virginity. In the mornings you make tea for her before she gets out of bed. You go to her·mother's for dinner on Sundays. She joins a book club. You join the Y.

She hooks up with some old friends. Dumpy-looking girls who creep into your apartment, two-year-olds tethered to their arm. Husbands you never see. Who probably spend their unemployment cheques on new parts for their ATVs. And there are others whom you've never met. That mousey wisp of a guy who has been living at home since high school. Taking care of his sick mother. Or that sad old piano teacher whose wife left him. Who Emm visits out in the sticks because he refuses to come to the city.

"God your friends are depressing," you tell her one night over Thai food. "What is it, something in the water?"

She laughs. Swats your arm. "James! Don't be mean."

"Well, they are."

"That's what marriage does to you," she says. She takes a swig of her Singha. Eyes you over the bottle. "See how much happier we are?"

Later, after several more Singhas, Emm tells you that she still loves everyone she has ever loved. She tells you no one ever stops loving anyone. You don't tell her you have stopped loving several people. Your high school French teacher, who appeared in nearly every one of your early fantasies. Your best friend's older brother, whose slapshot was like poetry, who gave you your first *Playboy*. Your last girlfriend, who packed sandwiches for you to take to work and cried after every orgasm. Every one of them, now empty fucking holes in your heart.

*   *   *

One afternoon, Daniel and Emily fall asleep together, curled up on his bed watching *Roman Holiday* on TV. They had just come back from a walk in the woods, where Emily slipped off a rock and into a brook, soaking her jeans to the knee. When they got back to the farmhouse, he lent her a pair of his pajama pants and hung her jeans by the wood stove to dry, and then Daniel put the kettle on while Emily sat cross-legged on the bed, talking to him through the open door: "I love Audrey Hepburn, don't you? Daniel? *Quale attrice preferisce?* That means who is your favourite actress? In Italian? Maybe I'll go to Italy and do a *Roman Holiday* remake. I'm not going to be a waitress forever, you know."

Daniel smiled and shook his head as he carried the mugs of tea to the bedroom. He set the mugs on the bedside table and Emily curled against him. "Ciao, bello," she said, yawning.

He wakes up before her. He watches her, amazed that she is asleep at all, the way she is contorted, her body clinging to his in odd spots like a sock electric from the dryer. He can just see the downy blonde hair on the small of her back peeking out from under her T-shirt, and he rests his fingers lightly on her spine – positioning them on the two exposed vertebrae, white and smooth as piano keys – half expecting them to bend under his touch, to send a bellowing chord into the silence. He laughs softly to himself, pressing them harder, and Emily lets out a sigh and shifts her body closer to his. He feels the hairs on the back of his neck stand up.

He is falling in love with her.

When Emily wakes up the light coming through the curtains has softened to dusk. She looks at Daniel and in a hoarse voice tells him she has loved him since she was twelve. "You were the first, Daniel," she says. "You are the only true, pure love I have ever felt."

"That was a long time ago, Emm," he says, his voice cracking.

"Don't call me that," she says sharply. She rolls away from him, and soon her little shoulders are shaking. Daniel feels a familiar panic rise in his chest. His ex-wife used to cry like that – a silent, gentle weeping he was excluded from, tears that came from old, creaking pain. He didn't know what to do for her then, and he doesn't know what to do for Emily now.

Eventually she turns to face him, with flushed cheeks and bloodshot eyes. "You never stop loving anyone, you know," she says, tucking her face into the crook of his shoulder. "No one does."

Daniel feels her warm breath on his neck and believes her.

*   *   *

"Emm's not the kind of girl you fuck and leave," your buddy Niall told you before he introduced you. "She's hot. She loves sports. She doesn't care if you check out other women." Emm and Niall had been dating for six months. Already living together, shacked up in Niall's twelfth-storey condo. Emm playing fucking housewife while Niall went to work. When you first met her, in a bar on College after a Leaf's game, you thought she was fairly ordinary. Until she started talking about hockey. Then she smiled and she had all these teeth that you fell in love with one by one, like pennies clinking in a jar. Niall was working for a law firm and even though you knew he loved her, you knew what kind of love he was capable of. The evenings-and-weekends kind. The all-inclusive vacations. Suburban whatnot. You thought you could give her something more. This is why you felt justified in taking her from him. That you were doing him a favour, actually.

All it took: four martini-fuelled conversations at four different parties. A couple of well-placed compliments. Emm laughing into her sleeve, never quite sure how serious you were. Finally you offered to take her to a Leafs' game. "I'd rather see the Raptors," she said. So you pulled out all the stops. Courtside seats and a VIP booth at a private after-party, where the two of you drank way too much and ended up dancing on a speaker to "Funkytown." A five A.M. pancake breakfast. A slow walk through the empty streets of Toronto. Back to your apartment just as the sun was coming up.

"I totally love basketball players," she said. Squinted her eyes against the light. "But I suppose a hockey player'll do in a pinch."

You kissed her on the forehead. Thought: *I've got her.* It didn't occur to you until later. Her cool, naked back pressed against your chest as you slept. That maybe it was the other way around.

When Emm told Niall she was leaving, he hit her. Split her lip. Cracked her tooth on his ring. She didn't seem surprised. A week after she had moved her things from Niall's apartment to yours, he came by. You were home alone. What you saw: his bloodshot eyes. Greasy hair. Jacket with the one pocket turned inside out. You realized you'd been wrong about him. But what was done was done.

He leaned against the doorway. "I never thought I would be the one standing here. And you probably won't, either," he told you. Eyes more tired than accusing.

*   *   *

"James is driving me crazy," Emily tells Daniel. The two of them are in the sunroom, playing gin rummy in the late afternoon glow. "I think I may breakup with him."

Daniel lays his cards face down on the table and crosses his arms in front of him. James. The journalist from Toronto with the eyebrow ring. In the pictures Emily showed Daniel he looked smug, always holding Emily's elbow protectively, resting his hand on her shoulder.

"Why?" Daniel asks nonchalantly.

"Oh, I don't know," Emily says. "Maybe it's just being back here, seeing him out of context. I feel bad. But he doesn't, you know, fit."

"Not small-town enough for you?"

"*Dan*-iel!" she says. "Come on. I'm not being mean, am I?"

"All I know," he says, "Is I wouldn't want to be on the end of that stick." She swats him with the back of her hand. He throws out the jack of spades. "Your turn," he says.

Emily picks up the jack. "Maybe I should just have an affair," she says. She watches Daniel while she says it. "An older man, with greying temples and a moustache, someone who will meet me for drinks in hotel lobbies, take me to Italy. Someone who will buy me jewellery, tell me he'll leave his wife for me even though he doesn't mean it."

"You don't wear jewellery," Daniel says, because he can't think of anything else.

"Maybe I would," she says. She gives him a wicked grin and lays her cards down.

"Gin."

*   *   *

One weekend, you fly back to Toronto for a story. You've got a regular column now, for a Halifax-based sports magazine. When you come home in the middle of the night, the bed is empty. You find Emm asleep on the couch in the living room. Under a blanket. Body curled around an empty bottle of Chianti. You leave her there on the couch. The next morning she wakes you up with her mouth on your cock. When you fuck she's like a hungry person. Digs her fingernails into your ass. Kisses you like you're strangers. You don't hate it, but you're uneasy. You start to have disturbing dreams where she's fucking you. A long hard cock rising up between her thighs.

She tells you she wants to go to Italy. She even tries to learn to speak Italian, with this set of CDs she bought at a yard sale. Listens to them in the car on the way to and from the grocery store. Leaves the CDs in the stereo so every time you start the car you hear this creepy, nasal Italian guy: *A che ora comincia il film?* What time does the film start? *Non sapevo che c'era il limite di velocità.* I didn't know there was a speed limit.

"I've never been anywhere, James," Emily says. Leans her head against the frame of one of those stupid Victorian windows. Looks sad. You're the one who wanted to come home, you think. But don't say. We could have gone anywhere.

*   *   *

Daniel's ex-wife once told him she wished her life had a soundtrack, like a movie. She wished her life was a movie, actually, with music swelling at the climax, important moments edited down into montage, an ending she could tell was an ending, as opposed to just this, this on and on, no rolling credits to tell her that the story was over.

One day he comes back from the market to find Emily in his kitchen, making coffee. She has her earphones on and doesn't hear him come in. He watches her for a moment, as she levels off the coffee grounds with the blunt edge of a butter knife. Then abruptly she throws her head back, slamming her hands against the counter in a spontaneous drum solo. Daniel bursts into laughter, and she spins around to face him, her hand over her chest.

"Jesus Christ. You scared the crap out of me."

Daniel takes one of her earphones and kisses the tip of her nose while "Knockin' on Heaven's Door," the Guns N' Roses version, plays in one of his ears and one of hers. He can see the line on her front tooth where she cracked it falling on the ice when she was first learning to skate.

"You know Bob Dylan wrote that," Daniel says.

"Bob Dylan didn't have Slash."

Daniel smiles and wonders how it's possible that he has fallen in love with a girl who prefers cover songs to the originals.

* * *

Something has changed. She wears her earphones all the time now. Stares at the wall in the bedroom when you come home from work. Vacant eyes. She goes to movies by herself. A couple of times a week. Stops coming to see your hockey games. Starts smoking weed again. "Hockey's so *boring*," she says when you confront her about it. When you stare at her, disbelieving, she shrugs.

"I never said I liked it," she says.

Once, when you both still lived in Toronto, you thought Emm was having an affair. She would disappear for long periods of time and when she came back she was flushed. Full of endorphins. Fucking *radiant*. One night you called her on it. You made her dinner. Poured her a glass of wine. Told her very quietly you knew what was going on. You stayed calm. Clenched your muscles into stone. You made sure she knew you were doing her a favour. That you could break her arm. If you wanted to.

As it turned out, she had been taking skating lessons so she could go to the rink with you. It was going to be your birthday present. She said. Calmly. Later you found her crying in the shower. Hair still full of shampoo. The next weekend, you suggested a trip to the rink. She said "James, I forgive you, but I will never, *ever* go skating with you."

Now, part of you wishes you *had* gone. Seen her glide across the ice. Arms outstretched. Just so you could stop thinking it was all a lie.

Now when you're in bed together she will only let you fuck her from behind. She tells you it's the only way she comes. You know this isn't true. She just doesn't want to look you in the eye. Your hands are all over her. While she washes the dishes. While she waters the endless number of plants that have somehow accumulated in your apartment. You start waking up in the middle of the night just to watch her sleep. Like some goddamn lovesick fucking puppy.

She reads *Under the Tuscan Sun*. At night before bed. Part of her book club, she tells you. Her suggestion. "Let's do it," you say. "Let's go to Italy." She just nods. Stares out the goddamn window.

You buy her a ring. "Not an engagement ring," you say. Feeling foolish. "Just a ring." Sapphire edged with diamonds. She kisses you. Tells you she loves it. Two days later you find it sitting in a puddle on the bathroom counter next to the open tube of toothpaste. This is it, you think. This is all we will ever be.

* * *

The night of the first snowstorm of the year Emily brings Daniel a Patsy Cline record and he dances with her, one arm around her waist, holding her hand in close to his chest. She sings, "I'm crazy for cryin', crazy for tryin'" at the top of her lungs as they waltz around the room.

"Hey, Daniel," she says. "I like the original best. Are you surprised?"

"This isn't the original," he tells her. "The song was written by Willie Nelson. But I guess people have pretty much forgotten."

"Poor Willie," says Emily.

Daniel's ex-wife once told him that he was too passive. "You don't take the things you want," she'd said. "And it pisses me off to watch you sit there and wait for things to happen to you." Later, Daniel watched her walk out the door and silently agreed with her.

James doesn't know how to love Emily, thinks Daniel. Why else would she be here, now, resting her cheek against his, listening to his heart race in his chest? James can't possibly be capable of feeling the way Daniel is feeling, or else he wouldn't let her go. I may actually be doing him a favour, Daniel thinks, reaching out and tilting Emily's chin upwards.

He kisses her, and she doesn't stop him. She may even be kissing him back, but he is so flushed with adrenaline he can't be sure. Then the kissing ends, their foreheads are pressed together and Daniel's cheeks are wet but he realizes it's Emily who is crying. She says his name once and then she is gone, he can hear her car tires crunching through the snow and he wonders, in an oddly detached way, whether he will ever see her again.

*   *   *

You and Emm fight. The night of the magazine's Christmas party. She is wearing a black skirt. A green silk halter top that offsets her eyes and shows too much cleavage. She has always known how to dress to drive you crazy.

"It's fucking ten below. You're going to freeze to death."

"I'm wearing a coat, James. Jesus."

At the party you drink too much. Ignore her on purpose. Fuck you, you think. People *like* me. You shoot tequila with some of the young guys from distro. You share a cigar with your boss. You dance with Shelley from Accounting. Lean over so your foreheads touch. Whisper to her as though you are saying something important. Something secret.

What you do say: "I think Brad from distro has a crush on you."

Shelley laughs loudly. Turns red. You look back to your table to make sure Emm is watching you. You see her get up. Walk out of the room. You feel childish. But vindicated.

On the way home, Emm drives. You lean against the window in the passenger seat. Stare at her. You wish she could see herself: that fucking slutty top. Sad fucking eyes. She doesn't even know who she is. You imagine throwing yourself on top of her. Twisting her body. Thumbs on her neck. Fucking her until she splits in two.

In front of your apartment you sit in silence. Listen to the engine tick. The air in the car growing cooler. You get out of the car. She starts it up again. The stereo blasts on. *Fa molto caldo oggi. Pensa che ci sarà un temporale?* It's very hot today. Do you think there will be a storm?

*   *   *

Emily shows up at Daniel's door dressed for a party. She knocks, even though she has been letting herself in for months. "Hi," she says. Her eyes are so light they are almost golden. She shivers, and she is beautiful shivering, her lips parting, her teeth trembling lightly. "Can I come in?"

He nods, even though he's not sure what she's really asking. She steps inside like leaves swirling in a windstorm, blows through the porch. In the kitchen Daniel puts on the kettle, but she asks if he has any beer. He opens his last two bottles and they sit across from each other, staring: she is still wearing her coat as she takes a long drink of the beer, setting it down on the table a little too hard. In the wood stove a piece of bark spits with a loud cracking sound, like something large and brittle breaking in two.

"Why do you come here?" Daniel asks.

"You have a TV in the bedroom," she says without missing a beat.

"Don't leave," he whispers. And this time, she doesn't.

*   *   *

On the way into your apartment, you slam the door. A piece of wood splinters from the frame. You rip it away. Throw it against the wall. It knocks down a picture, one of those stupid fucking framed puppy-pictures. You are seething. You want to destroy the apartment smash all the windows set fire to the furniture. Trash all those fucking things you thought that she cared about. Things you thought that *you* cared about. You want to throw all Emm's junk into the street. And yours too. You want to rip off your clothes sit naked in your fucking drafty empty apartment wait for her.

To come home.

To know *what she's fucking done to you*.

But you don't. Instead you watch an Arnold Schwarzenegger movie on TV. *Terminator* something. Put a significant dent in a bottle of Johnnie Walker Blue Label you'd been saving. For what? You can't even remember. Afterwards you jerk off. To a picture. Out of one of her lingerie catalogues. Immediately feel guilty. Throw the whole thing in the trash. By morning you have dissolved. You put on her old York University sweatshirt. Curl up. On her side of the bed. Stare at the wall. To avoid. The spins.

*   *   *

Daniel could never have imagined this: Emily's hair in his mouth, grapefruit-smell of her everywhere, her soft hands unstoppable on his body, taking possession of every joint, every crevice. He slips into her so easily he feels like he might come right then; he wants to bury himself inside her, as deep as he possibly can, until he can't feel anything but Emily, Emily, Emily. She convulses against him and in the split second before he comes, one thought enters his mind. *I've got her.*

The next morning Daniel makes breakfast for Emily. She is wearing his pajama pants again, and his favourite blue hooded sweatshirt. The sleeves of the sweatshirt cover her small hands to her knuckles, her fingers peeking out the end as she pulls apart her toast, peels her bacon into strips. On the radio, the Stones play "Wild Horses" and she hums along, pulling her feet up onto the chair and resting her head on her knees, watching Daniel. For a moment he wonders if she is watching him, or watching him watching her.

Whichever it is, he is so happy he doesn't care.

*   *   *

Emm shows up late in the afternoon. She is still wearing her black skirt. Instead of the halter top, an unfamiliar blue sweatshirt. Her hair is pulled back in a ponytail. Her face is scrubbed clean of makeup.

She doesn't tell you where she was. You're so tired you don't care. You hate him, whoever he is. But you know you can't blame him. For any of this.

That night you watch the Leafs' game on your new plasma TV. Instead of laying her head on your lap on the couch, she curls up in the armchair. Legs tucked up underneath her. An old batik blanket pulled up to her chest. She seems uninterested in the game. Halfway through she pulls a book out of her purse and starts reading. You offer her a glass of wine but she wrinkles her nose and doesn't say anything. So you spread peanut butter on a cracker for her. Which she takes but re-spreads with her finger. Swirls the peanut butter out to the edges. Licks off the excess. You wonder why she is reading what appears to be a biography of Neil Young. For some odd reason, you suddenly and sharply miss your old favourite Chinese restaurant on Spadina.

Talking About
The Weather

On Sunday mornings, Tom and Susannah can hear everyone in their building having sex. It usually starts around eight A.M., sometimes earlier if Monique in the apartment above them has had a late night at the clubs. Their Sunday morning is still Monique's Saturday night. Monique is thirty-six: three years older than Tom, five years older than Susannah. Susannah wonders if this makes them boring, or if it makes Monique ridiculous. The men she brings home are not men, but boys; Susannah sees them as they sneak out afterwards, looking slightly dazed as they stumble home for sleep.

"It's a shame, really," Tom says as he boils water for their tea. Below their kitchen window, Monique's latest baby-faced, bed-headed conquest scurries off of their front porch and into a waiting cab. "I mean, she sounds like a cat in heat. Imagine the things she must be teaching them. Corrupting the city's youth, one poor, unsuspecting boy at a time."

Susannah tries not to imagine. She thinks instead of the things Tom has taught her. How to move around him in narrow hallways, how to adjust her breathing to his while they sleep face to face, in and out simultaneously, so that neither of them are breathing in each others' used-up air. "Our youth could use a little more corrupting," she says. She wraps her arms around Tom

149

from behind, pressing her face between his shoulder blades and breathing in his clean-T-shirt smell. The kettle begins to boil. "I'm feeling incredibly uncorrupted, myself," she says over the screeching.

Tom yanks the kettle's plug from the wall. "It's nice that you still think of yourself as 'youth'," he says. He gently unlocks her hands, knitted together over his stomach. She lets them fall. She watches him pour the water evenly into two mugs, the little gauze tea bags floating pitifully in the steaming water. She reaches for the milk.

*   *   *

By nine A.M., Tom and Susannah are in their living room reading the paper and listening to the news on CBC, and Al and Katie next door are fucking in their shower. They have known Al and Katie for years – Tom and Al grew up together in New Brunswick, and Katie and Susannah have become friends politely, out of necessity, awkwardly trying to find common ground while their husbands watch hockey and reminisce about girls they dated in college. Truthfully, Susannah has always considered Katie to be a complete flake. And since he has been dating her, she secretly thinks Al has started to become a little flaky himself – joining Katie at her Winter Solstice drumming circles, shopping with her on weekends for organic, unbleached cotton shirts and vegan shoes. Still, he is one of Tom's closest friends, so Susannah makes an effort, inviting them over for dinner on weekends, helping Tom plan a party for Al's 30th birthday, even going with Katie to that silly paint-your-own-pottery place that she manages. When the apartment next door had come up for rent, Tom suggested that Al and Katie move in, joking that it would be perfect seeing as they didn't have to share a bedroom wall.

Tom and Susannah don't talk about Al and Katie fucking the way they talk about Monique. It is as though as long as they don't talk about it, it's not actually happening, and this is how they will get through the next dinner party, the next night at the movies with them, without thinking about Katie's face pressed against the shower tiles, Al's hands on her wet hips, their bodies covered in soap.

Tom turns up the radio. Susannah knows he is waiting to hear the World Report, but all the announcer can talk about is a hurricane making its way up the eastern seaboard. Beyond the wall somewhere, the sound of slapping flesh. "Jesus," Tom says. "We live in the fucking *Maritimes*. How is bad weather considered *news*?"

"It sounds like it might actually be kind of intense," Susannah says. She hears Katie moan. "Maybe we should at least shut the windows or something," she says, louder.

Tom just flips the page of the newspaper, runs his hand through his hair, unimpressed with the storm, with weather in general. Next door, the water shuts off, and Al and Katie are laughing. For a moment Susannah wonders if they can hear her and Tom, if it is their conversation they are laughing at. "They're talking about the *weather*," she imagines Katie saying, her skin glistening, her wet hair hanging limply around her face, her mascara running around her eyes, and the two of them wrapping themselves up together in one towel, their laughter melting into one unified sound.

*   *   *

Susannah first met Tom after a succession of boyfriends seemingly incapable of breathing through the nose. Tom's nose didn't emit so much as a whistle and his moist lips rested gently together when he wasn't using them. At the time, this appeared to be the pinnacle of male perfection. The first time they kissed was the first time Susannah had kissed in silence, and afterward she ran her finger over those lips and thought to herself, rather triumphantly, that this one just might work.

Tom was an artist like everyone else she knew, and they had met through a friend of a friend, all of them sitting around in a dimly-lit cigar bar with black and white photographs pinned to the emerald-papered walls, all Van Morrison and Nick Drake, thick cigar smoke and talk of American politics and Asian cooking. Tom sat next to her, chewing on the peel of a lemon fished out of a vodka tonic, following the conversation with his eyes. His hair was curly and he was wearing a grey wool coat over a blue turtleneck sweater, and his equally blue eyes were framed with long black lashes. He looked comfortable and warm, the human equivalent to a cozy blanket and a favourite book in front of a fire. Susannah imagined herself crawling inside him, curling up and falling asleep.

At some point in the evening, he turned to her. "So you're a photographer," he said. As if it was the most amazing thing in the world.

"I take pictures," said Susannah, staring at her hands.

They moved their chairs to face each other, and everything else faded into the background. They discovered they had both lived in Vancouver for the same brief period of time; had almost identical scars on their foreheads at the base of their hairline. Those two small pieces of shared history made it seem to Susannah as though they had the entire world in common. Tom told her about things that he painted, about places he'd traveled. He talked about books and music with a quiet reverence. "I am always just so amazed," he said, with a lick of his lips, "that someone was able to create this . . . this beautiful thing, just out of thin air." Susannah felt a familiar ache in her stomach, a feeling that made her move her hand to rest on his arm while she talked, to look into his eyes a little too long, to brush her knee against his under the table. These gestures came back to her almost without thinking about it and her body fell, awkwardly at first, into the rhythm of seduction. Afterward they kissed in the parking lot beside the bar, in the snow, maybe even under a street light: the warm, scratchy wool of his coat against her cheek, fat snowflakes sticking to his long lashes.

"My god, you're beautiful," he said, brushing her hair out of her eyes and looking at her as if he was the lucky one. And with those four perfect words, Susannah fell in love.

Two months later, they moved in together. Susannah brought Tom to the Annapolis Valley to meet her parents, and they walked down the street holding hands as she whispered her hometown stories in his ear. He listened attentively, laughed when it was appropriate, kissed her on the forehead in that precise spot where every girl wants to be kissed. She took photographs of him in her most important childhood places: her elementary school playground with the rusty merry-go-round, under the giant weeping birch behind her parents' house, the dam where she used to swim. Susannah felt as if the whole world was watching them, admiring them, envious of their youth, their beauty, their perfection.

Back in the city, they went to art galleries, watched movies, shopped together at the farmers' market. In restaurants they carried on intimate conversations in hushed voices, laughed together at inside jokes. At night they lay next to each other, their skin sparking as it rubbed together, their breath ragged, falling into sync. When Susannah got together with her girlfriends they all gushed about Tom, wondering why their own lazy, selfish boyfriends couldn't be more like Susannah's brilliant new man. Susannah laughed, told them there was good and bad in every relationship, and *of course* she and Tom had their problems. Didn't he always leave his socks on the floor, or forget to shut the cupboard doors in the kitchen after he was finished cooking? But inwardly, Susannah beamed, believing that none of her friends had what she had. The shutter of her camera clicked easily, continuously, everything around her bursting with beauty and light, with joy.

*   *   *

The potheads downstairs usually start having sex around eleven A.M., about the time Susannah is getting ready to head out for her run. She is in the bedroom putting on her sneakers when she hears them: none of Monique's over-exaggerated porn-movie squealing, or Katie's wet, feral moaning, but just a slow, rhythmic *thumpthumpthump* that rattles the bottles of nail polish on the dresser and ends in nothing but silence. Susannah can remember a time when she and Tom would still be in bed while the potheads were fucking. They would lie together, spooning with the duvet pulled right up over their heads, their bodies gently rocking back and forth in time to the rhythm crawling up the wall from the floor below until Tom would climb on top of her, pressing himself between her legs. But Susannah figures it has been months now since Tom has heard the potheads downstairs fucking, that long since they had stayed in bed on a Sunday morning.

She finishes tying her shoelaces and walks quietly into the hall. Tom is already in his office, his second cup of tea growing cold on his desk as he rifles through a stack of papers. Essays, Susannah knows, on Environmental Art or The Social History of Graffiti or The Progress of Visual Communication in Communist China – topics that Tom's black-eyelined, striped-kneesock-wearing students adore and Susannah has grown to despise. Susannah stands in the doorway and watches as Tom clicks the end of his automatic pencil, the brittle lead growing longer and longer before he carefully pushes it back in against the edge of his desk.

"Hey," she says. "Can you hear that?"

"Hear what?" Tom asks, without looking up.

Susannah crosses the room and stands behind Tom. She reaches her arms out on either side of him and takes his hands, pressing them against the desk, which is shaking almost imperceptibly. "Thump, thump," she says.

"Really?" says Tom. "You'd think they'd have grown bored of that by now."

"What? Bored of sex?" Susannah draws her hands away and stares at the back of Tom's curly head.

"Well, they *are* potheads. Short attention span."

"I see," says Susannah, zipping up her hoodie. "I'm going for a run."

Tom pushes his automatic pencil back against the desk, and the lead snaps. "Don't be gone too long," he says. "I hear there's going to be some kind of storm or something."

*   *   *

Tom started teaching at the art college about a year after Susannah moved in with him. Tom really likes teaching. He is good at it. Susannah can picture him walking around his classroom in his turtleneck sweater and jeans, his hands stuffed into his pockets, winning the students over with his quiet charm, smiling that smile at all the ponytailed girls with paint smudged across their foreheads. Susannah imagines them doe-eyed and wispy, touching Tom's arm when they talk to him, canvas after canvas splattered with their young, febrile passion.

"Joni started making comic books," Tom told her one night at supper, a few months into his first semester. He wrapped a piece of linguine around his fork, pausing as he raised it to his mouth. "No, wait. Graphic novels. Something about a lesbian superhero. I'll get you a copy, if you want."

"Joni?" Susannah asked. "Isn't she the one who skipped her evaluation?"

"No. Well, yes," said Tom.

"Right," says Susannah. "The evaluation where you're supposed to submit your portfolio? The portfolio you need in order to, you know, *pass the class*?"

"That doesn't make her any less brilliant though, does it?"

"Did you pass her?"

A pause. "Yes."

"Well, I suppose you would. If Joni is *brilliant* and all," Susannah said, shoving a forkful of pasta in her mouth.

That night after supper, Susannah shut herself into the small spare room, which she had turned into a darkroom shortly after Tom had taken his teaching job. She had blacked out the window and painted the walls, and set up her developing equipment on brand new shiny metal tables. The pictures she had

155

taken of Tom hung on a rope stretched across one corner of the room. It was such a calm, peaceful room, but lately every time Susannah went in there, her stomach started quaking even before she closed the door behind her. Susannah leaned her back against the wall, running her hands over the box that held her camera, that had held it for months now. She peeled off a piece of cardboard and shoved it into her pocket. Her camera – which had always been so friendly to her, so loving and comforting – now looked up at her scornfully. "You're not like them," it told her matter-of-factly. "Those girls, they're babies, it's still kind of attractive that they think they're going to be artists one day. But you." Her camera sighed. "You should know better."

Susannah turned off the overhead light and stared at the pictures of Tom through the blush of red: Tom's face glowing, burning, fiery arms, legs, skin bursting out of the deep crimson shadows. They looked so pretentious, so ridiculous in their complete lack of artistry. At that moment, she knew it was true. She was not like them. She never would be.

When Susannah came out of the darkroom, Tom was sitting on the couch, his feet propped up on the coffee table, marking. Susannah walked over to him and he looked up from his papers. "Is everything okay?" he asked carefully. Susannah shut her eyes, suddenly irritated, and imagined his skin on fire.

"My camera's broken," she said, sitting at Tom's feet. "Do you want some hot chocolate?"

That was the last time Susannah had been in her darkroom.

*   *   *

As soon as she steps outside, Susannah can already feel the storm, the atmosphere practically sizzling with the impending violence. Everything is still. On her way down the front steps, she passes the boy pothead, on his way up with a bag from the corner store. Susannah has always felt wary of the boy pothead. He smiles too much, is a little too overenthusiastic about everything. When he talks, it is as if every other word is in italics.

The boy pothead holds the bag up to her and grins. There is something black caught in between his two front teeth. "*Provisions*," he says. Through the plastic, Susannah can see several cans of baked beans and a package of hot dogs.

"That looks like camping food," she says. "You guys got a Coleman or something?"

"Nope," he says. "We're taking the *van* over to Lawrencetown. We're going to check out the *waves*, man."

Susannah grabs hold of the banister. Her hands are already clammy from the humidity. "That sounds kind of dangerous," she says. "Isn't there supposed to be a storm surge?"

The boy pothead laughs. "They *always* say there's going to be a *storm surge*. When has there *ever* been a *storm surge*?"

Susannah suddenly feels annoyed. She thinks about the potheads fucking in their stupid violet-coloured VW van, *thump thumpthump*ing in time to the waves breaking on the beach, their breath stinking like canned beans. "They're saying three feet. How tall is the breakwater at Lawrencetown? Less than three feet, I'd guess."

"Who the fuck are *they* anyway?" the boy pothead asks. "And who the fuck are *you*? The fucking *weathergirl*?"

"Watch out for your beautiful van!" Susannah calls after him as he shuts the front door behind him.

Susannah pulls up her hood and begins running down Inglis Street, intending to head for the park. But the air feels so thick that she stops after only a few blocks, already out of breath. She turns and walks down South Bland Street, the grain elevators to the south rising like a bleak yellow wall blocking out the sky in front of her. Susannah doesn't know if they still even use the grain elevators. She remembers hearing somewhere that years earlier, a woman walking her dog had found a murdered prostitute in one of the dumpsters in the back, although she realizes now that this might be one of those myths about the city that, as an outsider, she will never really know the truth of: underwater tunnels connecting the Citadel with George's Island, escaped mental patients jumping off the MacDonald Bridge, dead

prostitutes behind the grain elevators. She crosses the street anyway, trying to block out the images of ripped clothing and
twisted limbs that push their way into her mind. On the other
side, a man and a woman are fighting through an open window.
Their voices echo between the houses, their drama unfolding in
front of the whole world.

"Jesus, are you crying again?" she hears the man say. There
is no pity in his voice, just impatience. Susannah sees him as he
stalks by the window, his body taut, electric as the air. The
woman speaks, but her voice is muffled, choking on her sobs.
Somewhere in the distance, a dog barks. Susannah turns around
and heads for home.

Back at the apartment, Tom has moved his pile of essays
into the living room and is watching the Penguins game while he
reads. For a moment Susannah watches him, his feet up on the
coffee table, wiry toes flexed, soft dark hair covering all those
delicate bones. She squints and involuntarily sees a photograph:
Tom's pale feet in the foreground, ankles crossed; the shelf of
CDs in the background an unfocused blur, their combined musi-
cal tastes piled into a neat little stack. Even though it has been
over a year since Susannah has used her camera, she can't help
but sometimes see things in photographs, unconsciously com-
posing images in her field of vision. These artistic intrusions
feel, to Susannah, like waking up from an erotic dream about an
old lover: unasked for, unwelcome, and maddeningly beyond her
control.

Susannah greets Tom with a kiss on the top of his curly
head. "Can we check the Weather Network?" she says. "I just
want to see." Tom sighs, mumbles something about the self-
importance of meteorology, but hands her the remote anyway.
She flips the channel and watches as a perky blonde woman
points to a little white pinwheel spiraling across an expanse of
blue, then turns to the camera with a knitted brow, her eyes
pleading with everyone to take her seriously.

"She's in heaven right now," Tom says. "This is her moment to shine."

"I'm going to get the chili started," Susannah says, mesmerized by the little white pinwheel. "You know, just in case the power goes out."

"When did you start being such a little girl scout?" Tom asks.

Susannah tosses the remote into Tom's lap. "Always be prepared, that's my motto," she says. She is laughing, but in her stomach she feels something knot a little tighter.

*   *   *

Days without art are like clockwork, calm and surreal. And easier, without all that extra search for meaning. Susannah wonders how Tom does it. How he gives his whole soul every day and can still possibly have enough left over at the end for her. He is *invigorated*. He brings home paintbrushes caked with his own sweat, sketches drawn with blood, canvases riddled with shrapnel from his own exploding self. Tom still talks about Joni, but he also talks about Bella and Julie and Caroline, all these beautiful faceless names whose blossoming futures are as fragile as flower petals, cupped in Tom's hands for him to nurture and protect. It makes Susannah want to puke. It's not that she is jealous of Tom's students. The truth is, she is sickened by their mutual wide-eyed admiration, their self-righteous creativity, their unembarrassed passion. She just doesn't see the point anymore.

One night when Susannah arrived home from work, she found Tom sitting on the floor of the darkroom, fiddling with her camera. "I don't think it's broken," he said as she came in. "What did you say the problem was?"

Susannah looked at the floor. "I don't know. I put my eye to the lens, but I can't see anything."

Tom held the camera up to his eye. "I can see fine. The problem's not the camera. It must be your eye." He stood up and walked towards her, taking her face in his hands. "Let me take a look."

They pressed their foreheads together. Susannah could feel the heat pulsing from Tom's skin, could feel how similar its texture was to her own. "I see the problem," said Tom. "You only have one eye. That must make things difficult."

Susannah stared hard at Tom's eyes, melted together above the bridge of his nose. They were so blue, flecked with gold, and they quivered so earnestly, with something unspoken, a deeper meaning Susannah was supposed to understand. She realized, with a twinge of panic, that she didn't understand at all.

"I'll figure it out," she said, watching Tom's pupils dilate and contract. "I promise."

"Don't promise me," said Tom. "You should do what feels right." He stroked the back of her head with his hand. It was such a perfect tender gesture – one that Susannah suddenly found hilarious.

"Is that what you tell all the girls in your classes?" She meant it as a joke, but Tom pulled away, dropping his hand abruptly.

"Yes, I do," he said quietly. "The girls and the boys. But they understand what I mean."

"So do I," Susannah said. "Really." They both knew she was lying.

*　　*　　*

The power goes out late in the third period. The Penguins, Tom informs Susannah, were on a power play and only down by one goal. "Their first power play of the fucking game!" he says, pacing back and forth outside the kitchen door as Susannah lifts the pot of nearly-cooked chili into the oven she has already pre-heated to try to keep it warm.

"I told you the power was going to go out," she says. "Always be prepared, remember?"

Tom stops in the doorway and glares at her. "How is *being prepared* going to help me see if Malkin can finally fucking score?"

Susannah shrugs and leans against the counter. Even in the dimming light she can still see Tom's face growing redder. *Sports-frustration* crimson, as opposed to *finished-a-painting* vermillion or *angry-at-Stephen-Harper* scarlet or *good-day-of-teaching* burgundy – Tom has a slightly different shade of red for all his various passions. Which these days, it occurs to Susannah, seems to include everything but her.

"I guess you'll have to settle for the highlights," she says. She turns back to the oven, which is already starting to lose its heat. "You'll get the gist of it, anyway."

"The gist? Oh, great," says Tom. "There's nothing better than *the gist* of the beautiful slapshot that could be sending the game into overtime as we fucking speak."

Sure, Susannah thinks. The gist. What more does anyone really need than that?

*   *   *

Later, Al and Katie show up at Tom and Susannah's door with a jug of homemade wine, and the four of them eat chili sitting on the floor, bowls held under their chins, candles quivering on the coffee table in front of them. Al talks excitedly about the storm: knots per hour, storm surges, Doppler radar, the Saffir-Simpson scale. "Did you know," he says, "That the last time a Category 2 hurricane hit Nova Scotia was in 1893?"

Susannah takes a deep drink of her wine. It tastes like fermented gym socks, but Al and Katie seem to genuinely be enjoying it. They are like parents who think that their baby is the most beautiful baby ever born, and no one is ever allowed to tell them differently. Ugly babies and homemade wine, Susannah thinks: two things adored only by the people who make them. She takes another drink. "They had the Saffir-Simpson scale in 1893?"

"Well, no," Al says, pushing his glasses back up on his nose like a television caricature of a science geek. "But they can apply it, you know, *retroactively*."

"I don't think they can, Al."

"Sure they can. I mean, it just measures the amount of damage done. They had records."

Susannah puts down her wine glass. She doesn't really want to argue with Al, but he just looks so smug, sitting there with his little round glasses and ridiculous goatee. "I can't imagine they had the technology back then to record things like central barometric pressure."

"Jesus," Tom says. "What is with you?"

Katie takes a bite of her chili, her spoon clicking against her teeth. "None of it really matters, anyway," she says. "Science can't predict the moods and whims of Mother Nature. Meteorology really is just an illusion."

"Well, there you go," says Susannah. "Thank goodness they didn't try to predict this hurricane, like, 24 hours ago." She downs the rest of her glass of wine and reaches for the bottle. "Oh wait, *they did*." Katie looks as though she is about to say something, then stops. Al takes off his glasses and rubs them against the hem of his organic, unbleached cotton shirt. Tom grabs Susannah's empty bowl off the coffee table and, without looking at her, stacks it on top of his with a loud clatter.

When the wine is gone, Katie and Susannah go to the kitchen to look for vodka. Katie holds the flashlight while Susannah searches in the cupboard, holding one arm up to her face to try to mask the stench of Katie's patchouli.

"I'm sure we have some somewhere," Susannah says. "We have to. It's too dark in here and I'm not nearly drunk enough."

"I think we might have another jug of wine back at the apartment," Katie says, darting the flashlight around the kitchen.

Susannah feels her stomach turn. "No, it's here somewhere. Let's keep looking." Her hand passes over an assortment of random kitchen things: a hammer, extra paper towels, an indoor grill that they never use. "Maybe Tom drank it all. I always had a feeling he was becoming a closet alcoholic."

"Really?" asks Katie. Even in the dark, Susannah can see her eyes grow wide with concern. Fuck, thinks Susannah. Does she really not know I am joking?

"No," says Susannah, standing up and brushing off her hands against her jeans. "No, I think we just forgot to replenish our supply."

"Oh, dear." Katie leans down, moving the flashlight around inside the cupboard. "Hey, is that a George Foreman Grill? Al wanted to get one of those. Before we went vegan, I mean."

"Of course," says Susannah. For a moment she considers telling Katie that what she and Tom had told them was ground round in the chilli was actually ground cow. Instead she shuts the cupboard door, narrowly missing Katie's fingers. "Let's check another cupboard," Susannah suggests.

Eventually they find the vodka, which, as it turns out, Tom has stashed in the freezer. Relieved, Susannah takes a drink right from the bottle, her lips freezing and burning at the same time. In the living room, they all take turns with it, until the glass becomes a mess of fingerprints and condensation and the rim tastes vaguely of tomato sauce. No one says anything, they just keep passing the bottle back and forth as if it is some solemn, ancient, power-outage ritual. Al and Katie sit on the floor, far apart but facing each other, their eyes shining in the glow of the candlelight. Tom sits on the couch with a blanket over his legs. Susannah crawls across the floor to sit at his feet, and he adjusts the blanket to cover her bare shoulders, resting his hand on the top of her head for a moment before leaning back against the cushions. As Susannah nestles into the blanket, she hears a distinct wailing coming from the ceiling. Monique's little morning friend must have returned, thinks Susannah. Almost in unison, the four of them look up.

"What is that?" Katie asks.

Tom leans forward and grabs Susannah's shoulder. "I don't know," he says. "Could be a cat or something." Through her shirt, she feels his fingers dig harder into her skin. The couch begins to jiggle. Susannah realizes Tom is laughing.

"A cat?" Al asks. "Really?"

It's not even that funny, but Susannah feels herself start to laugh, too. "A cat," she says. "Sure, why not." Al and Katie keep staring at the ceiling, their faces confused and slightly concerned as they listen intently to Monique's howling. They look ridiculous. Susannah buries her face against Tom's leg and bites him gently through the soft wool of the blanket. The two of them shake together with silent laughter.

*   *   *

The hurricane hits just after midnight with a sudden rush of wind, moaning and screaming and tearing limbs from trees as it weaves down their street. The four of them stand by the rain-soaked window, drunk, and watch a tree topple on a neighbour's house, creaking and groaning over in slow motion, the top branches coming to rest between the two dormer windows on the top floor. Then below them, the door opens, and Susannah sees Monique and a young boy, barely old enough to drink, running out to the sidewalk. In the dark Susannah can't tell if it is the same boy from this morning. They are both barefoot and laughing, dressed in T-shirts and boxer shorts as they stand in front of the house face to face and hold onto each others' hands.

"Is that the girl from upstairs?" Al asks.

"Yeah," says Susannah. "Monique."

"Who's that with her?"

"Just one of the city's many corrupted youth," Tom says. He reaches his hand out to Susannah. She takes it.

Then Monique and the boy raise their arms above their head, throw back their heads, and start to scream. Susannah can hear them, even over the howling of the wind and the rain pelting against the window. They are screaming up at the sky, screaming along with the sound of a city's worth of car alarms set off by the force of the storm, screaming along with the wind and rain, against a backdrop of thick dark air bursting with light from the blue-smoke fizz of exploding transformer boxes and flashlights flickering out of windows.

Susannah presses her free hand against the rattling glass and wishes she and Tom could be out there with them: outside and away from here, the shell of their life cracking open, their arms raised, faces soaked with rain.

Where You Are

I f you had been born, Natalie, you would sit in the chair in the corner where the cats now sit and eat peaches, your favourite fruit. You would sit there and eat them and line up the pits in a row on the arm of the chair and Sid would say "Nat, please put your peach pits in the garbage" and then you would say "Okay, Sid" or "Peach pits go in the compost, not the garbage, *duh*" or "You can't tell me what to do you're not my father," because you are ten and Sid isn't your father, and then maybe you would go to your room and slam the door.

Except you wouldn't have a door to slam because if you had been born, Natalie, your bedroom would only have three walls as you would probably have to live in the pantry. There would be high shelves for our cans of soup and really pretty curtains to block off you from the kitchen, with fish on them, maybe, or airplanes, but I'm sure it would still not be as nice as your father's house, which is probably in the suburbs – the near-suburbs, not the far-off suburbs, but the suburbs nonetheless – where you would have a bedroom with these glow-in-the-dark stars on the ceiling. Not just stars, but a whole galaxy, with planets and moons and constellations, the Milky Way mapped out very precisely above your head and even though I would never see it, you would tell me about it, how at night after your father kisses you and calls you "Nutella" and puts you to bed, you wait for one of them to fall so you can make a wish.

I don't know why I imagine your father to be the kind of man who would map out a galaxy on the ceiling of his daughter's bedroom. Maybe he told me that he was. It seems like one of those things we could have·talked about: our Vegas wedding, our dog named Jack, our bed frame made of bamboo. A pool table for him in the basement, an office for me in a tree house. Sunflowers in the backyard. Stars on the ceiling.

*　　*　　*

If you had been born, Natalie, it would have rained while I was in labour. The contractions would have started and the sky would have opened up, raindrops the size of apples plummeting from the sky, and your father would have held an umbrella over my head as we walked to the car, but he would have kept forgetting and letting it fall forward, the drops rushing off the end of the little metal spokes and bursting in my hair like tiny water balloons. On the way to the hospital he would have taken us through the Tim Horton's Drive Thru because he was up late the night before and you, Natalie, would have wanted to be born before the sun came up.

In the hospital they would have put me in a room that was full of flowers from another new mother next door, whose co-workers kept sending her huge bouquets of them even though she was allergic. The scent of the flowers would have been so thick it would have made me tingle, each nerve ending rolling around under my skin as if it were trying to put out a fire, and after only an hour of this I would have felt a sneeze in my womb and out you would've come.

On the way home from the hospital, your father would have broken up with me. "I just think we're too young, Anna," he would have said, "and I think that I need to, you know, *experience* things." Bon Jovi would have been playing on the radio, and the rain would have stopped. I would have felt my toes go numb in my boots. I would have said "But what about Natalie?" and your father would have said "Who?" and I would have said "Natalie. Our daughter." And your father would have looked out the window as if he had never heard me.

Eventually I would have heard from him, a late-night drunken phone call and a bunch of scotch-soaked weeping about his "baby girl." Then he would have started coming by again, his glazed eyes staring past me to you, a beeline for the bassinette. You would have cooed and giggled every time he came near, squeezing your little fingers into fat baby fists. Your father would have held you against his chest and you would have both fallen asleep, and when he woke up he would have handed you to me without looking at my face, left without saying goodbye, because if you had been born, Natalie, he would have loved you like a fire in the wall, but it still wouldn't have been enough to keep us together.

*　　*　　*

If you had been born, Natalie, Sid might have been your primary teacher, and we would have met on the playground at recess instead of at a bar. He would still have asked me out, other people's children clinging to his arms, and I still would have gone, but I wouldn't have had sex with him until the third or fourth date, and I certainly wouldn't have done it in that restaurant bathroom, urgent and lightning-fast, with the metal waste receptacle digging into my hip, the line of people outside banging on the door to get in. If you had been born, Natalie, I would have had someone to set an example for.

You would have loved Sid, his brown skin and slender hands that always smell like curry, even though the other kids would tease you when you accidentally called him by his first name in class. He would make you balloon animals and pull coins from your ears, and you wouldn't be embarrassed by his accent until you were at least twelve or thirteen. By then you would have grown used to the taste of dhal, and the feeling of his hand on your head, and the way he called you his little *sahib*, but you would still roll your eyes when your friends came over after school and he was in the kitchen, dancing around to Madonna and wearing his *dhoti* over a pair of blue jeans.

Sid and I still might have bought this little one-bedroom house if you were born, Natalie, although you wouldn't really like it here, this rundown house like every other rundown house we've lived in. For one thing, the carpets are too thin. I think you would have preferred them thick, luxurious – or maybe you would've preferred hardwood, to slide around on in your clean little socks, getting the odd splinter wedged into the pink-soft skin of your foot. No, if you had been born, Natalie, you would have been a thick-carpet kind of girl, something you could lay your stomach on, feet in the air as you watched TV or talked on the phone. And we would have wanted to give it to you – the new house, the big backyard, the rec room in the basement, all the things a little girl should have. Maybe we would have tried harder. Maybe Sid would have stopped sending half his paycheque to his mother in India, or maybe I would have gone back to school, gotten a degree in business or IT, a nine-to-five office job instead of all these late nights behind a bar. If you had been born, Natalie, I would have had a reason to make my life better.

Sid says at least it smells better than the old place. That it's a better place for us to start a family. But I don't know. I think I have lost my sense of smell. If this is true, then it is certainly not the greatest thing I've lost, but I still miss it on occasion: the green and gassy smell of a freshly cut lawn, or the way the harbour smells in the fog, the way the fog can carry the scent for miles and miles. Sid says that since I remember these things, they will never be gone, the same way Tim Robbins reminded all those prisoners in *The Shawshank Redemption* that they can keep music in their head and no one can take it away. I don't know, it seems to me that a memory can never take the place of a real thing, and trying to make it that way will only drive you crazy. If I were one to argue with Sid about these things, I might have said as much, but at least I am spared the smell of the mildew in the bathtub that he complains about every morning.

*   *   *

Your father, on the other hand, would be able to give you these things. He would be married, I suspect, to a woman named Susan, or Janet, or Brenda. You would like her too, of course, even though she makes you eat tofu, which you hate, and doesn't let you stay up late. But she would take you to the park and teach you how to rollerblade, and on hot summer days you would make your own ice cream in their spotless stainless steel kitchen. Brenda would come in for tea when she dropped you off at our house, a vaguely disguised look of pity as she sits perched on the very edge of our couch, coolly sipping water from her hot-pink Nalgene bottle, telling me she's worried about your calcium levels and discreetly offering to pay for your gymnastics. And I would smile at her and pretend not to hate her, because there is nothing mysterious about her, nothing exotic, because I was never afraid of losing your father to a woman like her, and looking at her and her Nalgene bottle I wouldn't be able to help but wonder why it couldn't have been me, why he would have gone through all that trouble to find someone *like* me when he could have just had me all along.

*   *   *

If you had been born, Natalie, you would have trouble fitting in at school. You'd think the other kids were too loud, too childish, and instead you would like to spend time by yourself, writing letters or maybe drawing; you would be very artistic, and poised for your age. Your teacher would say you were withdrawn and call me in for meetings and I would sit in one of those child-desks in front of her and try not to feel small when she suggests you go for counselling. Then there would be meetings with all four of us, your father and Brenda, Sid and me, and maybe the teacher would make a suggestion about a change in custody arrangements, and maybe I would get mad, storm out across the soccer field, stomping my footprints into the grass.

Later, you would console me, tell me you like coming to my house, even though we only have three channels on the TV and you live in the pantry. You would tell me I was your mom and you loved me, as if you were the adult and I was the child, as if I was the one who needed looking after.

*   *   *

If you had been born, Natalie, we wouldn't have had to think about your name. We talked about naming you before you were even there to consider, your father and I in his parents' basement, with the stereo on, bored, stoned, looking at the cracks in the ceiling, lying there with our fingers linked but nothing else. "I wanna lay you down in a bed of roses," Bon Jovi sang, wiry carpet fibres digging into the small of my back.

Your father stretched his legs out. "One day I'll marry you," he said, his face flushed, eyes bloodshot. "We'll have ten absurdly adorable babies and call them all Jack."

"Jack is a dog's name," I said, "and besides, I want a girl."

I could feel his heart beating through his fingers. "Nutella," he said and I said "You can't name a baby girl Nutella," and he said "Why not, I love Nutella," and I said "Because you can't name anyone anything with *nut* in it, it's not right." "Well, how about *Nat*ella?" And I said "God no" and then "How about Nat*alie*?"

Then your father rolled on his side and pulled his hand away from mine, and I realized my fingers were asleep. "Okay," he said, "But I'll still call her Nutella when I put her to bed" and I said "Okay" and your father went upstairs to make some toast and I lay on my back smiling and still looking at the ceiling as if the entire wide expanse of my future was mapped out there in the cracks.

If you had been born, Natalie, I would have told you that story.

Or maybe not. Maybe some parts of your father I would have wanted to keep for myself.

*   *   *

If you had been born, Natalie, even though you would like Brenda and Sid – because you are the type of girl who likes everyone, all these adults around you with their earnestness, their good intentions, Brenda with her calcium supplements, Sid prancing around to Madonna – you would also secretly plan ways to get your father and I to do things together, like dragging him into the house to show him your new pillowcases when he dropped you off, or asking us both to chaperone your school field trip to New Ross Farm, where we would meet face to face in the parking lot, and I'd catch a glimpse of your impish grin before you turned your back to us as you pretended to search for something in your school bag.

Your father would look at me then with that distant look he gets now, the unfocused way he looks at my face as if he is trying to forget what I look like, and I would breathe in wishing I could smell the farm-smells, the manure and the sweetness of the grass, to have an excuse for the tears in my eyes.

"Anna," he would sigh. "Well, you're here, aren't you?"

And you would race up and grab his hand, skipping over the hay bales and cow patties, looking back over your shoulder at me with a smile and a look of vaguely disguised pity. And I would think back to that day ten years ago when I looked into your father's eyes and we asked ourselves Natalie or no Natalie, *yes* or *no* laid out on the table like playing cards, a ceiling-crack future waiting to be flipped over, our hopes and dreams and everything else that we thought was so important weighed against a life. This life, this skipping, ponytail swinging, knobby-kneed life, that would have changed nothing that I expected it to, and everything that I hadn't even imagined it would.

I would wonder at the ebb and flow of those two parallel worlds, at the way they would meet and diverge and meet up again, twisting around the sound of your name. If you had been born, Natalie, I still would wonder about those days in which I would only imagine you were there.

Yes, I would think, watching your father's back as he walks away. I am here. I am here.

Metathesiophobia

Even the day Bennett Briggs kidnapped me, I thought he was beautiful. He had these green eyes like something was alive and growing in his irises, and he shook and shook as he pointed this thing at us, this nail gun Maggie told me later. That Bennett, everyone always said with a shake of their head, who had moved into the house behind us the previous spring, whose yard was full of tires and tools and old pieces of wood and metal, whose dog howled on nights when the moon was hidden behind the clouds. Then suddenly there he was, standing in the early November snow wearing a flannel shirt and his hair all messed up and there we were, my friend Maggie and I in our parkas and woolen scarves, and him telling us with this feeble voice to get in the truck, and even though we were on our way to town we did it anyway, not because we were scared but because we were curious, and more than anything else I was just happy to get out of the cold.

Maggie tried to joke with him in the truck as he drove. "Are you going to try to ransom us? Cause I'm not really sure how much my husband is willing to pay." But Bennett wouldn't talk to us, he just kept those green eyes focused on the road like he was on a mission from God, and Maggie held my hand on the seat between us and I tried to keep my knees from rubbing

Bennett's arm as he shifted gears. His truck smelled like oil and dirt, but it was very clean, and there were books all crammed down behind the seats, there must have been fifty books back there, but I didn't have a chance to read any of the titles because before I knew it we were pulling up the long steep driveway to his house.

*　　*　　*

"You can't kidnap someone with a nail gun," my husband Mike said later, his cheeks red with anger as he washed the dishes, his apple cider pork roast congealing, uneaten, in a roasting pan on the counter. "How the hell do you kidnap someone with a nail gun? Did he keep the compressor running in the back of the truck?"

"The what?" I asked.

"The fucking compressor, Catherine. The fucking compressor that makes the nail gun shoot its fucking nails."

"He didn't have a compressor," I said. "He just had the . . . the *thing*."

"Oh, right. The *thing*." Mike yanked the plug out of the drain and looked at me with disgust. I don't know if it was because he thought I was lying, or if he thought I was stupid. He didn't even know what he was angry about.

That night, just before I fell asleep, I felt Mike's arm creeping across me as I curled up on my side. "I'm sorry," he whispered into my hair.

"About what?" I asked.

"You know." His hand strayed up to my left breast and cupped it gently, his fingers toggling my nipple like a switch. I could still smell the dish soap on his skin. "I just worry about you. Maybe you and Maggie should quit walking to town for a while."

"I like walking to town. It's the only remotely fun thing to do around here."

Mike's hand dropped abruptly. "Jesus, Cath, are you twelve?"

I turned my head and let a dark sigh escape into the pillow.

*   *   *

When I first moved to the town of Lakefield, I discovered I missed everything about the city that I thought I hated. "I mean, what kind of field is a 'lakefield,' anyway?" I joked on the phone with my mother, two provinces away and well within walking distance of a decent cappuccino. "A swamp, I suppose, named by a real estate company."

"Don't worry, honey. I'm sure you'll adjust. Maybe wonderful opportunities are hiding in that swamp." My mother always had a way of making me feel worse when she was trying to make me feel better. You know what really hid in swamps? Swampy things hid in swamps, vile creatures with slimy hands and beady eyes that came to me in my sleep like monsters hiding under my bed when I was a kid.

It was about a month after we'd moved to Lakefield that I developed metathesiophobia, which Mike, who is a Brilliant Young Doctor according to the Lakefield Church Bulletin, told me is the proper term for having an irrational fear of housework. Suddenly I was afraid of laundry, terrified of dirty dishes, immobilized by the thought of vacuuming, and even though I used to be a good cook I became incapable of using spices, inexplicably and uncontrollably adding cinnamon to my pot roast, oregano to my apple pie. I was really lucky that Mike was such a Brilliant Young Doctor and understood my illness; he never complained, not even while scraping curry-flavoured tomato sauce from the bottom of a frying pan, not even when he mopped the floors and I hid in the bathroom, the fear sneaking its hands around my neck like a swamp monster.

*   *   *

Being kidnapped is not something you ever really think is going to happen to you. It's a movie crime, with hundreds of hilarious possibilities for confusion and mix-ups, something you don't ever really worry about unless you are, say, the child of an heir to a media empire or an oil executive in a South American country in the middle of a military coup. So even though this potentially scary thing was happening to me, I will admit that I was mentally crossing off GET KIDNAPPED from my list of things to do in life.

As it turned out it was Maggie he wanted, not me. At the top of the driveway he stopped the truck and stared right past me to her, with those green eyes full of pleading and pain, and then they were gone. I shivered in the truck for a few minutes staring up at the old, rambling house and then got out and followed them. It never occurred to me to go home, even though from Bennett's front yard I could see my own house, nestled glowing and cozy at the bottom of the hill. It felt strange looking down on my house after looking up for so long. I wondered if Mike was in the kitchen then, watching Bennett's house over a pile of dirty dishes, wondering why that distant woman looked so much like his wife.

I caught up to Bennett and Maggie just as they were going inside. Bennett kept those green eyes trained on the ground as he led us down the cold, empty hallway, past rooms in various states of renovation and many handy-type things, with absolutely no evidence that anyone was actually living there. I watched Bennett's shoulder blades moving under his flannel shirt as we followed him into what I assumed was the kitchen, although it had been gutted and stripped to the beams, and was completely empty except for a pile of blankets in the middle of the floor. As we moved closer, I saw that writhing in the blankets was an enormous German Shepherd with three tiny puppies clamouring around next to her, trying to pin down a nipple as she squirmed. As she rolled away from us, I saw a tiny paw protruding from just under her tail.

"Oh, okay," said Maggie under her breath. She knelt down and Bennett knelt right next to her until she told him to move away, then he took a few crouching steps back with his eyes still trained on the dog. I stayed back, eyeing the dog warily, grappling against the wall with both hands and waiting to see what would happen.

*   *   *

When Bennett first moved in, I talked Mike into going over to say hello. He relented, and trudged over one Sunday after church, clutching a jug of homemade wine under his arm. I think he was a bit apprehensive. He always said that you'd have to be insane to buy that house, which had stood empty for almost ten years. I waited eagerly in the kitchen, drawing pictures of trees on a paper towel with my back turned self-consciously to the pile of laundry in the middle of the floor. Mike returned almost immediately, still carrying the wine jug.

"Well?" I asked impatiently. "Are you having him committed or what?"

Mike sat down at the kitchen table and slowly untied his hiking boots, threading the laces carefully back through the eyelets after he had slipped them off his feet. "No," he said finally, leaning back and rubbing his jaw. "He didn't want to talk to me."

"Did he say that to you?"

"More or less." Mike leaned back in his chair and made nervous little figure eights on the floor with his sock feet. "Anyway, one look at those dogs of his and I got the message."

"The dogs?" I asked, crumpling up the paper towel. "Mike, I didn't know you were scared of dogs. Are you scared of dogs?"

But Mike wasn't talking. He tucked his boots under his chair and picked up the *Lakefield Advertiser*, his face suddenly obscured by a photo of the mayor grinning as he cut the ribbon on the new Kwik Way.

Later I found out that Bennett had refused to join the congregation, according to Mrs. Jessome the pastor's wife, who showed up on our doorstep one evening, puffy hands strangling a jar of preserves, cheeks bloated with gossip. Mike was cleaning the oven; I was sifting loose tea through my fingers from a canister on the kitchen table.

"He was standing up on a ladder in that junkyard he calls a house, and he didn't even come down to speak with me!"

"How did you get past the dogs?" I asked, looking sideways at Mike.

"Dogs?" Mrs. Jessome frowned. "Oh, yes, I did see a sweet old German Shepherd asleep on the front porch . . . the poor thing was as fat as a pregnant sow! I ought to call the SPCA." She pulled out a chair and plunked herself down next to me, and I was immediately fogged in by the smell of baked goods and stale perfume. "You should have seen him, up on this ladder, looking down on me as if I was the mailman! I said, 'You mean you don't believe in God?' And do you know what he said, Catherine? He said 'I do believe in God, I just don't believe in church.' Then he went right back to caulking or priming or whatever he was doing."

"Caulking first, then priming, Judy," Mike said, snapping off his gloves. He wouldn't look at me.

Mrs. Jessome pushed a sweaty piece of hair across her forehead with an indignant thumb. "Well, whatever. I said 'Honey, if you don't believe in God, that's one thing. But in this community, we believe in church.' Am I right?"

I didn't say anything. I looked through the window at Bennett's house and thought he probably primed before he caulked. I thought he probably lived on the top of that ladder, I thought his junkyard was probably art, I thought he would never put up with uninvited visits from Mrs. Jessome.

"You're right," said Mike. "Cath?"

"Oh, yeah, right," I said, but as soon as Mrs. Jessome turned away, I stuck out my tongue at Mike, the big liar.

*   *   *

"What's her name?" Maggie asked. Her voice was low and calm, a professional vet voice, the voice she used for crises and speeches. She was so good at crises and speeches, with that voice. The thought of my own voice suddenly terrified me.

"Rosie," Bennett said quietly. His voice sounded like a violin.

"Good Rosie, good Rosie," Maggie murmured. She slipped out of her parka and pulled off her leather gloves. Then she bent forward and pressed her hand against Rosie's belly. Rosie moaned and bared her teeth at the same time, her hot breath fogging up the cold air. From where I was standing in the doorway I could see the whites of her eyes, wet and howling, and foam at her mouth as she snarled and snapped in the air. "Tie her mouth closed," Maggie said to Bennett, kicking a towel across the floor at him. Bennett hesitated, looking at her with the helpless desperation of a delivery-room father. "Tie it!" she said again, and Bennett did, clamping his rough looking hands over Rosie's muzzle.

Rosie let out a low growl that seemed to seethe straight from her belly and out her nostril, and then with a wet sucking sound Maggie's fingers slipped inside her as she writhed and moaned, violently throwing her hips in an effort to shake her loose. Then Maggie twisted her wrist, the fingers of her other hand dancing lightly over Rosie's belly, and with a gentle tug she released a tiny, slick puppy on a tide of whitish, fleshy grease.

"Catherine, get a mop, please," Maggie said, gently easing her fingers out of Rosie's womb.

I felt myself growing dizzy. "I can't," I whispered. "Meta . . . metathesiophobia."

Maggie sighed impatiently. "Fine," she said "At least get me a towel. There's another one in there." She raised her dripping hand in the air, and I felt my vision go dark as I turned around and stumbled down the hall, pushing my way through the first door I saw.

*   *   *

I did try to visit Bennett once before, in late summer, carrying a bag of potatoes dug up from our garden. I thought he would love the smell as much as I did, so dirty and clean at the same time. It took me a long time to walk up the hill, and the whole time I was convinced he was watching me, looking down at me from one of the upper windows of his house, or maybe on the top of the ladder, and wondering who this beautiful woman coming towards him could possibly be. But when I got to the top of the hill there was no one home, even though his old red truck was still in the driveway, and I left the bag of potatoes leaning up against his front door.

I spent the rest of the afternoon watching for him to come home, to pick up the bag of potatoes and look around, wondering who had left them there. All through supper I stole furtive glances out the window, until Mike closed the blind and asked if I could please just concentrate on having a nice dinner with my husband. It was when I told him I liked the light coming in through the window that he told me that I was crazy, because there was no goddamn light coming in at nine o'clock at night, and he wondered what I was trying to pull, acting like some unhinged soap opera housewife. And when I said maybe I wasn't acting at all, he laughed that bitter I-can't-fucking-believe-you laugh that always made me cry, so I spent the evening in the den reading old copies of *Canadian Living* and trying to drown out the sound of Mike vacuuming in the next room. The next morning, when I looked out the window again, the potatoes were gone.

*   *   *

When I opened the door I knew I had found Bennett's room because of all the books, piled in meticulous stacks against one of the walls in descending order of size. I wandered around, trying to walk off the dizziness and taking inventory of Bennett's life. Aside from the books, the room was nearly bare, except for a mattress, a hot plate and a bar fridge, and inside the fridge I found a bowl of rice and a bottle of medicine, which turned out to be de-worming medication for a cat named Jim. There were blankets tacked up on all the walls, and the windows were sealed with thick plastic.

I looked at the titles of all the books and only recognized a few. Some were books about carpentry and plumbing and the like, but most of them looked quite scholarly, authors with foreign-sounding names, lots of letters tacked on to the ends. I wondered if Bennett had gone to university, if he found God in those books, if he liked being alone. I suddenly felt myself swelling up with goodness, full of my own compassionate love for this boy, this sweet misunderstood boy who obviously needed me.

*   *   *

Back in the kitchen, Maggie was sitting with Rosie's head in her lap, murmuring into her ear. They looked oddly serene, sitting there in the bare room surrounded by the growing darkness. Rosie growled softly when I entered, and Maggie put her finger to her lips.

"She's exhausted," Maggie said. "But not sedated. So be careful."

"Is she going to be okay?" I asked, keeping my distance.

"Sure she is. And she's got four healthy little ones."

"But I thought . . ."

Maggie shook her head. "The last one didn't make it," she said. "She was in there too long."

I leaned against the wall and breathed deeply. "Where's Bennett?" I asked.

"He went out into the yard." She paused and looked down, stroking the inside of Rosie's ear. "He seemed pretty shaken up."

I walked slowly across the room and crouched down next to Maggie, peeking under the blanket at the four tiny puppies, their brand new mouths sucking reflexively, their brand new hearts beating under their downy fur. Rosie's ear twitched but she stayed silent, so I reached down and ran my index finger along the back of one of the puppies, who let out a shuddering sigh and tucked its head under his paw. "I'm going to go find him," I said.

"Okay," said Maggie, smoothing out the blanket around her black-stockinged knees. "Can you tell him something for me? Tell him next time, all he needs to do is call the clinic."

*   *   *

I found Bennett behind the shed in the backyard. He was just standing there, staring off beyond the junk, beyond the trees. Then I watched as he dropped to his knees and started digging through the snow with one hand.

I walked toward him, my footsteps crunching across the snow. "What are you doing?" I asked.

He didn't look up. His left hand was red and raw from the snow, and in his other hand he held the dead puppy, its eyes still glued shut, its pink tongue lolling to one side. "I want to bury her," he said hoarsely, pawing at the snow.

I knelt down beside him and grabbed his hand, damp and freezing against my own. "Okay," I said. "But you can't do it like this. Once the snow melts . . ." He drew a sharp breath and looked at me, and suddenly I realized he was young, just a boy really, and he looked so sad. I let go of his hand. "Do you have anything we can put her in?"

Silently Bennett slipped out of his flannel shirt and held it out to me, his body shivering under his thin T-shirt. I opened the shirt and Bennett gently placed the puppy in the centre, and I held it there in front of me, already stiff and lifeless cradled in the soft flannel, its tiny puppy paws curled under its body as if it was sleeping. Then Bennett and I both looked up at the same time, and when I saw those chlorophyll eyes filled with tears I felt a familiar glow filling my stomach, growing hot and sore like a bruise, and before I could stop myself I leaned in and kissed him. Bennett's lips were frozen, and he didn't kiss me back.

When I pulled away and looked at him, he was looking at the ground again, his cheeks flushed. I felt tears pricking the back of my eyes. "You kidnapped me!" I whispered.

"I didn't mean to," he said without turning around.

We stood there for a long time, not speaking, our shadows growing longer in the snow. I could see Bennett's breath forming little clouds in the air, could hear his teeth banging together violently and suddenly I thought of Mike, two years younger and standing in an icy parking lot outside the city hospital, holding out the Lakefield Real Estate Guide to me with shaking hands, the way a child might hold a butterfly whose wings they had accidentally crushed. I remembered his eyes, pleading with me not to leave him, that desperate look that made me want to hurt him, that made me want to break his heart.

When Bennett turned around and looked at me, his eyes were sad, but calm. "Fear of change," he said softly.

"What?" I murmured.

"Metathesiophobia. It means fear of change." He dropped to his knees next to the grave, slowly resuming his digging.

I should have been upset, angry, at least surprised. But all I felt was calm. Slowly, I folded the flannel over the puppy, wrapping its stiff little body in the soft fabric. Then I knelt down next to Bennett and placed the puppy in the hole, and with frostbitten hands we both started to fill it in, watching the red of the flannel gradually disappear under a pile of white. When we were finished, Bennett pushed a stick down into the snow. A marker, our secret hidden beneath. A proper burial.

"This isn't a fantasy, Catherine," Mike said to me in that parking lot. "You can't always control what happens next." I didn't know what he meant then, but kneeling there in the snow with Bennett I thought maybe I was starting to understand.

*　　*　　*

A few nights later, I stood in front of the mirror naked, something I hadn't done since before Mike, since I lived by myself. I ran one hand over the opposite shoulder and down my arm, a line on my body I had once loved, skin taut and soft as an earlobe. I cupped my hands under my breasts, trying to imagine Bennett looking at me. But all I could see was sags and wrinkles, the vague outline of what was once there, now flattened in some places, bulging in others, signs of wifeness, of oldness everywhere I looked.

When Mike came in, he ran his hands over my back and told me I was beautiful, but I was starting to think maybe he only saw me for who I used to be, and not who I had become. I turned around and pressed my body against him, suddenly cold, folding myself into his warmth. "Let's have a baby," I said, running kisses along his jaw.

He laughed softly. "Do you really think we're ready for that?" he asked, but by "we" he meant "me," I know he did. I turned away from him, folding my hands over my belly the way I had seen pregnant women do, and thought about Rosie's puppy frozen and wrapped in flannel under the snow. I wondered if Bennett would find it there in the spring, or whether maybe a wild animal would get to it first, leaving nothing but toenails and teeth and a few scraps of red material strewn across the yard.

Post Mortem

Jeremy

It is Christmas Day, and we are driving to the place off the 103 where my brother Gavin died in a car accident five months ago. In the car there is my father, in his new suit, driving with hands firmly at 10 and 2. There is my mother, straight-backed in the passenger seat with her hair freshly curled. There is my younger sister, Millie, sitting behind my father, ears plugged with earphones, slouched down in her seat with one leg bent so that her bare knee is touching my elbow. She and my mother fought about this before we left.

"It's December, Millie. Put on some stockings forthelove ofgod . . ."

"Fuck you," Millie said. Millie has an extensive vocabulary, she is fond of telling us. She just chooses not to use it.

There is Theresa, Gav's wife, sitting behind my mother, wrapped in a blanket with her eyes closed. Then there is me in the middle, in a too-thin T-shirt, not thinking about Millie's knee, about the layers of skin pressed between our bones, not thinking about Gav, not thinking about anything, really. Just staring out the front windshield so I don't get carsick.

It is six o'clock. I wonder how long we will have to stay. Gav was my brother but I'm thinking about turkey. My mother says I should have grown out of this by now, that I am no longer a Growing Boy In Need Of Constant Sustenance but a Young Man Who Should Practice Restraint. But I am hungry all the time, and still too skinny, even though it seems like all I ever think about is food.

"Look," Millie says. "They put up a guard rail."

In the rear-view mirror I can see my mother is beaming. "I wrote a letter," she says. Millie rolls her eyes and sticks her earphones back in her ears.

Theresa

You have seen my ass. You have seen it being flossed by thong panties in magazine ads for a certain line of skin firmer. You have seen it wiggling away from the camera, tanned and bathing-suited, in commercials for a certain men's body spray. You have seen it bent over in tight-fitting jeans on billboards pushing a certain brand of beer. If you have been to Europe, you have even seen my ass in all its bare glory, slathered in bronze paint and airbrushed to remove the mole at the base of my tailbone, in subway posters for a certain line of Mediterranean resorts. My ass *sells*. It is smooth, it is firm, it is perfectly symmetrical, each cheek round and hard as an apple. It defies gravity. Maybe, it even defies logic.

People love my ass so much it sometimes seems a waste to sit on it. At clubs I always stand, bent at the hips, elbows resting casually on the bar or the table. I shift my weight back and forth from leg to leg, slowly, almost imperceptibly. I pretend not to notice when you lock your eyes on me, or when your girlfriend yanks you away by your arm. But I do notice. Even without turning around I can feel your eyes on me, the electricity in the air, the building intensity. I can feel your muscles tightening, your pulse quicken, your mouth water. I can feel your cock stirring in your jeans. This is desire. This is what I do. It's the same story, over and over: you want me, you feel your hands running over those perfect, hard apples, your mouth pressing against that bronzed skin. Or you want to be me – you clench your own ass, suck in your stomach, press your shoulders back, widen your eyes, moisten your mouth. Your breath grows heavy. You go home and you fuck your boyfriend better than you ever have before, you pin him to the bed and ride 'em cowboy, both of you imagining my perfect ass bouncing up and down, suspended in the air, waiting, open, ready.

This is desire. This is what I do.

When we first met, at that club in Vegas with the potted palm trees and the jungle cats in cages all around the edges of the dance floor, Gav didn't even notice my ass. So completely predictable. I told him what I did for a living and he just smiled and said he was "more of a breast man," himself. Let his eyes drop to my chest. My breasts are okay in a push-up but they are a little small, with these puffy pink nipples that can never quite stay hard enough. So I leaned forward and pushed my tits together with the tops of my arms, but Gav wasn't even looking, he was smiling at the waitress with the huge rack, he was letting his eyes melt all over her, and I felt such a *rage* brewing in my stomach, I felt my body shake with it. That was *my* look. That was the one look, the one out of the hundreds of thousands of looks, that meant anything at all to me.

And I never, ever got it from him.

Jeremy

Gav died in the summertime. He and Theresa were on their way home from a party. Theresa was driving. It was raining. The car hydroplaned off the highway. Theresa was wearing her seat belt. Gav wasn't. This is how these things go.

I don't know why we're making this trip on Christmas Day. "Gav loved Christmas," my mother said when Millie and I complained about having to get out of our pajamas and leave our Christmas presents and the shabby-sweater comfort of the family room. "Gav loved Christmas!" she wailed, and my father glared at us, and we dragged ourselves upstairs to get changed.

"It's not true," Theresa said when I went to her room to get her. Her room. Gav's room. Her voice was flat, bitter. Far away. "Gav didn't love Christmas. He just loved the presents. Almost as much as he loved himself." Theresa had come back to Halifax five months ago with Gav for a summer vacation. She probably pictured sailboats and lobster. In the five months since his death, she had barely left his room.

"You loved him, too," I said. *And so did I*, I wanted to say, but the words stayed unformed in my mouth. *So did I. So did I.*

We're coming up to the spot when my father starts slowing down. Way too early. "Paul," my mother says. "What are you doing? Don't you remember the spot?"

"Of course I remember the spot, Pauline," my father says. Paul and Pauline. My parents. He puts on his blinker.

"Paul!" my mother says, a little louder. "You're confusing the car behind you!"

"They can go around," my father says.

"But this is a no passing zone!" My mother takes out a wad of Kleenex from her pocket and begins to shred it in her lap. "See? It's a solid line. It's a solid line, Paul!"

My father mumbles something, but he turns off the blinker and speeds up.

"Paul!" my mother screeches. "Slow down! You're going to miss it!"

My father slams on the brakes and jerks the wheel to the right. The car behind us honks and rips out into the opposite lane. The Rabbit skids across the gravel shoulder towards the ditch, scraping along the new guard rail. My father spins the wheel, and the Rabbit veers back towards the highway. We are now half on the shoulder and half on the road. Theresa's half is on the shoulder. I watch through her window as trees whiz by, the gravel spitting out from under our wheels. Finally, my father gets control of the car and eases it back onto the shoulder.

"You didn't put your turn signal on," my mother says.

My father says nothing.

Theresa

Four months after Gav's death and I'm still here.

You have probably heard *this* story before, too. Grieving young widow lying in the bathtub contemplates letting herself slip under the water, to stop the pain forever, imagines serenely dying with her hair floating all around her like a golden halo, her eyes closed as if she is only dreaming, her eyelashes kissing the tops of her cheeks. Then maybe actually doing it, feeling her back slipping against the smooth porcelain, the water rising up over her face, her hands floating gently to the surface as life fades from her, as she drifts off to join her beloved in the after-life.

So romantic. So *Grey's Anatomy* or something. But *that* grieving young widow did not have Pauline Russell as a mother-in-law.

I hear Pauline's voice before I see her, a watery mush of muffled words seeping into my ears. I open my eyes and see her blurry face in the air above me, her mouth moving, her hands waving in the air as she rolls up the sleeves of her sweater – then feel the water ripple around me as she reaches down and grabs my shoulders and heaves me upright. The water drains away from my body, sight and sound now dripping, waterlogged, painfully sharp. Her fingers dig into my skin.

"Theresa," she says, shaking me. "Theresa!"

I keep my head down, trying not to move. I wonder if I close my eyes and hold my breath, if she will believe I'm already dead.

"Theresa!" she says again. She puts her hand under my chin and tilts my face up to hers. I close my eyes, I'm dead, I'm dead. "Oh, for heaven's sake. Must we go through this every day?"

"Don't be so dramatic, Pauline," I say, keeping my eyes closed. Pauline lets go of my shoulders and I draw my knees into my chest. "Leave me alone."

I feel her move away from the edge of the tub. Hear her rustling around. I open one eye, just a crack, and see her rummaging through the jumbled pile of makeup on the counter. Pauline: she was beautiful once. I know, not just because of the picture that Gav has, no, *had* of her in his wallet – her graduation from nursing school, all big dark eyes behind horn-rimmed glasses, finger-waves curling around porcelain skin – but because you can still see it in her face, beneath the layers of fat that have accumulated on those cheekbones, in the way she holds her head like she was the queen of the fucking world.

I never understood why a grown man would carry a picture of his mother in his wallet.

"Do you wear foundation?" Pauline asks, holding up a half-empty bottle to the light and examining it.

I close my eyes again and rest my head on my legs. "Yes," I mumble to my knees.

"I see," says Pauline. Her breasts wobble beneath her sweater as she shifts against the counter. "You know, you really should use something lighter, what with your dry skin. Maybe a tinted moisturizer . . ."

"Pauline," I say. "Gavin's dead."

Pauline stares at me. "Yes," she says. I don't know Pauline well enough to tell if it's pity that is building up behind her eyes, or something else, but I keep pushing it anyway.

"So why the fuck are you talking about foundation?" I slide back down into the water, my neck pressing against the hard porcelain, my knees poking out above the water. Make an intense study of the cracks on the ceiling. I can feel Pauline's body tense, push back against the sink. It's not pity, I think. It's rage.

"Theresa, why are you still here?" she asks.

"You know," I say, "When Gav would kiss me, he used to put his hands on either side of my head, first, like this . . ." I bring my hands up to my cheeks. They are pruney and wet and nothing like Gav's used to be.

"Your . . . people have been calling you."

But I'm on a roll. "Sometimes," I say, "It would be all warm and tender. And then other times . . . all desperate and rough."

My hands rake up the sides of my cheeks, into my hair, pulling my head side to side.

Pauline sighs. "Yes, yes. You'll never meet another man who held your head the way that Gav did . . ."

She stops. My hands drop to the water. Neither of us breathe. Silently, I slide back under the water, holding my breath until I hear muffled footsteps, the click of the door.

Jeremy

I'm too old for all of this family shit, anyway. Six more months and I won't even be a teenager anymore, even though my mother says I still act like one. Even though I still live in the same room, decorated with the same Foo Fighters and Our Lady Peace posters, my one hockey trophy sitting on a bookcase, an Anna Kournikova calendar from 2001. Gav gave me that calendar. He told me one day I would appreciate it. When I was as old as him, which, when I was ten and he was eighteen, seemed like an eternity away.

"You're younger than Gav ever was," Theresa said to me once. "He was an adult before he could even walk."

I wanted to tell Theresa that someday I will be *older* than Gav ever was. But talking to Theresa has been hard these days. "Don't tell me these things, Jeremy," she would have said to me, anyway. "You make it sound as if this is all about you."

The car finally stops by the side of the road, and my father shuts off the engine. None of us make a move to get out. I look over at Theresa. Her eyes are dull, and she still has the blanket wrapped around her shoulders. She is sucking on the tip of one of her fingers. I watch her for two seconds and instantly get a hard on. This is what sucks about having Theresa around. I breathe in, stare straight ahead. In the rear-view I catch Millie's eye. She is grinning from ear to fucking ear.

"Do you two need a minute alone?" she asks.

I feel my face turn red. "Shut up, Millie," I mumble. Theresa just keeps staring out the window.

"Hello, Princess?" Millie leans over me and waves a hand in front of Theresa's face. "Anybody home?"

"Millie!" my mother says. "Enough."

"Fuck you, mother."

My mother sighs. "You know, for someone with such an extensive vocabulary, you seem to use the same two words a lot."

"Fuck you *rancorously*, mother. Fuck you *unremittingly*. Fuck you . . ."

My father leans on the horn. This seems to startle Theresa into the present. She pulls on the handle of the car door, but it won't open.

Theresa

In the four months I have been living at the Russell's, I have caught Jeremy jerking off to pictures of me exactly eight times. The first time was an accident, the inevitable result of sharing a bathroom with a nineteen-year-old boy. The next seven times, I will admit, I went looking for it. They say a person's nose itches when they sense that someone else is thinking about them; well, something sort of similar happens to you when you sense that someone nearby is getting off while imagining you naked. This time, I catch him on his bed, magazine spread open across his knees, hand moving fitfully under his track pants. I stand in the doorway in my bathrobe with my hair wrapped in a towel and watch, his baby face screwed up in concentration, so like Gav in the way his tongue pokes out between red lips, so like Gav but younger, more innocent. More alive.

"Jeremy."

He jumps up, and the magazine falls to the ground. "What?" he said loudly. He reaches his hand around the back of his neck and rubs. "Don't you knock? Civilised people *knock*!"

I lean against the door frame. "What are you doing?"

"What? What do you mean?"

I shrug, then walk over and pick up the magazine. It is still folded open to Jeremy's page: an ad I did a few months before Gav died, some kind of beer-company-sponsored golf tournament that required a lot of bending over in short skirts. In it I am looking over my shoulder, one piece of hair falling across my forehead, my lips airbrushed into plump little pillows. Looking at it, I suddenly feel like throwing up.

"My face looks weird," I say. "Doesn't my face look weird?"

"Huh?" says Jeremy. He is still standing, shifting his weight awkwardly from left foot to right foot.

I run my hand over the page. "I'm smiling. It's weird. It's horrible." It *is* horrible. All teeth and gums and vacant eyes. I slowly crumple the page under my fingers.

"Don't . . . what are you doing?" Jeremy sits back down on the bed. He looks confused. He's not equipped to handle this sadness, I think. He lost his brother, and his grief is out there: it is tangible, it is there for everyone to see. It's a proper kind of grief. I sit down next to him.

"Jer," I say. I shift my leg closer to his.

He clears his throat. "Um," he says. I reach up and run the tip of my finger lightly along the outside fold of his ear. His leg begins to shake. "We should order a pizza for supper."

"Jer," I say again. I slowly unwind the towel from my head. Then I put my hands over his hands. Slowly lift them to the sides of my head and then drop my hands away. He keeps his hands there, awkwardly. They feel hot and clammy and nothing like Gav's used to be. I try not to think about it.

"I like pepperoni," he says.

"Me too," I say. "Now, kiss me."

He looks terrified, but he does what I tell him to. His mouth tastes fizzy. Like soda. I kiss him back, hard. Push him back on the bed and climb on top of him. His whole body is shaking now, but I can feel his hard-on pressing into me, and I reach my hand down the front of his track pants. He stops kissing me. I can feel his breath growing heavy as his hands slide down over my back to my ass.

"Oh my god," he says. He stares at me, eyes wide, incredulous.

I freeze. I feel a weird calm settling over me. Jeremy is grinding up against me, he's ready to go. But I can't even feel him anymore. I'm on a beach in Cuba, doing a photo shoot, two months after Gav and I started dating. He is sitting on a beach chair watching me, his pant legs rolled up to his knees, sunglasses pushed up on his head. I'm rolling around at the edge of the shore, my body covered with wet sand, my hair matted into dreads from the sea water, and he is watching me, watching me wrap the shoot, watching me pull my hair back over my shoulders into a pony tail, watching me cross the beach to where he is sitting.

"Oh my god," he says. He pulls me down onto the chair. "If you don't marry me right now, I'm going to drown myself in the pool." He's smiling, he's reaching his hands up to the side of my face, but it's his eyes. There's something missing.

I shake it off. "I'm all yours," I say.

"What?" says Jeremy.

I sigh into his neck. "I'm all yours," I say. I stand up, undo my bathrobe, let it fall to the floor.

Jeremy

Of course I've had sex with girls before. I'm almost twenty years old, for Christ's sake. But Theresa was different. Or would have been different, if Millie hadn't walked in.

At first, all I heard was a weird sucking noise. Then a laugh. I was there, Theresa had her hand down my pants and I had my eyes all screwed shut trying to think about school, about hockey, anything to keep me from, well, you know. Then I opened my eyes and over Theresa's head I saw Millie standing in the doorway, eating a freezie the colour of antifreeze. Her lips and mouth were stained dark blue. She looked like a corpse.

"Gross," was all she said.

I jumped up, pushing Theresa to the side. "Jesus Christ," I said. I pulled up my track pants, started randomly picking clothes up off the floor. "Doesn't anyone knock anymore?"

"The door was open, Jer," Millie said. "Oh, I'm sorry. Should I have bought a ticket?"

"What do you want, Millie?" My heart pounding. Blood pricking with adrenaline. Dots forming behind my eyes. I have never wanted to punch anyone more than I wanted to punch my little sister in that moment.

Millie shrugged. "I heard that the Princess got the pea unstuck from her ass and finally left her room." She took a long, pointed suck of her freezie.

"Please leave, Millie," Theresa said softly. She was still lying on the bed where I had pushed her, naked, her arms stretched up over her head. It was like she didn't even care. I picked her bathrobe up off the floor and spread it across her body like a blanket. She didn't move.

"Holy shit," said Millie. "It speaks."

"Millie!" I said.

"Yeah, what?"

I crossed the room and stood in front of her. I had a good two feet on her, but when I looked down at her, all of a sudden I was the one who was scared. Scared of my own fucking sixteen-year-old sister. I tried to stare her down, you know, I wanted to be there for Theresa. But Millie stared back at me and I just kind of froze there. She raised the end of her freezie into the air and ran her fingers down it, squeezing out the last of the juice. Then she gave a little belch and turned around to leave.

"Why are you so mean to her?" I blurted out as she walked away.

"Because she's a fucking fraud," Millie answered before she went into her room and shut the door.

Theresa

I don't know how long I stay lying there on Jeremy's bed. It may have been hours. After Millie leaves, he sits on the bed watching me for a while, then gets up. At some point I think I hear his car start outside, engine revving before he peels away. Eventually, I shuffle back to Gav's room and close the door. It isn't until I'm standing in front of the mirror that I realize my bathrobe is on the wrong way, hanging open at the back like a hospital gown. I vaguely remember Jeremy tucking it around me. I feel like I somehow should be touched by this. But all I feel is a draft up my back.

After Gav died, I took everything in the room that was his and piled it on his bed. Then I crawled under it and stayed there. It was all old stuff, soccer jerseys, old school books, T-shirts with band logos on them, shoeboxes filled with god knows what – Pauline had kept everything. I didn't look at it. I just wanted to feel it. I wanted it to press up against me, to dig into me, to smother me.

At one point, I shifted and knocked over one of the shoeboxes, spilling the contents onto the floor. It was soap. Bars and bars of it. Hotel soap, mostly, but also regular soap too, bars of Ivory, of Dial, of Irish Spring. The smell was nauseating. I stared at the little pile beside the bed, trying to process what it meant. It was like I had discovered a secret stash of drugs, or gay porn or something. No, it was worse. At least that would have made sense.

How could I have ever been in love with a man who collected fucking *soap*?

Gav always said I was a terrible driver. I was only driving that night because he was drunk. We had been at someone's housewarming party in some godawful suburb half an hour outside of the city. Gav and I had fun at the party. He didn't get too drunk and make a fool of himself. I didn't get jealous. We didn't have a huge fight that ended in tears, and we didn't say anything horrible to each other that we now can't take back. I was driving, we hydroplaned. He went right through the windshield. It shattered. Shards of glass everywhere. Flying through the air. They said it was a total fluke. The sheet of glass, clean through his neck. It was a total fluke. A fluke decapitation. I was planning on leaving him. He didn't know it yet. He had no idea. He never did. All this grief, all this sadness, it is a lie. I was going to leave him anyway. So, Millie was right. I am a complete fraud.

When they found me after the accident, I was sitting on the side of the highway with Gav's head in my hands. They said I wouldn't let go. They had to pry his head away from me. It was the way he was looking at me. His eyes were open, he was dead, his eyes were open. And he was looking at me. Like he wanted me. Like he wanted me more than anyone else in the world. He looked at me like . . . like his insides were on the outside, raw and throbbing, completely naked and vulnerable. Like my name was spelled out in blood across his chest for everyone to see, and he didn't care. Like his whole body was screaming "Look at me, Resa. I love you." The way I wanted him to look at me while he was alive.

Everyone says it wasn't my fault. The police, the firemen, the insurance people. They say it was an accident. They say that I hit a trough of water and lost control. But I don't think that was what happened. I think I lost control long before that.

Jeremy

We all get out of the car and trudge to the side of the road. My mother is carrying a giant wreath made out of fake brush and pine cones painted silver and covered with fake snow. She thinks it is beautiful. She leans it up against the guardrail and then starts to cry. My father places his hands on her shoulders, at 10 and 2. Next to me, Millie shivers in her bare legs. Theresa stands apart from us, the blanket now dragging on the ground behind her as she walks along the gravel shoulder and caresses her hand along the edge of the guardrail. I want to touch her, but I know it won't make things any better. Instead, I push my hands into my pockets and try to remember Gav's face, try to picture him as a kid opening his presents on Christmas morning, his excitement, his wicked smile. But no matter how hard I try, my mind wanders back to turkey dinner, and I wonder how long it will be before even the trying stops.

The Church of Latter-Day Peaches

1.

There is nothing more unseemly than a pregnant widow at a funeral. That bulging belly under black, skin glowing beneath a thin film of tears, life stubbornly bursting from every pore. Georgia wears a veil, even though it is summer, even though her mother, Lilly, says "No one wears veils anymore, Gigi," says it without a hint of malice, just stating a fact, as though the dazed look on her daughter's face was due to her lack of funeral-fashion etiquette. Since Georgia has no idea how to wear it, Lilly fastens it carefully to the front of her pillbox hat – asking "where on earth did you find this, dear?" as she delicately maneuvers an ancient artifact called a hatpin through the fabric with her swift fingers.

When she is finished, she steps back to survey her work. For a moment, Georgia thinks she sees some sort of recognition in Lilly's eyes: that this is not a dress rehearsal for some school play, that this hat, this veil are more than just a costume, that the event that they are preparing for has some kind of meaning attached to it. But then it is gone, and she pats Georgia lovingly on the shoulder and says "You look beautiful Gigi," humming a little as she packs up her sewing kit, and Georgia just wants to smack her, pull her hair out, pinch her earlobes, just anything, anything to make her cry.

Georgia drives them both to the funeral. Lilly still has a driver's license, but Georgia has not let her use it since that day last summer when she drove her car off the road and into a sunflower field just outside of Truro. It was beautiful, Lilly said. All that yellow. Like being underwater. Georgia only remembers what she left behind, the crushed flowers, the churned-up dirt. The farmer had been very understanding. He had even given Lilly a little bottle of sunflower oil, but when Lilly wasn't looking, Georgia threw it in a garbage can at the Tim Horton's in Stewiacke when they stopped on the way home for coffee and a Danish. Just looking at that bottle had made Georgia feel angry.

On the way to the church, Georgia runs two red lights in a row. The second time she nearly hits a pedestrian, who yells something indiscernible and gives her the finger. Lilly rolls down the window and says, "Young man, your shoelaces are untied." Georgia rests her head against the steering wheel and starts to cry.

2.

What would you do if I died?
Oh, you know. Wear lots of black. Wander around the house all day like my life had lost all meaning. That kind of thing.

Like a small-town cheerleader from the 1950s, Georgia married Marty Peach right out of high school. All the other girls she graduated with were moving to Toronto to do pre-law or becoming au pairs in France. Neither of these appealed to Georgia, so when Marty proposed to her on the swing set at the Commons she said yes, on the condition that she didn't have to change her last name.

"Look what being Lilly White did to my mother," she said, leaning back, swinging so high the chains went slack.

"What's wrong with your mother?" Marty asked, pumping his legs furiously, trying to catch up with her. "I love your mother."

Marty Peach was the son of chocolate magnate and well-known Halifax politician Hugh Peach. When he transferred to Georgia's high school from private school in grade ten, everyone already knew who he was – had seen him on TV, positioned behind his dad and next to his younger sister Angela in the Peach & Sons Fine Chocolate commercials, or in a campaign ad, or at the now-famous press conference where Hugh denied any knowledge of the insider trading scandal at his company. There were a lot of rich kids at Georgia's school but none as rich as Marty, so at first he was invited to those parties at the mansions down along the Arm, kids with parents who went away for weeks at a time in the winter – condos in Aspen or Whistler, yachts in the Caribbean – and he briefly became the new door prize in the ongoing competition between two certain blonde-highlighted, SUV-driving, Oakley-wearing archrivals. But it became immediately clear that Marty wasn't interested in girls, or parties, or even being rich. When word got out that he took the bus to school, Marty Peach faded into the oblivion of high school obscurity, a place all too familiar to Georgia.

"I hear he's planning on giving his inheritance to charity," Georgia's best friend Mairi McIntyre told her one afternoon, as they were drinking coffee at the Ardmore Tea Room instead of reading sonnets in fifth period English.

"Oh yeah? I hear his parents disowned him for helping to organize their chocolate factory employees," Georgia said. It wasn't true, of course, but she liked to contradict Mairi.

"Nice try," Mairi said, sipping her coffee. "You know, you should marry Marty, Georgia. Then you could be Georgia Peach."

"Ha ha," Georgia said, sticking out her tongue.

A few weeks later, Mairi and Georgia went to a party at The Rock, a clearing on a cliff above the railway cut in the South End where most of their high school congregated on the weekends to get drunk, have sex and fight. Georgia drank two of the beers that Mairi had stolen from her older brother and wandered through the crowd, most of whom she didn't recognize. Strangely enough, she didn't feel awkward or uncomfortable, even though she had been dragged there and basically ditched by Mairi, who was after the new star of the boy's soccer team – a wiry kid named Will who had just moved with his family from Scotland. The way Georgia felt – half-drunk, breathing in the tangy granite air and listening to the general cacophony of so many teenagers following their own predestined path of rebellion – was oddly detached, as if she were an alien scientist sent down from another planet to observe the ritual rites of passage of humans in transition from child to adult. Or something like that, she thought, staring up at the stars as if one might be beacon calling her to a far-off home. She wasn't a part of this business; she was an interloper, a casual observer, and so convinced was she of her own lack of involvement in the situation that when the cops eventually showed up with their flashlights and dogs, believing they couldn't possibly be there for her, she almost forgot to run.

Eventually, however, instinct overtook. At first she ran in the same direction as everybody else, on the path that would eventually lead down to the train tracks and across to the School of Theology on the other side. But she could feel the crowd peeling away silently, kids instinctively shucking backpacks and beers and dipping into the eerie silence of the woods as if part of some secret, pre-planned tactical mission, as if how to run from the cops was programmed into their DNA.

Georgia veered off into the thick of the trees, her long skirt tangling around her legs as she tripped through the exposed roots and deadwood. In the distance she could see the lights of the houses lining the edge of the woodcut, and she aimed her body in that direction, her heart pounding as she realized she could still feel footsteps behind her, light bobbing through the trees. She hiked up her skirt and jumped over the first fence she came to, and stayed on her back in some random garden waiting for the footsteps to pass by, which they did, the sound peaking and then receding along the edge of the fence, the light skipping back towards the path. Georgia pulled her knees to her chest and tried to catch her breath. She could feel thorns digging into her back, but the stars up above, they were beautiful, they were sparkling, they were symbols of her hard-won, newly-appreciated freedom.

"Hello," someone said to her. She jumped to her feet, feeling the thorns ripping through her T-shirt, and saw Marty Peach standing there, with a headlamp strapped to his forehead, holding what looked like a tape recorder. He looked at her curiously. "What are you doing in my aunt's garden?" he asked.

Georgia could feel a draft breathing through the newly-formed hole in the back of her shirt. "What are *you* doing in your aunt's garden?" she asked.

"Looking for bats," Marty said.

Georgia raised both her hands to her head. "Bats?"

"They won't hurt you," he said. "They're actually really interesting. They make the neatest sounds." He held up the tape recorder. "Would you like to listen?"

Georgia stared at him. He didn't look like a gazillionaire. He was wearing jeans that were too short for him and a black T-shirt with a green Mr. Rogers cardigan hanging loose at his sides. "Sure," Georgia said. "I'd love to listen."

"Really?" Marty's face lit up, and then he was beautiful. Georgia followed him out of the garden to the gazebo, where they drank iced tea and ate Oreo cookies and listened to bat noises. When it was time for Georgia to leave, Marty wrapped his green cardigan around her shoulders and asked her if she would like to come back the next weekend and look for owls. She said yes, and then ran all the way home. *Georgia Peach*, she thought, lying in her bed, noticing for the first time the way the light from the moon shone in through her window. *Georgia-frigging-Peach*.

Later, after they were engaged, Marty offered to change his last name to White, but the Peaches said no, never, over their dead bodies. The Peaches were a very influential family. The Whites, as it turned out, were not.

The wedding was held at the Peach family's boat club, but Georgia's parents still insisted on taking care of the reception. For dinner they served salmon, and Angela Peach choked on a bone and fainted. "There are no bones in that salmon," Georgia tried to tell Kitty Peach as she sobbed over her daughter's wilted body. "Those Whites," the Peaches grumbled. "Probably bought that salmon in a can."

When Angela came to, murmuring for water through paper-white lips, Georgia's bridesmaids (cousin Peaches, all dressed in aquamarine) bore her to the boat club kitchen on a wave of taffeta. "My baby is so delicate, you know," Kitty said as she followed them, loud enough for anyone who cared to listen. "These Whites, they're so . . . sturdy." The rest of the guests – the Montreal Peaches and the Mississauga Peaches, business associates and other various Influential People – gathered in little pockets on the boat club lawn, leaving the possibly-from-a-can salmon virtually uneaten on their china plates, while the one lone White table – Jack and Lilly, Grandpa Jim, and Mairi and Matthias, a German cellist with whom she was leaving for Australia the day after the wedding – all stayed seated, prodding with various utensils at the food on their plates.

"Do you think that Hugh and Kitty would like some more wine?" Lilly asked, pushing her chair back and standing with the wine bottle in her hand and the tablecloth somehow tucked into the waist of her painstakingly chosen Mother-of-the-Bride outfit.

Georgia found Marty under the head table reading a comic book. She hoisted up the skirts of her Peach-family-heirloom dress and crawled under there with him. "Do you want me to do the voices with you?" she asked. Marty nodded. So she tucked herself under his arm and they whispered *The Watchmen* into each other's ears, and when they heard Kitty say "Now where have those two gone off to?" they only giggled softly, holding each other tighter on the boat club dining-room floor.

3.

Sometimes, Georgia catches herself thinking: if I were dead, we'd be together. Georgia White and Marty Peach, R.I.P. Of course, if she died, so would her baby. Baby Peach. Peach Pit. Heir to the Peach chocolate fortune. Georgia imagines a great pile of gold-wrapped chocolate discs locked up somewhere in a giant refrigerator.

Georgia and Lilly reach the church two minutes before the funeral is scheduled to start. The parking lot is overflowing with cars, so Georgia parks her old Corolla at the back of the lot on a patch of grass. Her belly is so swollen it barely fits under the steering wheel, and she has to put the seat all the way back in order to squeeze out the door. She sits there in the car for a moment, trying to catch her breath, while Lilly slips out of the car and floats through the parking lot towards the church.

The Peaches have made all the funeral arrangements. The service is being held in the Peach family's church, a plain, modern building on the edge of the gated community where Hugh and Kitty live. Georgia knows that Marty never went to church, and doubts any other Peaches do either, but now here was Angela, in huge dark glasses, gripping the minister's arm and wailing as though the volume of her grief could get her closer to God.

When she sees Georgia, the wailing fades to snivelling. "Georgia," she says, dabbing her eyes. "You're wearing a veil." She resumes her sobbing, albeit quieter, against the minister's arm.

Lilly reaches into her purse and pulls out a tissue, placing it in the palm of Angela's hand. "Use this instead, dear," she says.

"This man needs his sleeve." Angela feigns a swoon, and the minister struggles to hold her as she bends backwards. For a moment, they look like they are dancing, the minister dipping Angela to the floor.

Georgia grabs her mother's hand and pulls her down the church steps. Under her veil, she can feel sweat forming on her hairline. "I'm not ready," she says.

Lilly reaches up to adjust Georgia's veil. "Well, now, Gigi," she says. "Of course you are. Just put a smile on your face, and the rest will come."

Georgia looks at Lilly, who is smiling widely, her pale eyebrows arched hopefully above her milky blue eyes. Georgia's eyes fill with tears as she stretches her mouth into what she knows must be the thinnest, most desperate smile.

Georgia holds Lilly's hand as they walk into the church. Everyone turns to stare at them, and Lilly waves, cupping her hand and rotating her wrist like a pageant queen riding a parade float, whispering, "Everyone's here, isn't this exciting?" They shuffle down the aisle, Lilly waving, Georgia holding her belly as if it might drop to the floor and shatter if she lets it go. If it weren't for Mairi pulling them into the pew next to her, they might have kept on walking, up the stairs to the altar, past the table holding Marty's ashes, his smiling high school graduation photo, past the choir, the organist, straight to the front of the church.

As soon as they sit down, Mairi wraps her arms around Georgia. She is with her boyfriend, Matunde, a Kenyan basketball player on scholarship to the University of Connecticut, where Mairi is studying pre-law. Matunde smiles at Georgia, his teeth shocking white, as he tries to tuck his long limbs under the tiny pew.

Georgia is so relieved to see them there she starts to cry all over again. "I don't know where I was going," she says.

"It's okay," Mairi says.

Matunde reaches over and touches her shoulder. "I am so sorry, Georgia," he says in his deep, soft voice. "It is so beautiful to see this full church. Your husband had many friends."

Georgia's chest heaves with a sob, which somehow dissolves into a laugh. "Who are these people?" she says. Mairi touches Georgia's hair under the veil. Next to her, Lilly is humming under her breath. *Que Sera, Sera.* Her head sways back and forth.

"Hi, Lill," Mairi says, reaching over and squeezing Lilly's arm.

"Mairi, you look lovely," Lilly says. She fingers Mairi's sleeve. "Is this silk?"

"I think so," Mairi says. "I got it at an outlet store."

"Oh, I bet Australia is just wonderful for shopping." Mairi opens her mouth then closes it. Lilly picks a loose thread from Georgia's blouse. "Gigi, you should have worn silk," she says. "And those shoes, they're so frumpy . . ."

"Mother, I'm pregnant."

Lilly stares at her. "That doesn't mean you can't be fashionable. You should always try to look your best, Gigi, otherwise . . ."

"Lill," Mairi says. "This is my boyfriend, Matunde."

Lilly looks at Matunde. "My goodness, you've got long legs," she says.

The church is sweltering, and Georgia can feel the sweat gathering behind her knees, beneath her swollen breasts. On the opposite side of the aisle, Angela and Kitty grip each other while Hugh sits, straight-backed, his hands splayed on his thighs. Georgia inexplicably, wishes she could be with them. They hate her, she knows, and they always have. But they are connected now, whether they liked it or not. Georgia is sure that out of everyone else in the church, Hugh and Kitty are the only ones who come close to hurting as much as she is.

4.

> *Or maybe I'd just die along with you. You know, cast myself on the funeral pyre.*
> *You could always just build a shrine to me. Or start a*

new religion. Ever notice that "Marty" is only one letter away from "Martyr"?

The Peach chocolate fortune was built on a punchline.

The story – as told to Georgia by Kitty one afternoon just after Georgia and Marty were engaged, sitting in Hugh's office overlooking the South Terrace – went like this: Marty's great grandfather, Franz Pietsch, had founded the company in Germany in the 1880s with a partner, Gerhard Bindler. They started modestly, selling chocolate in cloth bags around their town using a formula that Franz had adapted from an old recipe belonging to Bindler's grandmother, who claimed it came from a water fairy who lived in the river behind her house.

In 1887 Bindler invented a machine that put caramel inside a chocolate bar, which he called the Bindler Binder. With the success of their new invention, Franz and Bindler decided it was time to expand their business. They formed a partnership with the notorious John Cadbury, under the impression that he would help them export their chocolate to England, and maybe even to pre-Hershey America, a nation with a steadily growing sweet tooth. What actually happened was, John Cadbury stole the design and prototype for the Bindler Binder and used it in the manufacture of his own caramel-filled chocolate, which he called the Caramilk bar.

Franz and Bindler tried to reclaim their design and expose Cadbury in the form of a strongly-worded letter, but never received a response. The following year, Bindler traveled to England to confront Cadbury himself. He was never heard from again. When Franz learned of his partner's mysterious disappearance, he quickly packed up his family and his shop and braved the trip across the Atlantic to Canada. Along the way he changed his name to Frank Peach, hoping to live in relative obscurity with his new, anglicized name. He opened Peach & Sons Fine Chocolate in Halifax in 1896, a full four years before Hershey began bringing milk chocolate to the masses, and using Bindler's method, began producing what he called Chocomel bars.

The lawsuit that Cadbury brought against Frank Peach was well-publicized at the time, although the details of the case were kept under wraps. Whether as a result of the trans-Atlantic prosecution, or the four British ex-military goons who, legend has it, showed up on Frank's doorstep with crowbars, the outcome was that Frank Peach ceased production of his Chocomel bars and destroyed his copy of the Bindler Binder design in exchange for an extremely generous settlement – a settlement that was to be paid to any male Peach heirs, on their thirtieth birthday, for as long as they kept the Caramilk secret.

Mairi was wrong about Marty – he hadn't donated his fortune to charity, although it was true that he didn't care about it at all. His parents were disappointed to discover that Marty wasn't interested in business or boating, the two things his father loved above all else. Hugh and Kitty, to their credit, did try to indulge Marty's interest in biology, building him a state-of-the-art greenhouse adjacent to the east wing of their mansion. But Marty still preferred wildflowers to orchids, maple trees to bonsai. Often Kitty would find her son helping Jake, their gardener, trimming the hedges around the perimeter of the property, his hands disturbingly covered in dirt. But they let Marty do what he wanted, knowing that before his thirtieth birthday, he would have to come back to them.

"So you see," Kitty told Georgia, "Martin has a great responsibility in this life, one that, like any great responsibility, is both an honour and a burden. When Martin turns thirty, he will, like his father, and his father before him, become the keeper of a great secret."

Georgia stuck the end of her ponytail in her mouth to keep from laughing. "I see," she said, with a mouthful of hair.

Kitty sighed. "I would love to tell you the secret, Georgia. But I'm not sure you're ready. Even I wasn't told until Hugh and I had been married for almost ten years. I suppose, once you've demonstrated your loyalty to the Peach family . . ."

Georgia spat out her ponytail and stared at Kitty: her skin sagging around her eyes, her thin lips pinched into a tiny O, the deep lines on Kitty's face, beyond the reach of all the expensive skin creams in the world. Georgia wondered what Kitty had had to do to demonstrate *her* loyalty to the Peach family.

"I am marrying your son," Georgia might have said, if she cared even the slightest bit about the Caramilk secret. Instead she sighed and nodded, wishing Franz Pietsch had kept his German name.

5.

The service begins and Georgia drifts in and out, vaguely aware when the minister is talking about "the bereaved" he is referring to her. Even more unfathomable is the fact that he seems to be talking about Marty as if he were dead. Every time Georgia thinks of him now it hits her in a wave of panic: dead, dead, dead. Marty is dead. Marty is dead. Dead. Marty. She wonders how long it will be before she can stop reliving Marty's death every time she wakes up in the morning, every time her mind comes back to the present after drifting back into the past.

At some point the minister stops talking and stoops to light a candle. Georgia can hear a quiet buzz in the church, people shifting in their seats, sniffling, fanning themselves with their programs. Everyone in tears, murmuring "so young, so young," turning to stare at Georgia, at the life bulging obscenely beneath her dress.

"Maybe you should go up and say something, Gigi," Lilly says.

Georgia looks at her. "Are you fucking insane?" she says, a little too loudly. Mairi puts a hand on Georgia's knee, but Georgia pushes it away.

"Oh Gigi," Lilly says. "There's no need to be angry. I just think you need to grieve. You know, for Jack."

"Marty," Georgia whispers. "I need to grieve for Marty."

Lilly stares at her. "Marty. That's what I said. Marty." She turns away and starts humming again, a high-pitched, discordant melody that exists solely in her head.

6.

*Yeah, right. "Peachism." A religion totally devoted to
the worship of comic books and Lena Horne.*
*Actually, I prefer "The Church of Latter-Day Peaches."
Has a nice, cultish ring to it.*

Before she and Jack were married, Lilly White was Lilly Stern:
normal Lilly Stern, with a slight lisp and coffee-coloured hair,
Lilly Stern who was a soloist in the church choir, who loved
poetry and Ricky Nelson and her mother's homemade straw-
berry-rhubarb pie. No one laughed at her when she told them
her name, no one gave her a second thought when she made a
doctor's appointment or filled out a form at the bank. She was
Lilly Stern, just like Betty Smith or Janet MacDonald or Brenda
Jones or any one of the other moderately pretty, likeable girls
she went to high school with.

But then she met Jack, tall and handsome, with an armful of
books and hair below his collar, and on a late spring day, when
the apple blossoms were past full bloom and casting their petals
into the air like soft, fragrant snowflakes, she married him in
bare feet on the steps of the Grand-Pré church. "Will you love
him forever, sister?" the minister asked, and she said "I will," and
the next day when they went down to the courthouse to sign the
papers, her whole life changed along with her name.

"Your mother loved being Lilly White," Jack told Georgia
just before he died. They were sitting together on the back
porch watching the sunset. Somewhere inside, Lilly was singing
along to Brenda Lee on the record player, the scratchy music
wafting out through an open window into the warm night air.

"She still does," Georgia said, frowning. Jack stirred more
sugar into his coffee and smiled. "Seriously, Daddy. I don't
know if it's a good thing."

Jack patted Georgia's shoulder. His hand was still strong,
despite being knotted with arthritis. "When your mother was
your age, she was a great singer," he said.

"I know. People came from miles around, blah, blah, blah."

"Before we were married, we had planned on moving to Toronto. But things, well, you know how it is . . . things came up. We never went. Then she got that throat infection. When the doctor told her she couldn't sing anymore, your mother smiled and said thank you," Jack said, sipping his coffee. "But it was like she had no idea what to do with herself anymore."

"Daddy," Georgia said. "Maybe she should, you know, see someone."

Jack waved his hand in the air. "Bah!" he said. "All girls think their mothers are crazy."

Georgia closed her eyes. "So when you hear it thunder," Lilly sang from inside. "Don't run under a tree. There'll be pennies from heaven for you and me."

7.

"The Church of Latter-Day Peaches," huh? Does that mean that you have to be a Peach in order to join?
Oh, I'll make you a Peach yet, baby.

After they were married, Georgia and Marty moved to Wolfville, an hour from Halifax, five minutes away from the church where Jack and Lilly were married. They had a two bedroom apartment with a view of the dikes, where Georgia would walk every morning with their dog, Rorschach. Marty worked "at the university," as Kitty wrote in the Annual Peach Family Newsletter, although the nature of his job – cutting grass, shovelling snow, clipping hedges – was never mentioned. Georgia was "working her way up in the film industry," beginning with a job behind the counter at the video store.

They were happy in Wolfville. No one asked them anymore when they planned to go to university, when they planned to move to Toronto like everyone else. When they had nights off together they would make pizza and listen to old Broadway show tunes, which Marty inexplicably loved and Georgia hated, but was learning to appreciate. Once a week, they drove to the city to visit Jack and Lilly, and Jack would load their trunk with groceries, check under the hood of the Corolla, and slip money into Georgia's purse when she wasn't looking. Lilly would sit at the kitchen table doing a crossword puzzle or darning a sock, with one pair of glasses on her face, and another hanging on a chain around her neck or nestled in her hair. Occasionally, she would forget that Georgia didn't live there, and would ask her if she had finished her homework, or if she needed to borrow the car.

"My goodness," Lilly would say, after they all laughed uneasily. "I just don't know where my brain is today."

"It's okay, Mother," Georgia would say, glancing sideways at Jack, who would always pretend to be engrossed in the television, or a spot on the carpet – anything to avoid looking at Georgia.

Then one week two years ago, they skipped their visit to Jack and Lilly to see Mairi, who was back in town with her new boyfriend, Hermano, an Argentinean revolutionary she had met working on a kibbutz in Israel. Marty and Georgia and Mairi and Hermano drank cheap wine in Mairi's parents' basement, where they played poker for cigarettes and danced the tango, which Hermano taught them, dragging Mairi, then Georgia, across the room, grinning wide enough that Georgia could see that several of his back teeth were missing.

Later, while Marty and Hermano were locked in a heated debate about the economic impact of the Argentinean Occupied Factory movement, Mairi and Georgia snuck out into the backyard to share a smoke. "I'm glad you're home, Mai," Georgia said, sitting down on the back step.

Mairi cupped her hand around the cigarette and lit it, blowing slow smoke rings up to the sky. "Hermano wants me to go back to Argentina with him," she said. "He said the movement could use more women like me." She flicked an ash into the air. "Not really sure what that means."

"Are you going to go?" Georgia asked.

"I don't know," Mairi said. Her short hair was sticking up straight, and her cheeks were flushed from the wine, but otherwise she looked exactly the same as she did in high school. "I'm actually thinking about going back to school," she said. She handed the cigarette to Georgia. "Maybe I'll be a lawyer."

"That sounds great, Mai."

"Remember when we were in high school we always said we would live together in university? And we would paint our kitchen purple and make a documentary about all the people who came to visit us?"

"My kitchen's purple," Georgia said. "You should go to Acadia. Live with Marty and me."

Mairi stared at her. "You have no idea, do you?" she said. "Jesus, Georgia. You think the whole fucking world starts and ends within an hour's drive from home." She shoved her hands into her pockets.

"Maybe I just don't have to run away to feel like I'm doing something important," Georgia said, staring back. *These are the things we're not supposed to say to each other*, she thought. She wasn't angry, she just felt sad. She held the cigarette out for Mairi. After a minute, Mairi took it.

"I hope Hermano and Marty haven't come to blows," she said.

Later, after they had all crashed on the floor, Georgia and Marty made love silently in their sleeping bag while Mairi snored softly into Hermano's armpit. They were drunk, but still it was a familiar thing, comfortable and soft. "Georgia, Georgia," Marty whispered into her ear. *There is nothing more than this*, Georgia told herself over and over as she drifted off to sleep.

A few days later, feeling guilty about not seeing her parents, Georgia drove to the city alone. The night before there had been flurries, and the roads were slippery, especially passing through Mount Uniacke where it seemed, in the winter months, to be perpetually snowing. Georgia was relieved to finally get into the city, and stopped at her favourite coffee shop on the way in, where she drank two espressos and read a day-old copy of the

Globe and Mail. She made a trip to the drugstore to fill a prescription, and then stopped at Mairi's house to pick up Marty's
jacket.

When she finally got to her parents' house, she found Lilly
in the backyard raking the freshly-fallen snow. "Goodness, all
these leaves!" she said when she saw Georgia, working her fingers up and down the rake handle as if it were a flute.

"Where's Daddy?" Georgia asked, feeling her skin turn to
ice.

"Your father is taking a nap. He is taking a nap." Lilly said
firmly, her eyes unable to meet Georgia's. Then she went back
to raking.

Later, the coroner told her that Jack had been dead for at
least twelve hours. The smell alone should have told her, the
purplish colour of his skin, the raw-clay feel of his hand in hers.
But Georgia's first thought, seeing her father lying peacefully in
bed at three o'clock in the afternoon, was that the poor man
really did deserve some sleep. The bedclothes were rumpled on
Lilly's side of the bed, and Georgia knew that her mother had
slept there, Jack's body lifeless and heavy next to her. Instead of
panicking, Georgia found herself wondering if Lilly had kissed
him when she woke up that morning, had felt the waxy cold of
his cheek.

After the screaming of sirens and the rush of dirty feet up
and down the stairs, Georgia and Lilly sat in the living room,
Georgia with her knees tucked under her on the sofa, Lilly in
her rocking chair with her hands folded primly on her lap, Jack's
armchair swaying back and forth slightly, as if he had just gotten
up to put on the kettle. The room was so silent Georgia could
hear the tap dripping in the kitchen, the creaking and groaning
of the house as the wind blew around the eaves. Twilight crept
in, but neither of them got up to turn on a lamp. They sat that
way, in silence, not looking at one another, until Marty showed
up and gently took Lilly, then Georgia, up the stairs to bed.

The next morning, Georgia woke to the sound of screeching. She ran downstairs to find Lilly in the kitchen with her face

pressed up against the window screen, screaming out into the backyard where a murder of crows was cawing in a tree. "They're here to take Jack," Lilly cried when Georgia and Marty tried to pull her away. "They can't have him!" Then she passed out, her limp body hanging between them like a sleepy child.

Lilly spent three weeks in the hospital, sedated, refusing to eat, unable to talk. After everything had been looked after, the funeral, the internment, the endless amounts of paperwork, Georgia and Marty brought Lilly home. And even though it took only days for them to uproot their lives – to quit their jobs, pack up their things, and move into Lilly's house – it was months before Georgia could look her mother in the eye without thinking about Jack's dead body lying cold and heavy on the bed next to Lilly while she slept.

8.

That morning, before the funeral, Georgia woke to a gentle fluttering in her stomach, and for a fleeting moment she imagined it was Marty inside of her, making love to her. She arched her hips gently against the covers, feeling Marty's weight on her, even as the remembering came to her, even as she became aware of her belly straining against her nightgown, of the incessant pressure on her bladder, the ache in her back.

Now, Peach Pit is awake and in full form, pounding against her back with what Georgia imagines are angry little fists, screaming to be let out. She knows the baby can feel her grief. Her entire pregnancy Georgia has been the picture of health, taking her folic acid faithfully every day, drinking gallons of milk, doing everything she was supposed to do. And ever since that surreal morning Georgia told him he was going to be a father, Marty had spent hours reading to her belly, playing music, whispering secrets. Months of being soothed by Marty's voice. And now that voice was gone.

One of the Mississauga Peaches is at the podium, talking about Marty's early love of baseball or something equally generic and untrue. Georgia shifts in her seat, trying to get at the dress fabric that has bunched up underneath her. She turns and sees Mairi and Matunde both watching her with a softness that, since she has been pregnant, Georgia has learned to recognize. Georgia takes Mairi's hand and places it on her belly, and Matunde reaches over Mairi and places his huge hand over hers. Georgia's belly is stretched so tight she can barely feel the pressure from the two clasped hands. Next to them, Lilly has her eyes closed. The humming has stopped, but her head still sways back and forth to some silent rhythm in her head. Georgia, in a momentary surge of guilt, takes her mother's hand and places it over Matunde's, but Lilly only keeps it there a moment before absently pulling it away.

When Lilly found out Georgia was pregnant, she kissed her on the cheek and told her congratulations, her eyes distant and sad. Later, Georgia found her standing in her bedroom in front of the mirror, her hand over her diaphragm rising with each breath she took. When she saw Georgia, she smiled and slowly twirled around on her toes.

"I've been thinking about singing again," she said.

Georgia leaned against the doorway. Although Lilly sang constantly around the house, she hadn't sung in public since before Georgia was born. "You mean in church?" she asked. "I think that's a nice idea."

"Well, maybe." Lilly turned sideways and studied her profile. "Or maybe I'll try to make a record. That's always what I wanted to do, you know."

Georgia reached up and grabbed a piece of her hair. "Well," she said, clearing her throat. "That's a lot of work, you know, Mother. It's not easy."

Lilly's eyes began to flutter. "I didn't . . . say it would be easy. When I was . . . there were . . . you probably don't know this, but I had agents coming up to me. And there's all these . . . television programs now . . . people sing and get recording contracts . . ." Lilly turned to look at Georgia. She was smiling, but her eyes were watery.

Georgia felt a lump forming in her throat. "Mother, that's . . . those shows are for young people."

"I'm young," Lilly whispered, tears running down her face. "I'm young. I'm young."

9.

After an hour or so, it appears that the service is over. "Unless there is anyone else who would like to speak," the minister says, folding his hands on the podium in front of him, "Then I would like to invite you all to join Hugh and Kitty for a reception . . ."

Georgia shifts in her seat. That's it then. This is her closure. She stares at the photo of Marty on a table at the front of the church. In the picture, his hair is combed, and he is wearing a shirt with a collar and a tie. Nothing about him is familiar except his eyes, deep blue and looking slightly startled, the same way he looked in every picture, as if he couldn't believe someone was actually taking a picture of *him*. With a stab of pain, Georgia thinks about Marty's green Mr. Rogers cardigan. She wishes she had worn it, the itchy wool scraping against her shoulders, strangling her with its warmth. She suddenly wishes she had worn all of Marty's clothes, wrapped herself up in them, his jeans, his tennis shoes, his "Ornithology is for the Birds" T-shirt, his Chicago Cubs baseball cap, instead of this ugly hat, this stupid veil . . .

"I would like to say something," Lilly says, standing up beside Georgia.

Georgia feels her hands grow numb. A slow wave of nausea rolls across her stomach. She watches as Lilly sweeps down the aisle and climbs the stairs to the podium.

"Should we do something?" Mairi asks. "Georgia?"

Georgia doesn't reply. The numbness has risen to her face, and even though she wants to cry, can feel the tears brewing behind her eyes, they just will not come. She feels as though her whole body is swelling – lips like beach balls, fingers like little sausages, skin stretching tight, about to snap. Without turning her head, she can feel Kitty's stare from across the aisle. *It'll be okay*, she tells herself. *Everything's going to be fine.*

"Hello everyone," Lilly says breathlessly. Her face is flushed, and even though she is too far away to tell, Georgia knows she is blinking feverishly. The church is silent, but Georgia feels like she can hear the thoughts of everyone in the room: *where do we look, what do we do with our hands?* Then Lilly's mouth is open and – oh God – she is singing, her voice soft at first, then growing louder, until the microphone begins to whine.

"I've got you under my skin," she sings. She pulls the microphone from its stand and dances out from behind the podium, one hand clutching the microphone handle, the other in front of her snapping her fingers to the beat. Georgia feels the air in the church starting to curdle, a pressure on her chest as it rises and falls. "I've got you deep in the heart of me . . ."

"Georgia!" Kitty hisses from across the aisle. "Georgia!" Next to her, Angela starts wailing, her cries oddly harmonic with Lilly's wavering soprano. The crowd in the church erupts into a low, muttering buzz as people flip through their programs, looking for something they might have missed. Hugh rises to his feet.

Somehow, Georgia forces her body to move. She turns to Mairi. "Do you see my purse?" she whispers.

"Oh, no, Georgia," Mairi says. "Don't leave. It's not that bad. She sounds good."

It's true. She sounds like summer evenings, like childhood, like flour on an apron, curtains blowing in a crisp breeze. It is the first spontaneous, genuinely emotional thing that has happened at this funeral, and Georgia can't bear to watch. She pulls herself to her feet. "I'll meet you outside," she says to Mairi.

When she reaches the aisle, she sees Kitty staring her down. "Sit down," Kitty hisses, the skin trembling around her lips. She looks like she might crack, like a crushed Caramilk bar: small

221

fissures running along the contours of her face, leaking honey-coloured liquid onto the church floor. "Sit down," she says again. "Don't make things worse."

"You know what, Kitty?" Georgia says. *Fuck you, Kitty.* The words are on the edge of her tongue, waiting to roll across the space between them and do their damage. She swallows them down and turns away instead, not towards the door but towards Lilly, whose eyes are now closed, who is lost on some other, imaginary stage, in New York or Paris, in some other, imaginary life.

Georgia waddles up the aisle, gripping the pews for support. As she passes the photo of Marty, she stops and looks at him for a moment. *My mother is singing Cole Porter at your funeral*, she tells him. Marty just stares straight ahead. Georgia kisses the tip of her index finger and presses it to the glass.

She makes her way to the podium and she stands next to Lilly. For one terrifying moment she looks out into the crowd, looks out to all those unfamiliar faces – Hugh's business associates, all those chocolate industry bigwigs, Kitty's fellow Junior Leaguers in their tailored funeral suits, Angela's sorority sisters, members of the subdivision neighbourhood committee, the country club, various boards and charities, upstanding members of the community. They are all watching Lilly and Georgia with a mixture of disgust and pity, curiosity and horror. Kitty has her head in her hands, and Hugh is nowhere to be seen. Then she sees a flash of white, and looks over to see Matunde, smiling broadly with his arm around Mairi, who is giving Georgia the thumbs up.

Georgia smiles back. Then she takes a deep breath.

10.

> *Over your dead body.*
> *Isn't that supposed to be "over my dead body?"*
> *Um, yeah, that's what I said. Over* your *dead body.*

222

Georgia gently pushed the dog off the bed and turned out the light. Down the hall, she could hear the television blaring from her mother's room. Involuntarily, she thought of Jack, imagined him still decomposing next to Lilly, of the smell that never really seemed to go away, even after years of trying to forget.

"I take it back," she said, curling herself towards Marty. "I like your body better alive."

Six weeks later, head buried in a newspaper, Marty walked into a parking garage elevator that wasn't there and fell four long stories down the shaft before landing on the roof of the elevator. It was Georgia's birthday. They were on their way to see the new *Star Wars* movie. The people in the elevator at the time said they felt a thud, but that the elevator never stopped moving.

Georgia, right behind Marty, felt the baby head butt her back, and leaned against the doorway to catch her breath. Rather than seeing the hole beneath her, she felt it: felt the emptiness, the tempting pull of gravity. When she realized what had happened, her whole body started to shake. She could feel the baby squirming inside of her, the smell of grease in the cold elevator air as it rushed past her, the sudden emptiness beside her, an aching in the spot where Marty should have been. She lifted one foot off the ground.

If only Marty had looked down. It could have been one of those moments, moments that pass. Maybe they would have cried, held each other. Maybe they would have laughed. Maybe it would have struck them, halfway through the movie, how absurd it all was – the empty elevator, their families, baby growing impatient in Georgia's belly.

Even now, Georgia has to try hard not to think about it.

She almost followed Marty into the hole. She almost did it. Almost.

About the Author

Originally from Halifax, Amy Jones is a graduate of the Optional Residency MFA Program in Creative Writing at UBC. Her short fiction has appeared or is forthcoming in several Canadian publications, including *The New Quarterly, Grain, Prairie Fire, Event, Room of One's Own, The Antigonish Review*, and *08: Best Canadian Stories*. In 2006, she was the winner of the CBC Literary Award for Short Story in English. Amy currently lives in Toronto.